HIS FACE SUDDENLY TWISTED WITH PAIN.

He reached out and grabbed my hand.

And held on.

I resisted my first impulse. Which, I'm ashamed to admit, was to pull away.

I know, I know. I'm an unfeeling clod. And yet, you have to remember, this was the very same guy who'd publicly questioned my integrity in yesterday's paper. And who'd been running around for months now telling a pack of lies about me and the way I did business.

You should also remember that I did somehow manage to resist my first impulse and that I went with my second. Which was to grip Bartlett's hand even tighter.

The man may have been a weasel, but poor old Bartlett didn't look as if he would be too long in this world. I hurriedly asked the question I knew the police would've wanted me to ask right off the bat. "Who did this to you?"

CLOSING STATEMENT

A Schuyler Ridgway Mystery

Tierney McClellan

A SIGNET BOOK

SIGNET
Published by the Penguin Group
Penguin Books USA Inc., 375 Hudson Street,
New York, New York 10014, U.S.A.
Penguin Books Ltd, 27 Wrights Lane,
London W8 5TZ, England
Penguin Books Australia Ltd, Ringwood,
Victoria, Australia
Penguin Books Canada Ltd, 10 Alcorn Avenue,
Toronto, Ontario, Canada M4V 3B2
Penguin Books (N.Z.) Ltd, 182–190 Wairau Road,
Auckland 10, New Zealand

Penguin Books Ltd, Registered Offices:
Harmondsworth, Middlesex, England

First published by Signet, an imprint of Dutton Signet,
a division of Penguin Books USA Inc.

First Printing, July, 1995
10 9 8 7 6 5 4 3 2 1

 REGISTERED TRADEMARK—MARCA REGISTRADA

Printed in the United States of America

PUBLISHER'S NOTE
This is a work of fiction. Names, characters, places, and incidents either are
the product of the author's imagination or are used fictitiously, and any resemblance to actual persons, living or dead, events, or locales is entirely
coincidental.

To my ex-husband, John McCafferty,
with much affection

ACKNOWLEDGMENTS

I wish to thank Detective T. Hightower of the Louisville Police Department, for taking the time to answer my questions; my twin sister, Beverly Herald, for serving as my first reader; my editor, Danielle Perez, for her thoughtful assistance; and my agent, Richard Parks, for his invaluable guidance. I would also like to thank my fellow Sister in Crime, Lynn S. Hightower, for all the encouraging words.

And, especially, I'd like to say how very much I appreciate the kind assistance I was given by Juanita Holder, an associate real estate broker with Steve Hall and Associates, a Century 21® agency.

CLOSING
STATEMENT

Chapter 1

It was only nine a.m. on a beautiful September Wednesday, and already I was not having a good day. In fact the only way my day could've gotten any worse was if, when I showed up for work, Mike Wallace from *60 Minutes* was waiting for me. Microphone in hand, camera crew at the ready.

As it was, instead of Mike Wallace, I had Jarvis Arndoerfer—the man some people might call my boss—waiting for me just inside the front door of Arndoerfer Realty.

The front door of the real estate office is always kept standing wide open during the day in order to encourage walk-ins, so I spotted Jarvis through the storm door the second I turned off Taylorsville Road into the Arndoerfer Realty parking lot.

In his late fifties, with a good-size gut hanging over his belt, extra-thick lips, and a nose reminiscent of W. C. Fields, Jarvis is not exactly the sort of thing you want to lay eyes on first thing in the morning.

I've often wondered how his wife could stand it.

And, technically speaking, no matter what anybody might call him, Jarvis is not my boss. Jarvis does happen to be co-owner—along with his wife—of the firm I work out of, but as a real estate agent, I'm supposed to be an independent contractor. Who, for all intents and purposes, works for herself. Sans boss.

What this means, I do believe, is that I actually get

to make my own decisions. It also means that, while Jarvis does take a percentage of all the commissions I earn, he does not have any kind of final authority over me. I needed to remind myself of this as I walked in and immediately noticed that Jarvis had planted himself directly in my path—and that two of the veins in Jarvis's forehead looked close to bursting.

I also needed to remind myself that I was a forty-two-year-old grown-up, and *not* a six-year-old first grader about to be reprimanded by her teacher.

Since the front door of the office opens into one huge room with four metal desks in each corner, you can see at a glance exactly who is there at any given time. At this particular moment, for example, I could plainly see that there were two other real estate agents present—Barbi Lundergan and Charlotte Ackersen.

Neither of these women, however, even glanced my way. In fact, it looked as if both were trying their best to look totally absorbed in whatever happened to be on top of their respective desks. Barbi, for instance, appeared to be mesmerized by a large, cut-glass ashtray.

I turned back to Jarvis. "Good morning," I said cheerily. I already knew, of course, that the morning wasn't good, but, hey, I thought I'd give it a shot.

"Schuyler," Jarvis said, "thank God! *There* you are! I've been trying to phone you at home!"

Apparently, a "Good morning" in return was out of the question.

"Something awful has happened!" Jarvis hurried on. "SOMETHING AWFUL HAS HAPPENED!" Lately, whenever Jarvis gets excited, he repeats himself. The second time Jarvis says something is always quite a bit louder than the first time. It's sort of like watching an instant replay with the volume turned up a little higher.

I'm not sure why Jarvis started doing this. I do know this past year Jarvis became terribly absorbed in the

NBA and NFL playoffs. Maybe all that time in front of the tube has affected his mind. Maybe he's become convinced that every exciting moment in his life has to be replayed at least once.

It must be doing wonders for his love life.

"It's terrible, Schuyler! IT'S TERRIBLE!"

During the first play and the replay of "IT'S TER-RIBLE," Jarvis had started waving in my face what looked to be an entire newspaper section. Even though he'd wrinkled it badly, clutching it that tightly in his fist, I knew exactly what newspaper it had to be. Yesterday's *Courier-Journal.* I even knew what section it was. Section B—the Metro Section.

Call me psychic.

"Have you read this?" Jarvis was now saying. "HAVE YOU READ THIS?"

I opened my eyes very wide, stared for a long moment at the newspaper, and then finally shook my head. "Have I read the entire paper? No, Jarvis, as a matter of fact, I don't believe I have."

I was being deliberately obtuse. I've always thought one of the advantages of being a woman is that, if you want to, you can act incredibly stupid, and sure enough, some man will actually believe you're really that dumb.

One of the veins in Jarvis's forehead now appeared to be doing a pretty good imitation of Mt. Vesuvius just before that Pompeii incident. "No, NOT the EN-TIRE paper!" Jarvis said. "Have you read the article about this firm?"

Actually, it wasn't exactly an article *about* Arn-doerfer Realty, but I could see how Jarvis might look at it that way.

I shrugged, trying to look as if he were talking about something inconsequential. "Oh, that," I said.

"That? THAT?" Jarvis really needed to do some-thing about those veins. Siphon them off. Have them removed. Something. "I got home very late last night, after writing and rewriting a contract on one of my listings, so I didn't read yesterday's paper until this morning," he said. "I was eating breakfast when I saw it. God, I almost choked. I ALMOST CHOKED!"

I was tempted to say, "No kidding. NO KIDDING!" But I resisted.

Jarvis's eyes were now bulging out a little more than his veins. "Your mess is splattered all over the paper for the entire WORLD to see!"

I just looked at him. Was Jarvis actually suggesting that at this very moment there were people in *Bosnia* perusing the Louisville *Courier-Journal*? Somehow, I doubted it.

Jarvis might also give you the impression that "my mess," as he called it, had made front-page news.

This was far from the truth. The article to which Jarvis was referring was in the second section of the paper, on page B5, toward the bottom of the page, and it couldn't have been more than four inches long.

It didn't even rate a picture.

Under the headline LAWYER SUES REAL ESTATE AGENT, there were a few extremely brief words that detailed how a local real estate agent by the name of Schuyler Ridgway—that's me—was being sued by a local attorney by the name of Edward Bartlett—that's slime—to whom the agent had sold a house a couple of months earlier. The article also mentioned that Bartlett alleged that the aforementioned Schuyler Ridgway of Arndoerfer Realty had known about several defects in the house she sold him, *and* that she'd knowingly and deliberately not told Bartlett about these defects before the sale had been closed.

That was just about all the article said. Other than, toward the end, where whoever wrote the article had thought to mention that lawsuits only tell one side of a case.

When I'd read the article last night, it had distressed me a little that the *Courier* hadn't even called me up for my reaction before they'd printed the thing.

It was probably just as well, though. I would've called Bartlett "a lying weasel" at the top of my lungs. Which would've been a big mistake.

Not, of course, because this was an inaccurate assessment.

Bartlett *was* a lying weasel. Make no mistake about that.

Inaccurate assessment or not, however, in a couple of days, there would've been—no doubt—yet another article detailing how local real estate agent, Schuyler Ridgway, was once again being sued by local attorney, Edward Bartlett. This time, for slander.

I suspect one reason the *Courier* didn't call me was that they didn't want to waste any more time reporting this thing than they absolutely had to. Because it was obvious, if you glanced over the entire page on which my little article appeared, that even the people at the *Courier* realized it made for pretty boring reading. They'd put it right next to a news item headlined UTIL-ITY POLE REPLACED. The utility pole headline was in significantly larger type than mine.

I cleared my throat. "Look, Jarvis, this thing is not exactly splattered all over the—"

Jarvis interrupted me. This is something Jarvis does a lot. Standing five feet five inches in his stocking feet—and that's only when he wears very thick socks—poor Jarvis has been suffering from SMD, Short Man's Disease, for as long as I've known him. One of the symptoms of this affliction is that its suffer-ers feel compelled to dominate every conversation. They also labor under the delusion that they know everything there is to know about everything, and they feel as if they must demonstrate it. Frequently.

Jarvis was obviously in the throes of his illness.

"This thing could end up costing a small fortune! A SMALL FORTUNE!"

I just looked at him. To hear Jarvis talk, you might've thought the money would be coming out of his own pocket. The truth was, everybody at Arndoerfer Realty carries insurance for just this sort of thing. It's called E and O insurance, which stands for Errors and Omissions, and it's supposed to cover us in case some client ends up doing exactly what Bartlett was doing—taking us to court over some error or omission that he thinks occurred during the sale of his property.

E and O insurance is not the least bit cheap, and this is yet another way in which it's a lot like the malpractice insurance doctors carry. "Jarvis," I said, trying to be patient, "I believe our insurance would—"

Jarvis interrupted me again. Hardly a surprise. "Even if it didn't cost anybody a dime personally, it's the worst kind of publicity!"

Jarvis is not only short in stature, he's also a little short in the hair department. He only has this furry brown border left just above his ears and around the back of his head. I have to hand it to Jarvis, though. At least, he doesn't do what a lot of bald guys do—let his hair grow very long on one side, and comb it across. What Jarvis does do, however, is constantly swipe at his forehead as if there's this great mass of hair there that he's brushing out of his eyes. He was brushing nonexistent hair out of his eyes now, as he did his replay. "IT'S THE WORST KIND OF PUBLICITY!"

I tried for a placating tone. "Now, Jarvis, some people say that any kind of publicity is okay as long as they spell your name correctly."

This was evidently not the best thing in the world I could've chosen to say. Jarvis's eyes and veins suddenly seemed to be engaged in a bulging contest.

"Well, now, Schuyler, they certainly spelled *my* name correctly, didn't they?" Jarvis punctuated this by waving the *Courier* in my face all over again.

What Jarvis was referring to here was one other tiny detail that the newspaper article had mentioned. This particular tiny detail had been mentioned in the very last sentence, and there was every chance that most people didn't even read that far.

Still, to give Jarvis his due, I have to admit that the few people who did happen to read that far would find out that, since he was the broker I represented, Jarvis had been named as co-defendant in Bartlett's lawsuit.

This was not exactly news to me. As a matter of fact, I'd been meaning to tell Jarvis about it myself. I'd been meaning to tell him ever since yesterday morning when some guy from the sheriff's office had dropped by Arndoerfer Realty to serve papers on me.

If Jarvis had been in the office, the guy would've served papers on him, too. As luck would have it, however, I had been the only one in the office at the time.

Like I said, I'd been meaning to let Jarvis know. I'd just been waiting for the most opportune time, that's all. Like, for example, a time when I felt particularly in the mood to poke a tiger.

Of course, if I'd known this article was going to appear in the paper, I certainly would've gotten into a tiger-poking mood right away.

Jarvis's voice had reached a crescendo. "OH YEAH, SCHUYLER, I'D SAY THEY SPELLED MY NAME CORRECTLY, YESSIRREE—"

I took a deep breath. "Look, Jarvis, I'm sorry about this, I really—"

Jarvis brushed nonexistent hair out of his eyes. Again. And interrupted me. Again. "You're sorry? *You're* sorry? Well, *I'm* sorry, too! I'm sorry you didn't do what I told you to do!" Jarvis had gone back to waving the *Courier* again. "I'M SORRY YOU DIDN'T SETTLE THIS DAMN THING OUT OF COURT!"

Jarvis, as much as I hated to admit it, did have a point. Last night, as I sat reading that horrid little article in the comfort of my living room, I'd realized that settling out of court probably would've been the prudent thing to do.

Actually, I probably would have settled—just as Jarvis had suggested—except for one thing.

"Jarvis, how many times do I have to tell you? Settling out of court is *exactly* what Bartlett wants us to do! It would be playing right into his hands!"

Indeed, settling was what Edward Bartlett himself had been telling me to do ever since he first threatened to file a lawsuit. For months now, the little weasel had been phoning me on and off to remind me that he had a witness who was prepared to testify in court that I'd mentioned in her presence that I was well aware that the basement of Bartlett's new house leaked, that the plumbing in the bathroom was faulty, and that the fireplace in the living room was not usable. Moreover, according to Bartlett, I'd said all this to his alleged witness before we'd even written up a contract.

It had taken Bartlett almost a month before he'd finally told me who his witness was. Gloria Thurman, his girlfriend.

Uh-huh.

That was believable. Bartlett's own girlfriend certainly wouldn't lie for him. Oh no. Not a chance. What an outlandish idea.

Once I found out who his witness was, I had trouble believing that *anybody* would take Bartlett's accusations seriously. Why on earth would I admit to Bartlett's girlfriend, of all people, that I intended to deceive Bartlett? Were we supposed to be sharing girl-ish secrets, or what?

Not to mention, sharing anything with Gloria Thurman would've been a little difficult, since I'd never even met her, for God's sake.

I took another deep breath. "Jarvis," I said, "Bartlett is trying to pull a scam, and I, for one, am not going to let him get away with it."

Actually, I'd had my doubts about Bartlett the second he'd walked into Arndoerfer Realty. I'd taken in the cheap polyester suit, the two pinkie rings, and the way Bartlett's tiny brown eyes never quite met mine, and I'd thought, this guy is a weasel. No joke. That had been my first thought.

My second thought, unfortunately, had been: So what? Even weasels need to buy and sell their houses every once in a while.

I should've known better.

I should've realized that weasels need to stick with their own kind.

The entire time I was showing Bartlett houses, he'd kept grumbling about the 7 percent commission he had to pay me to sell the house he presently owned. More than once, he'd whined, "That sure is a lot of moolah just for herding a few folks through a house." Bartlett had made it sound as if my job could easily be confused with an episode of that old sixties' television show, *Rawhide*.

Now there wasn't a doubt in my mind that the slimy little jerk had decided to take me to court to recoup the commission he'd paid. Not to mention, to get his new house repaired for free—if, indeed, repairs really did need to be made, a thing I questioned as much as everything else.

"Jarvis, if I settle out of court, it would be the same as admitting that I'd done something wrong when I sold Bartlett his house," I said. "Well, I didn't do anything wrong, and I won't say I did!"

Jarvis's eye-bulging, vein-bulging contest looked to be a dead heat. *"Instead,"* he said, "you let this Bartlett guy drag this firm's name through the mud! This article makes us all sound like a bunch of crooks!"

"Nonsense. *He's* the one that's a crook. Bartlett's not only a crook, he's a lying, cheating, little weasel that deserves to be hit by a truck!"

"I don't care if he's a woodchuck!" Jarvis said.

It was at this point that a muffled sound reminded me that there were other people in the room. I glanced in the direction of the noise. Over at her desk, Barbi Lundergan was snickering into her hand. Charlotte Ackersen, at *her* desk, immediately turned away, but not before I saw the smile twitching at the corners of her mouth.

Jarvis didn't seem to care who heard him. "You need to settle this thing!" he was going on. "And you need to settle it FAST!"

I took still another deep breath. I was on the verge of telling Jarvis that I was about as likely to do that as I was to go bungee jumping. Then it occurred to me that, given the choice, I was a *lot* more likely to plunge headfirst off a very high platform, head screaming toward the ground while most of my internal organs headed toward my throat, and then be snatched from certain death by a thin elastic cord that bounced me around until my eyes rattled in my head like marbles, than I was to give in to Bartlett.

What's more, now that I really thought it over, there was no actual choice about it. "Jarvis," I began, "I would sooner—"

At that moment, I was interrupted by someone other than Jarvis, believe it or not. Walking through the storm door in back of me was a young couple in their early twenties. I couldn't help staring.

The two of them looked exactly the way I pictured the Bobbsey twins looking, once they'd grown to young adulthood. That's the younger set of Bobbseys I'm talking about—Freddy and Flossy, the ones always described in the Bobbsey twin books as having "fair, round faces, light-blue eyes and fluffy, golden hair."

The young woman and young man walking into Arndoerfer Realty had fair, round faces, all right. They also had light-blue eyes, and short, wavy blond hair that could easily be described as both "fluffy" and "golden."

The younger Bobbseys in the Bobbsey twin series were also always described as "plump," and while neither the young woman nor the young man walking into Arndoerfer Realty even came close to meeting this particular description, the young woman was nicely rounded. I gave her a quick, envious glance.

By letting Jane Fonda—through the magic of videotape, of course—torture me three times a week, I had managed to finally get down to 128 pounds. At five feet six inches, I probably would not be confused any time soon with the *Goodyear* blimp. The young woman, in front of me, however, looked as if she not only didn't have to worry about having the word *Goodyear* stenciled on her side, she probably didn't even know what the word "cellulite" meant.

The young man probably didn't, either. In fact, both of these two looked as if they spent a significant part of their lives in a gym somewhere.

Of course, since in all those books I read as a child, the Bobbsey twins really didn't seem to do anything but play, spending a large part of their young adult lives in a gym was, no doubt, exactly what the Bobbseys themselves would do.

The young man and woman in front of me were even dressed the way you might dress boy and girl twins. The woman was wearing a white short-sleeve polo shirt and a khaki-colored skirt that ended just above her knees, and her companion had on an identical white short-sleeve polo shirt and khaki-colored shorts. Both were wearing white Nike Airs and no socks, and both had identical golden tans.

I blinked again. If I hadn't already had a pretty good idea who they were, I would've taken them for, if not fraternal twins, then at least brother and sister.

Last night, however, a woman by the name of Amy Hollander had phoned me at home, and had started off the conversation by telling me that she'd just picked my name out of the Yellow Pages. A first, I do believe. Up to that moment, I'd been under the impression that I paid to have my name listed in the Yellow Pages just because all the other real estate agents in Louisville seemed to list theirs in there, and I didn't want to be the only real estate agent in town who didn't.

Last night, Amy had asked if I'd show her and her fiancé, Jack Lockwood, a few listings in the immediate area, and we'd agreed to meet at the office around nine.

Well, it was around nine. Freddy and Flossy here had to be Amy and Jack.

Sometimes, I suspect Jarvis can smell a new client. His bulbous nose actually started quivering a little the moment the Bobbsey twins walked in, and Jarvis's manner immediately underwent an abrupt transformation. Jarvis's veins even stopped pulsing. "Why, hello," he said, taking a quick step forward and extending his hand toward the young man. Jarvis's voice could've been mixed with vinegar and poured on a salad. "May I help you?"

The young man shook Jarvis's hand, but he was looking directly at me. "We're here to see Schuyler Ridgway?"

Jarvis's face fell.

I smiled.

Chapter 2

Five minutes later, I was still smiling as Amy, Jack, and I got in my car, and we headed away from Arndoerfer Realty. I almost felt like thanking them for getting me away from Jarvis.

Even if I'd intended to thank them, though, I probably wouldn't have had the chance. Jack Lockwood kept up a running chatter the entire time we were on the road.

It might not have been so bad, but Amy had immediately deferred to Jack, letting him have the front seat. In fact, she'd scrambled into the back of my Tercel without so much as a moment's hesitation. I gathered from this that Amy was one of those women who believe that The Man should always come first. He should always have the biggest piece of fried chicken, he should always get the last dinner roll, and by all means, he should always have the front seat in the car.

My mother would've loved Amy.

Whatever Amy's reasoning, Jack ended up sitting right next to me. More's the pity, I might add. Once I pulled out into the crowded traffic on Taylorsville Road, there didn't seem to be anything to do but drive and nod, drive and nod, drive and nod.

While Jack talked and talked and talked.

Lord, he had real staying power. That's youth for you.

I hadn't driven a mile when I began to be very glad that the first house I intended to show these two was only a few miles away.

"Amy and I have been looking for a house quite awhile now," Jack started off saying, "and frankly, Amy has not been at all happy with the level of service we've been getting from the real estate agent we were working with." Jack gave me a pointed glance. "That's why we've come to you."

I gave him a quick smile, but I couldn't help wondering if this was Jack's way of telling me that he expected if either he or Amy said, "Jump," I should immediately respond, "How high?"

"Amy and I are both twenty-two," Jack said, "we've both just graduated from college, and frankly, we're getting a little tired of being treated like two kids."

I gave him a quick sideways glance. This probably was not the time, then, to mention that he and Amy reminded me of the Bobbsey twins. Not the older pair, either. The younger ones.

"I mean," Jack went on, "we're not exactly babes in the woods, you know."

This last statement might've carried a little more weight if he hadn't immediately gone on to say, "I mean, just because you've never held a full-time job doesn't mean that you're still wet behind the ears. I did work summers, you know. At my dad's hardware store. He owns a chain, you know, stretching all across Kentucky and Tennessee and Indiana. Three hardware stores in all."

I was obviously supposed to look impressed, but I couldn't help thinking: Do three stores make a *chain*? "No kidding," I said.

That was all I had time to say. Jack was hurrying on. "Working summers for my dad gave me an inside view of the hardware industry, and with my BA in marketing, well, I think when I start next week as district sales manager, I'm going to bring some real innovative ideas to the job."

Jack was now sounding as if he were on a job interview.

"Terrific," I said, smiling. No doubt, all the people who worked for Daddy would join me in my sentiments. Goodness, yes, I'd just bet every single one of Daddy's employees were practically champing at the bit to hear Junior's innovative ideas.

Jack returned my smile. "That's right," he said, "I'm not your average college grad. I've been around the block a few times."

I wouldn't have thought it possible, but Jack actually managed to look as if he were strutting, sitting down.

I gave him another smile. I hoped it looked admiring, but to tell you the truth, I was wondering, Exactly where was that block you've been around? It wasn't one of those little wooden alphabet blocks, was it?

Having established himself as the World's Authority on Hardware, however, Jack evidently was ready to move on to more personal topics. "With my professional life all settled, I decided I was ready for the next big step." Here Jack paused to direct an adoring look into my backseat. "Amy and I are getting married in two months," he said. "Yes, in just eight short weeks, she and I are going to be Mr. and Mrs. Jack Lockwood."

Jack said this last with a kind of awed reverence.

I gave Jack an even wider smile. "How wonderful," I said. I tried my best to sound sincere. As somebody, however, who herself had gotten married in her early twenties—only to divorce eight years and two children later—I probably wasn't the most likely person in the world for either Jack or Amy to hear hearty congratulations out of.

Particularly since the two children I just mentioned, Nathan and Daniel, are today twenty and twenty-one themselves. The very idea of either one of my sons—at their present level of lofty maturity—actually walking down the aisle with some unsuspecting female would be enough to have me waking in the middle of the night in a cold sweat.

In fact, if either Nathan or Daniel were to even *try* to tie the knot, then at the point in the ceremony where the minister asks if anybody knows why this couple should not be joined in holy matrimony, I'd probably have to stand up. And wave their last grade reports from the University of Louisville as proof of what I was about to say.

Nathan and Daniel, you see, have both managed to flunk out of college in the last year. At *my* expense, Lord love them. They have also both assured me that they are going to return to school just as soon as the university forgives them their transgressions. And that, yes, by gum, the next time they will actually pay their own way, instead of flushing my money down the drain.

I only wish I could say I believed every word.

I also realized, as I was listening to Jack go on and on beside me, that perhaps my experience with my sons had prejudiced me a little. Maybe I was being too hard on Jack here. After all, unlike my sons, Jack did have a college degree. And he *was* a little older than they were.

Maybe Jack was that rare thing. A truly mature grown-up at the age of twenty-two.

It could happen.

I tended to doubt it, though. Particularly since I wasn't sure I myself was a truly mature grown-up at the age of *forty*-two.

I also doubted it even more when Jack said, "You

know, Amy and I have been engaged now for six whole months, and we're just as much in love as ever."

He just blurted this out. As if I'd asked.

I stared at him, thinking, Do you go around telling this sort of thing to strangers all the time? I was also thinking, of course, Oh, sure, *six months,* now there's a real test of lasting devotion.

"How nice," I said.

Jack nodded and brushed a strand of blond hair out of his eyes. "I fell in love with Amy the minute I saw her," he said.

I stared at him again. This was probably also not a good time to mention that I don't happen to believe in love at first sight. I realize it's unromantic of me and all, but I actually think that you can't truly love somebody unless you know them very, very well. And getting to know somebody very, very well seems to me to take quite a bit of time. Strangely enough.

As a matter of fact, I myself had been dating one man exclusively for three months now, and I still couldn't tell you whether or not I was in love with him. I loved Matthias's company, I was completely nuts about him in bed, and right now, just knowing we had a dinner date later on tonight was enough to make my heart beat a little faster.

But was I in love with Matthias? How can you know a thing like that after only three months?

I had yet to tell Matthias I love him, and I certainly hadn't heard the words out of him. As a matter of fact, if he did say such a thing, I probably would look at him as if he were out of his mind.

I guess that's one of the differences between me in my twenties and me in my forties. In my twenties, if I felt this terrific urge to crawl into bed with some guy, I assumed it had to be love.

Now I knew there are other words for it.

Jack apparently hadn't thought of any. He was strutting, sitting down, again. "I really think Amy and I were predestined to fall in love."

I guess, if I don't subscribe to all those other romantic notions, it won't exactly be a surprise for me to admit that I really hate the term "fall in love." It makes love sounds like something akin to a hole in the ground. As if maybe one day you're just walking along, minding your own business, and then all of a sudden, whoops, there you are. Stumbling, tumbling, and ultimately finding yourself at the bottom of an extremely deep love, unable to get out.

Maybe divorce has made me a cynic, but I just don't think love works that way.

Besides, there's no telling who you might find at the bottom of that hole.

"One day I saw Amy walking across campus, and I said to myself, 'there she is, there's my future wife,' " Jack was now saying. He directed yet another look of adoration into the backseat of my Tercel.

Listening to Jack was actually beginning to make me cringe. It was also beginning to make me long to turn around, look Amy right in the eye, and ask, "Why the hell do you want to marry this yo-yo?" Not to mention, "Why the hell do you want to get married so young?"

For a fleeting moment, I actually felt like doing what the robot in that old *Lost in Space* television show used to do—wave my arms frantically in the air, and yell, "WARNING, Will Robinson, WARNING! WARNING!!"

These two Will Robinsons probably wouldn't have listened, anyway. From what I could see in the rearview mirror, Amy was returning Jack's look of adoration, oh, about a hundredfold.

"For our wedding present, my mom and dad are giving us the down payment on a home of our own," Jack said.

Uh-huh. Well, now, that might answer my first question to Amy. Marrying a chain of three entire hardware stores and getting a new house could possibly be a powerful incentive to matrimony. Particularly when you were only twenty-two.

"Of course," Jack added, "it's just going to be a 'starter' home, but Amy and I want it to be just right."

I gave Jack another sideways glance. Amy had indicated over the phone three specific listings they were interested in seeing. All three were in the hundred-fifty-thousand-dollar range. This, then, was their "starter" home. Lord. I would've dropped to my knees and thanked God for such a start.

Jack seemed to be taking it in stride, however.

"The house had *got* to have two baths, at least," he was going on. "I certainly won't settle for anything less. In fact, I told Mom and Dad that if it didn't have two baths, well, you could just forget it."

Apparently, Jack believed in looking a gift horse in the mouth.

Amy, on the other hand, did seem to be another story. While she hadn't said so much as a word while her fiancé prattled on, every once in a while, when I glanced at her in the rearview mirror, I thought I saw the sort of look on Amy's face that you might expect to see on Cinderella's. Right after the slipper fit.

Jack had now returned to more personal topics. "I've been looking for a truly nice girl all my life," Jack said, "and I've finally found her." He gave Amy yet another adoring glance. "Fact is, all you have to do is just look at Amy's parents—honest, decent, the salt of the earth—and you know there's a terrific pedigree there," he said.

I was, by this time, biting my tongue to keep from saying anything. My God, the guy was making it sound as if he chose his wife the way he would a cocker spaniel. I gave Amy another quick glance to see how she was reacting to all this.

Believe it or not, she looked tickled pink to have been given such an endorsement. In fact, Amy looked close to drooling as she stared transfixed in Jack's direction. I took a deep breath. The two of them must be made for each other.

What could I say? Rots of ruck.

I turned my attention to locating the house I intended to show the happy couple. A charming two-story English Tudor on Lakeside Drive that hadn't even been on the market a week, the house was in a prime location, it was in pristine condition, and its price was lower than market value.

Mainly because its owners, Marvin and Denise Carrico, had already found a new house in an even more expensive neighborhood, and were more than a little anxious to move.

I'd already had quite a bit of interest in this particular house—in fact, I'd shown it twice the day before—and frankly, I was anticipating an easy sell. If not to Jack and Amy here, then to somebody else very soon.

The second we all piled out of my Tercel, I headed straight to the front porch and the small ceramic cat that lay curled on the porch to the right of the front door.

Lifting the cat, I found the door key underneath it.

Okay, I admit it. This isn't the way it's supposed to be done. I'm supposed to use a lockbox, or something like that, but for some reason, Denise Carrico wouldn't hear of giving me one of her keys. I haven't been able to figure out why. Maybe she was afraid one day I'd sneak in while she was out and try on her clothes.

In fact, when I'd asked for a key right after I'd taken the listing, Denise had actually looked at me as if I'd suggested she give me the key to her safety-deposit box. "I really don't think that will be necessary, my dear," she'd said.

The woman couldn't be any older than thirty-two or thirty-three, tops—some ten years my junior—and yet, she always talked to me as if she were twenty years' older. Of course, the way Denise behaved might've had a little something to do with how much older her husband was than she was. In my estimation, I'd say Marvin was, if not in his early sixties, at the very least, in his late, *late* fifties.

Marvin hadn't just robbed the cradle. He'd practically lifted Denise from the womb.

You could tell Denise thought she was being terribly clever leaving the key under the cat, instead of under the doormat. "Nobody would ever think of looking for it there," she'd told me.

Uh-huh.

Now, as I unlocked the front door, and stepped aside to let Jack and Amy go in first, I started my usual sales pitch. Having shown this house just the day before, it was almost like turning on a tape recorder and pressing PLAY. "The present owners absolutely *hate* to leave," I said brightly, "but they've outgrown this house. It is, in fact, *perfect* for a young couple just starting out. It has a lot of charm, as you'll see—"

With Amy at his heels, Jack paused before he went by me, and held up his hand. "Now, it's not just charm Amy and I are looking for," he said in the tone of an instructor correcting an errant student. "Amy and I want to make sure we're not buying somebody else's troubles." He gave me a quick smile. "Matter of fact, I was very glad you told Amy last night that the owners were going to be away this morning. Because we intend to make sure all the toilets flush, all the shower heads work, and . . ."

I didn't pay attention to the rest of it. I just looked

at him. Last night, when I'd phoned to make the appointment, Denise Carrico had indeed told me that she and her husband Marvin were going to be out shopping this morning. Usually, I don't care one way or the other whether an owner is home when I show a house. In fact, sometimes I'd prefer them to be present so that they can answer any questions about the cost of utilities, garbage pickup, that sort of thing.

Last night, however, I'd been happy that the Carricos weren't going to be home, and now I was even happier. Particularly after I heard how Jack intended to spend his morning.

Denise Carrico, you see, was something of a housekeeping fanatic. When I'd first taken the listing, Denise had actually suggested that I make everyone I showed her house to remove their shoes before they entered. Really. I'd had to convince the woman that it was entirely possible that such a move could result in God knows what ghastly germs being introduced into her immaculate home. "Athlete's foot," as I recalled, were two words I'd repeated several times during our little discussion.

Now I could only imagine how Denise would react to having two strangers go through her house on a toilet-flushing binge. Denise would probably have insisted that Amy and Jack wear rubber gloves.

I returned Jack's smile, and as Jack and Amy went on by, I resumed my little speech. "Now, if you'll turn to your left, into the living room, you'll notice the hand-rubbed oak mantel and the antique light sconces on either side of—"

Just as I was saying this, Jack and Amy came to an abrupt halt directly in front of me, not two steps inside the arched doorway of the living room.

And they both did this quick intake of breath.

I thought at first that the two of them had stopped

and gasped like that because they were so impressed with the room.

That, however, was before I myself stepped to one side, getting ready to point out the genuine brass outlets and the like-new beige wool carpet, and I saw what had caught Amy and Jack's attention.

Sprawled in the middle of the aforementioned like-new beige wool carpet, flat on his back, so that you could plainly see the ugly crimson smear in the middle of his chest, was a man in his late forties wearing a white pullover shirt and blue plaid slacks.

It was—of all people—Edward Bartlett.

Chapter 3

I stood there for a split-second, just inside the Carrico's living room doorway, listening to someone scream. The sound seemed to be coming from a place far away.

And then, I realized it was coming from me.

It certainly wasn't coming from Jack or Amy. Both of them were standing motionless right next to me, staring at Bartlett in absolute, total silence. I couldn't even hear them breathing.

I started moving. I tried to cross the room as fast as I could, but my legs suddenly felt oddly heavy. It seemed to take forever to keep putting one foot in front of the other until I reached Bartlett's side.

As I went, I yelled over my shoulder, "Jack! Amy! Call 911!"

A quick glance told me that there was no phone in the living room, so I pointed toward the door leading into the hall. "Jack! *Quick!*"

Jack did this little jerk, as if maybe an invisible someone had just yanked his chain. "Uh, *right!*" he said, and ran out of the room.

I was finally at Bartlett's side, and I dropped to my knees on the floor beside him. From a distance, the crimson stain on the front of Bartlett's shirt had looked as if he might've been careless with a bottle of ketchup.

Up close, you could tell it wasn't ketchup.

I stared at the wound, horrified.

What in the world did you do for a thing like that? When my boys were little, and they'd come running to me, bleeding from some scrape or another, I'd always reached automatically for the Mercurochrome and the Band-Aids, and started patching them up.

I could be wrong, but I was pretty sure that Mercurochrome and Band-Aids were not going to do the trick for Bartlett here.

I glanced up at his face. Bartlett's eyes were closed, and his skin looked awfully pasty. He was still breathing, though.

I took a deep breath of my own, steeling myself. Then I moved even closer to Bartlett and leaned over him, trying to get a better look at his wound. There was a hole about the size of a quarter in the middle of the crimson smear staining the front of Bartlett's white knit shirt.

I swallowed, and peered at the wound even closer. Did you press on a thing like this? Like what you do for a deep cut or a puncture wound? Or would adding pressure do even more internal damage? Particularly if the bullet was still in there?

The wound didn't seem to be bleeding much, but maybe that was just because Bartlett was lying on his back.

I thought fleetingly of the first-aid chart I had taped on the inside of one of my kitchen cabinets. Fat lot of good it was doing me now.

Of course, it was probably highly unlikely that, on a chart called "Common Household Accidents and Their Remedies," a gunshot wound would be among the traumas listed.

Although these days you never could tell.

I settled back into my original kneeling position, and yelled in the direction of the hall. "Jack! When you talk to 911, ask them what you're supposed to do for a gunshot wound!''

I didn't get a reaction from Jack, but I got one from Amy. Still standing, more or less frozen in the doorway, she let out all the air she'd evidently been holding. She sounded like a tire going flat.

"It's okay, Amy," I said, trying to sound reassuring. "This guy's going to be fine."

Amy didn't look reassured. Her frightened eyes never left Bartlett's face.

I'd been looking over at Amy, and that's why I didn't realize right away that Bartlett had opened his eyes. When I saw that he was looking directly at me, I actually gave a little start.

Bartlett, for his part, looked as if he would've given an identical start except that he didn't quite have the strength. His eyes widened in recognition, though, and then, would you believe, he actually grimaced. In fact, I believe I could assume from the expression on his face that Bartlett would've preferred to have seen just about anybody else in the world kneeling beside him.

I knew exactly how he felt.

Bartlett apparently changed his mind a fraction of a second later, though. He must've decided that I was better than nobody. When his face suddenly twisted with pain, he reached out and grabbed my hand.

And held on.

I resisted my first impulse. Which, I'm ashamed to admit, was to pull away.

I know, I know. I'm an unfeeling clod. And yet, you have to remember, this was the very same guy who'd publicly questioned my integrity in yesterday's *Courier-Journal*. And who'd been running around for months now telling a pack of lies about me and the way I did business.

You should also remember that I did somehow manage to resist my first impulse, and that I went with my second. Which was to grip Bartlett's hand even tighter.

The man may have been a weasel, but poor old Bartlett didn't look long for this world.

"It's going to be okay," I repeated to Bartlett. Amy may not have believed me, but Bartlett here didn't look in any condition to argue. I hoped I sounded a lot more convinced than I felt. "We've called 911, and they're going to be here soon. They'll fix you right up."

Bartlett might not have felt like arguing, but he didn't seem to believe me any more than Amy had. His response was to turn his head away and moan.

Bartlett's moan didn't exactly sound robust. In fact, it sounded extremely weak, and fading fast.

That's when it occurred to me that Bartlett might not last until an ambulance or the police or somebody else arrived. Lord. This might very well be the last chance for anybody to ask him any questions.

I leaned closer to the ear facing me, and asked the first question that came to mind. "What happened?" I spoke into Bartlett's ear as if it were a microphone.

Bartlett's head turned toward mine again. His eyes were getting sort of vague-looking, and you could tell it was taking every bit of the strength he had just to form words. "I—I was—I—I was—"

At this point, I realized that Bartlett's answer to this particular question was going to take too much effort, and maybe too much time. Which, judging from the way Bartlett was now looking, we might not have a whole lot of. I waved my hand as if to erase my first question. "Never mind, never mind," I said, and I hurriedly moved to the question I knew the police would've wanted me to ask right off the bat. "Who did this to you?"

Bartlett grimaced and for a second, just stared me. Looking agonized. I couldn't tell if he was looking this way because he really was in pain right that second, or if he was miffed because I'd changed questions on him more or less in midstream. I decided it would probably be better not to ask. Instead, I repeated a little louder, "WHO DID THIS TO YOU?"

I was starting to sound like one of Jarvis's replays.

Bartlett swallowed. "It—was—" His voice was getting more and more strained. "It—it—was—"

Here Bartlett actually gasped out a name, but his voice was so ragged, I couldn't make it out. "Who?" I said. I leaned over, this time trying to position my ear right next to his mouth.

Bartlett apparently felt that the communication gap was all my fault. The look he gave me this time was one of unmistakable annoyance. He swallowed yet again, and finally gasped, "Porter's girl."

I just stared at him. I really hated to press for details at a time like this, but let's face it, the man was not making himself clear. *"Porter?"* I asked. "Porter who? You mean Porter, as in a name? Or porter, as in a job?"

I started to lean down even closer, practically putting my ear into Bartlett's mouth, but when I did that, I noticed that my hair on that side was hanging right into his face. It seemed kind of cruel to be tickling the nose of a man in his condition. My right hand was occupied, holding his, so I reached around awkwardly with my left, trying to pull my hair back as I leaned forward.

While I was doing this, Bartlett didn't just look annoyed. He looked disgusted. He closed his eyes for so long that I started to suspect he might not ever open them again. Finally, however, opening his eyes and looking straight at me, Bartlett choked out with tremendous effort, "It—was—Porter—Meredith's—girl."

I blinked. My God. I knew a Porter Meredith. Porter Meredith, like Bartlett, was an attorney. In fact, the Porter Meredith I knew had handled quite a few closings for Arndocrfcr Realty over the years.

Bartlett was now grabbing at my sleeve, obviously trying to tell me something else.

In fact, he was almost raising up off the floor in his effort to make me understand what he wanted to tell me.

"Groan," he said.

At least, that's what I thought he said. "Excuse me?" I said.

I pulled away and looked at him.

Bartlett had evidently said all he was going to, though, because now he began to do exactly what he'd just said. Groan. He let out a couple long, shuddering groans that made the hairs on the back of my neck stand up.

It didn't help any to see blood trickling out of the side of his mouth.

Oh, God. I couldn't seem to pull my eyes away. I wasn't a doctor or anything, but this didn't look like a good sign to me.

Something else also occurred to me. I hate to admit it, since it does make me sound pretty shallow, but it did cross my mind that I was probably going to be held accountable if Bartlett bled all over the Carricos' like-new beige wool carpeting.

The blood on Bartlett's front seemed pretty much confined to his chest, but this latest was headed directly for the carpet.

Blood, I've discovered—mainly while cleaning up after all those scrapes my boys had had—does not come out easily.

I also couldn't help recalling Denise Carrico's suggestion that I make everybody remove their shoes before they come into her house. What Bartlett was about to do was probably a bit worse than having her carpet *walked* on.

While blood still trickled slowly out of Bartlett's mouth, I glanced quickly around for something to wipe it with. Bartlett's shirt didn't have a collar, and his sleeves were too short to be of any use. I could probably use the hem of his shirt, but since his shirt was tucked in, it would require pulling his shirt out from his slacks. That didn't seem like a good idea, since I wasn't at all sure I could do it without moving Bartlett at least a little.

The only things within reach seemed to be three needlepoint pillows, arranged carefully on the sofa to my left, and a Battenberg lace doily under the lamp on the antique end table next to the sofa.

I was fairly certain that Denise Carrico would not appreciate my using either the pillows or the doily to wipe Bartlett's mouth.

"Amy!" I yelled. "Get me a towel from the bathroom!" Amy was still standing, more or less frozen, in the doorway, her eyes the size of saucers—the expression of a deer caught in oncoming headlights.

Amy was still motionless after I yelled at her. Her eyes appeared to be glued to Bartlett's face.

"Amy!" I yelled again. "I mean it. Get me a towel out of the bathroom. Now!"

The blood trickling out of Bartlett's mouth was now getting very close to dripping off the side of his face. In another second, I was going to have to stop it with my skirt. A white linen, mind you.

Which was regularly $138, but which I'd found on sale for $33.

As you can imagine, I adored this skirt.

"Amy!"

Amy jerked to attention much like her fiancé had done earlier. Still looking over her shoulder at Bartlett, she ran out of the room, down the hall, pulled open a door and disappeared inside. In less time than it takes to blink your eyes, she reappeared with a burgundy hand towel.

I must say, a towel that color was perfect for the purpose I had in mind.

By the time Amy handed the towel to me, Bartlett had lost consciousness. His head lolled to the left just as Amy reached my side.

Bartlett's head-lolling, evidently, was too much for Amy. She stood there and screamed. Actually holding her hands curled against her cheeks, exactly the way the heroines always did in those classic black-and-white mystery movies I used to watch when I was a kid.

I hadn't been expecting the sudden noise. I nearly jumped out of my skin when Amy let loose.

Amy didn't stop, either. She just stood there, screaming and screaming. I considered getting to my feet, and slapping her exactly the way they also always used to do in all those old movies, but thank God, Jack suddenly reappeared.

I was almost as glad to see him as Amy. I was fairly certain that slapping a client silly is not recommended as a real estate sales technique.

"Jack, what did 911 say? What are we supposed to do for a gunshot wound until they get here?"

Jack was heading straight toward Amy, and when I spoke, he gave me the sort of look you might give a bothersome gnat. "What? What are you talking about?" Before I could answer, he turned to Amy. "Amy, darling," he said, "are you okay? Oh, you poor baby, come here, sweetheart, come here to Papa."

I don't know. I've never thought of a twenty-two-year-old who looks like Freddy Bobbsey as the Papa sort, but Amy apparently didn't agree. She moved into Jack's arms without hesitating.

Once there, Amy gave up on screaming—thank

God, I might add—and mainly concentrated on whimpering.

"It's okay, darling," Jack said, "I'm here. Everything's going to be okay, sweetheart."

I hated to interrupt this touching moment, but Bartlett did seem to be dying. *"Jack!"* I said. "What are we supposed to do?"

Jack just looked at me. "Wait for the ambulance," he said. His tone implied that this was a conclusion I should've reached on my own.

"Jack, did you hear me earlier?" I said through my teeth. "I asked you to ask 911 what we were supposed to do for a gunshot wound."

Jack was in the midst of repeating the words. "Oh, you poor baby, oh, you poor baby," but he did somehow manage to hear me.

His response was a shrug.

I just looked at him. Apparently, on Jack Lockwood's list of priorities, "Comforting Amy" rated quite a bit higher than "Saving the life of a dying man."

"I didn't hear you," Jack was now saying. He gave Bartlett a quick look. "I guess I should've thought to ask, but I didn't. They'll be here in a minute." Then the subject evidently discussed to his complete satisfaction, Jack turned back to Amy. "Oh, you poor baby, I would never have left you so long, except that I couldn't find a phone! I must've looked everywhere before I noticed one hanging *under* one of the cabinets in the kitchen. Can you believe that? You had to bend over to even see it was there—"

Actually, this wasn't hard to believe. Denise Carrico probably considered a phone something that marred her perfect walls.

"I looked in the bedroom, and the study, and the bathroom, and the—"

While Jack went on and on, elaborating his telephone quest, I sat there on the floor next to Bartlett, still holding his hand. And wishing I'd taken one of the first-aid courses they're always offering at the YWCA.

I'd never felt so helpless. And yet, what was there for me to do? I was afraid to add pressure to Bartlett's wound without being told it would be okay. I was afraid to move him. In fact, I was afraid to do anything.

Except hold Bartlett's hand, and wait, and while I waited, go over in my mind what Bartlett had just told me.

My God, was it really possible that Bartlett's Porter Meredith and *my* Porter Meredith were one and the same?

I supposed it wasn't all that unlikely that Bartlett, an attorney himself, and *I*, who probably knew most of the attorneys in Louisville—having worked in real estate for the last nine years—would be acquainted with the same one. Bartlett and I probably knew a lot of the same attorneys. I just hadn't been aware of one until now.

If it were true that we both knew this one, then I happened to know our mutual Porter Meredith pretty well.

In fact, I'd even dated him. For about two months. Porter Meredith, in fact, was the last man I'd dated seriously—that is, for more than just a couple of dates—before I'd started dating Matthias. You remember Matthias, the man I'm dating now, the one I'm not sure I'm in love with.

Of course, when I thought about it, my having dated Porter wasn't all that unlikely, either. Porter had probably dated every eligible woman in Louisville at one time or another. He was something of a ladies' man. That, in fact, had been what had finally convinced me not to see Porter anymore. That, and Porter thinking that his going out with me gave him some kind of authority over me.

When he'd started actually telling me what shade of lipstick I should wear, I decided I'd had all the instruction I needed, and broken it off.

Bartlett hadn't just said, "Porter Meredith," though. He'd said "Porter Meredith's *girl*." Was it possible that whoever Porter was now dating had actually shot Bartlett here?

I didn't have much time to think this over, because right then, the police suddenly arrived. And an ambulance.

I, of course, was so glad to hear the sirens outside, I almost started whimpering as much as Amy. Which was saying quite a bit, since Amy was *still* making little snuffling noises.

When I saw the two policemen open the Carricos' front door and head my way, though, I felt suddenly even more like whimpering. For an entirely different reason.

It was Murray Reed and Tony Constello.

Two cops I'd met a little over three months ago.

Back then I'd had the rare privilege of having these two question me at length regarding the shooting of Ephraim Cross, a wealthy nursing home tycoon who'd left me over $100,000 in his will. At the time, I had not had a whole lot of answers for them. In fact, as I recall, all I could tell them was that I'd never even met Ephraim Cross.

Reed and Constello had not been all that impressed with my story. In fact, they'd definitely homed in on me as a suspect in Cross's murder. They'd kept asking, over and over, "You're trying to tell us that some guy you never met left you a small fortune?"

As it turned out, that was exactly what had happened.

I also wish to hastily add that I'd been cleared of

all suspicion—and, as a matter of fact, I'd been instrumental in bringing the real culprit to justice. All of which, you'd think, would make Reed and Constello look at me somewhat fondly.

I watched them, as they stalked into the living room and spotted me.

Nope. That didn't look like fond looks on their faces.

Matter of fact, the two of them didn't look any happier to see me than I was to see them.

Oddly enough.

Chapter 4

Murray Reed and his partner, Tony Constello, have always reminded me of salt and pepper shakers. Reed, with his white-blond hair cut in a flattop and a squat, weight-lifter's body, would, of course, be the salt, and Constello, with his swarthy skin, thick, black mustache, and heavy-lidded black eyes, would be the pepper.

Standing now in the Carricos' foyer, just outside of the living room, where the paramedics worked on Bartlett, I was amazed at how intimidating salt and pepper shakers could be. "Well, well, well," Reed—the salt—said. Somehow, he made those three words sound accusing.

Of course, I might've gotten that impression just because Reed was speaking in the flat, staccato tones of Jack Webb, the guy who played the detective in the old *Dragnet* television series. Jack Webb could make ordering a Big Mac sound accusing.

You'd think the one thing a cop wouldn't do was try to talk like Jack Webb. As I recalled, however, Reed had also sounded exactly like this during our first charming encounter. At the time I'd been convinced that the man had to be faking, but Reed's voice had never varied. Now I wondered. Maybe Reed really did talk like Jack Webb naturally. Maybe Reed had been talking like this ever since he was in diapers, and that's why he'd become a cop.

With a voice like that, he would never really have had a choice.

That might also explain his bad mood. Maybe old Reed here had really wanted to be a dentist. Or a preacher. And yet, with his voice, he'd been predestined to be what he was. A Jack Webb rerun.

A thing like that could make a person a bit touchy, I suppose.

Reed was frowning even now. "What do you know, it's you again," he said. "You do keep popping up, don't you?"

I don't believe Reed intended me to confuse this last comment with anything even close to resembling "Nice to see you again."

Amy and Jack had moved from the living-room entrance into the foyer when the paramedics arrived, and even though the foyer of the Carricos' home is about the size of my dining room, Amy and Jack were standing not three feet away, taking in every word. I didn't particularly want to give *clients* the impression that I run into the police on a regular basis.

"What do you mean—I keep popping up? It's been over three months," I said.

Constello—the pepper—shrugged. "Time sure flies, you reckon?" Tall and thin, Constello may have looked like somebody who could be an extra in one of the *Godfather* movies, but he sounded like somebody who hailed from eastern Kentucky.

Reed was running his hand over his white-blond head. For anybody else, this gesture would've amounted to running his hand *through* his hair, but with that Marine flattop, Reed was going to be hard put to find enough hair up there to even wiggle his fingertips in. "Seems like everybody you know gets themselves shot," Reed said. Jack Webb now sounded even more disgruntled.

Amy's and Jack's eyes were getting very round.

Their eyes were also bouncing between the salt and pepper shakers and my face. Amy and Jack could've been watching a tennis tournament.

"Now, wait a minute," I told Reed, "if you'll recall, I did *not* know Ephraim Cross. In fact, the only shooting victim I've ever known *before* the actual shooting is this one here." I waved toward poor Bartlett.

Reed, Constello, Amy, and Jack all looked in Bartlett's direction, as if everybody actually expected Bartlett to back me up on this.

I followed everybody's gaze. It looked like we were all going to have to wait quite a while for Bartlett's input. Perhaps, even, *forever*.

The paramedics had torn open Bartlett's shirtfront, and they now seemed to be in the process of connecting about a hundred tubes and wires and bottles to Bartlett's chest and arms. I wasn't sure what it was that the paramedics were doing to him, but it didn't seem to be working. Bartlett's head was still lolling to one side, and if anything, his face looked even more pasty.

Reed and Constello turned back toward me. Reed's eyes seemed to have shrunk a little. "You know this guy?"

I swallowed before I answered. Let me see now. The last time I'd talked to Reed and Constello, I hadn't even *met* the shooting victim, and yet, I'd gotten accused of his murder. I believed that I could assume from this that I needed to be careful what I said. "I don't know him very well," I hedged. "Edward Bartlett was just a business acquaintance of mine, that's all. A few months ago I sold him a house, and I handled the sale of the one he was moving out of. That was it. I haven't seen him for months."

I had, of course, talked to Bartlett a few times on the phone, during those occasions when he'd felt like calling me up and threatening me, but at the moment this didn't seem all that necessary to mention.

Besides, what little I had already said seemed to be getting enough attention all by itself. As soon as I'd started talking, Reed had taken out a small, spiral notebook, and started scribbling furiously in the thing with a Bic. Seeing Reed do that gave me the same sort of sinking feeling I'd gotten when I'd taken my driver's license test years ago. Even at sixteen, I'd known that every time the cop seated beside me in the front seat of my father's Chevrolet Impala had started scribbling on the form attached to his clipboard, it meant I'd made some kind of infraction.

Today I must've made quite a few infractions because Reed suddenly seemed to have quite a lot to write.

My stomach knotted up.

It knotted up even more when I noticed that Jack and Amy were now not even bothering to pretend that the two of them weren't eavesdropping. In fact, they were both openly gawking. First at me, then at Reed and Constello.

Constello must've felt Jack and Amy's stares. Abruptly, he turned his dark head toward Jack, and cleared his throat. "Would you two mind waiting for us in the dining room? We'll be talking to you in just a few minutes."

Jack and Amy both looked startled when Constello spoke to them. I decided they looked this way because either the very idea that the police would be interested in talking to them at all was fairly alarming, or else they were afraid that eavesdropping on a police conversation was something you could get a ticket for. Jack and Amy wasted no time moving through the living room and into the adjoining dining room.

I did notice that Amy directed an unflinching stare at Bartlett as she went by the scene in the living room.

She looked at Bartlett the way a lot of people look at car accidents. With a mixture of horror and fascination.

I realized immediately, of course, that it wasn't just to keep from being stared at that Constello had moved Amy and Jack to the dining room. Constello was isolating the witnesses. I'd seen this done often enough on the roughly a million television mystery movies I've watched in my lifetime. The police in the movies always separate everybody at a crime scene so that they can see if everybody's stories match.

Which meant that Reed and Constello were not exactly assuming that what had happened here today had not involved me nor Jack nor Amy. In fact, it actually looked as if the salt and pepper shakers had not completely ruled out the possibility that all three of us could be in cahoots.

I stared at Reed and Constello, disbelieving. Did they really think that Amy and Jack and I had all ganged up on poor Bartlett? Did they think we were some kind of roving band, going around, shooting people in houses currently for sale?

Lord, if Reed and Constello even thought that for a second, the two of them not only looked like salt and pepper shakers, they had the brains of salt and pepper shakers as well.

Having gotten off on a terrible foot once before with these guys, though, I decided that this time I was going to be so cooperative it wouldn't even cross their minds that I could've done anything wrong.

As it turned out, I was probably being a bit optimistic.

Standing there in the Carricos' foyer, Reed and Constello waited until Amy and Jack were completely out of sight before they resumed questioning me.

By that time I was sitting rather demurely, I thought, on a church pew.

That's right. In the Carricos' foyer, in front of the wide, floor-to-ceiling window in the middle of the wall to the right of the front door, Denise Carrico had carefully placed a small, oak church pew. Denise must've looked high and low for this particular piece of furniture, because it was the exact width of the window in back of it. As soon as Amy and Jack were gone, Reed directed me to the pew, guiding me there by the elbow as if I might not be able to find the thing without his help.

The second I sat down, I started feeling more and more uneasy. It seemed particularly inappropriate to be talking to these two while perched on a church pew. Certainly, the last time the three of us had had a little chat, I'd felt as if I didn't have a prayer.

Reed seated himself next to me, placed his notebook on one knee, and began scratching away with his Bic before either he or Constello said another word.

What Reed was writing was beyond me.

He could've been making out his grocery list, for all I knew.

Constello, who'd remained standing, was the one who started things off. "So," he said, "what's the story here?"

I would've preferred him to put that another way. "The *truth* is," I began, "Bartlett was lying on the floor when we walked in."

I told them both every single detail I could remember. While I talked, Constello paced in front of me and smoothed down his black mustache. Constello petted his mustache the way some people absentmindedly pet their cats. When I got to the part where I repeated what Bartlett had told me, Constello came to an abrupt halt.

And Reed stopped scribbling.

" 'It was Porter Meredith's girl?' *That's* what he said?" Reed asked.

I glanced over at him and nodded.

Reed's next question was not exactly an ego boost. "Did anybody else hear him say this?"

Evidently, my word alone was not going to be enough. I gave Reed a level look. As I recalled, Jack had gone to phone 911, but Amy had still been there, standing in the living-room doorway. "Amy Hollander, the girl waiting to talk to you out in the dining room, might've heard it," I said.

"Uh-huh," Constello said. I couldn't be sure, but that "uh-huh" sounded skeptical.

If I thought, however, that Reed and Constello seemed skeptical about the Porter Meredith comment, it was nothing compared to the way they looked when I told them what Bartlett said next.

" 'Groan?' " Constello said.

I nodded. "Bartlett said 'Groan,' and then he really did groan. Just before he lost consciousness."

" 'Groan?' " Constello repeated. He was petting his mustache again.

I nodded even more emphatically. "That's what he said. I'm pretty sure of it," I said.

Reed blinked. "You're *pretty* sure?"

I shrugged. "Well, his voice was getting kind of weak by then, but that's what it sounded like."

Reed blinked again.

I blinked right back at him. "Look, Bartlett didn't volunteer any of this, you know," I said. "I had to ask him. Otherwise, he wouldn't have told me a thing."

I'm not sure why I said this. I guess I was hoping that it would give me a little more credibility. And that maybe I'd get a little credit for having the foresight to question Bartlett before he lapsed into unconsciousness. More or less, helping the salt and pepper shakers with their jobs.

Reed and Constello, however, did not look the least bit grateful.

"He said, 'Groan,' and then he groaned," Reed said. "*That's* your story?"

This was getting irritating. The next time I ran into a gunshot victim, see if I asked him so much as his name.

I lifted my chin. "That's the truth. Maybe Bartlett was the sort of guy who liked to announce what he was going to do just before he actually did it?" I tried to look as if this last made perfect sense, but to be honest, as soon as I put it into words, this particular theory sounded farfetched even to me.

Reed apparently agreed. He was now looking at me as if mentally measuring me for a straitjacket. "Is there anything else?"

All the time I was telling them about finding Bartlett and what he'd said, it had been in the back of my mind to just tell them that, and nothing else. That there was really no use mentioning anything that might make the shakers think that Bartlett and I had not exactly been buddies. Now, though, it occurred to me that it would probably be better for them to hear it from me than from somebody else.

"Well, there was one other thing," I said. "I feel silly even mentioning it."

Reed and Constello exchanged a look.

I didn't like the looks of that look.

"Go ahead," Reed said encouragingly. "Feel silly."

I took a deep breath. The two of them were bound to find out what I had to tell them soon enough. And, if I omitted it, the whole thing would assume a significance it didn't really have. I plunged in. "Edward Bartlett was suing me," I said very fast. "Coincidentally enough."

Reed and Constello both suddenly looked a great deal more alert. You could get the idea that neither of them believed in coincidences.

"Well, well, well," Reed said. I believe I've already

mentioned how accusing he could make those words sound. He started scribbling with that damn Bic even more furiously than before.

I tried to sort of slouch a little in Reed's direction, in order to get a better view of what he was writing. Almost immediately, though, I began to feel as if I were cheating on a test, trying to sneak a peek at the paper next to me.

The look Reed gave me did nothing to put this idea to rest.

I sat up straight again, and hurried on. "Bartlett was *alleging*"—here I put a little extra emphasis on this last word—"that I deliberately misrepresented the house I'd sold him." I tried to follow up this little statement with a careless shrug that more or less said how truly idiotic this idea was.

Reed and Constello did not look convinced that the idea was all that idiotic. They gave me identical level stares.

"It was all lies!" I said. "Bartlett was making everything up!"

"Uh-huh," Constello said.

Reed gave me a tight-lipped smile. "Of course."

I looked first at Reed and then at Constello. "Look, I'm trying to be totally honest here. So that you two will know that I've got absolutely nothing to hide."

"Uh-huh," Constello said again. I was beginning to wish he'd stop saying that.

I was also beginning to wish I'd just stayed in bed all day today. At the very least, that I hadn't gone into work. Because, of course, there was still one other thing I had to tell them. Particularly since they could easily find out about it from everybody who'd been at Arndoerfer Realty around nine this morning.

This was going to be even more difficult than telling them about the lawsuit. "In the interest of being totally honest, totally up front, there *is* one more thing,"

I said. "It was just a passing comment, believe me, and at the time I said it, I was feeling a bit irritated with Bartlett for suing me."

I'd gotten Reed's and Constello's attention again. Reed stopped scribbling and Constello stopped petting his mustache, and both just looked at me.

"Yes?" Constello said.

"I didn't really mean anything by it," I went on.

Beside me, Reed took a deep breath. "Okay, okay," Reed said. His tone was impatient. "We understand."

I was almost sure by then, of course, that not only did Reed not understand, but the odds of his understanding were probably roughly equivalent to the odds of my winning the Kentucky lottery this week.

"I mean, I wouldn't want you two thinking that it was something when it was nothing—"

"Okay, okay," Reed said again.

I took another deep breath. "Well, I have to admit that this morning I did call Bartlett a 'lying, cheating, little weasel that deserves to be hit by a truck.'"

As soon as the words were out of my mouth, I decided I probably should've just taken my chances on anybody at Arndoerfer Realty telling the police what I'd said. Because this time Reed and Constello didn't just look alert. They looked fascinated.

"It didn't mean anything!" I hurried to add. "I was just blowing off a little steam, that's all!"

I had probably picked a bad time to bring all this up.

As I spoke, the paramedics had apparently just finished doing whatever they'd needed to do to Bartlett before he could be moved, and they'd gotten Bartlett all loaded onto a stretcher. So that, as luck would have it, Constello was repeating the words, " 'Hit by a truck,' you say," just as the paramedics carried Bartlett right past us and on out the front door.

It was not exactly a Kodak moment.

Neither was the one right after that.

Just as Bartlett was sailing out the front door, two other people were sailing in.

My heart sank when I saw them.

It was Marvin and Denise Carrico.

The people, no doubt, soon to be described in Reed's notes as "the owners of the crime scene."

I took one look at their outraged faces, and I began to wish that *I* was the one who was being carried out of here.

"What the *hell* is going on?"

For a man in his sixties, Marvin Carrico still had a yell strong enough to rattle the panes in the window behind me.

Chapter 5

Marvin Carrico's voice was like a sonic boom. *"What are all these people doing here?"*

A real estate agent is supposed to be adept at dealing with all sorts of ticklish situations. You're supposed to be able to more or less roll with the punches, think fast on your feet, and handle everything that comes your way with tact and diplomacy.

In fact, when you take a real estate course, your instructor often will give you several helpful tips on "Selling a Residence Because of Death or Divorce" and "What to Do When the Loan Is Refused," that sort of thing. I don't believe however, in any of the training manuals I've read, or in any of the real estate courses I've taken over the entire nine years I've been in this business, I have ever heard mentioned, "How to Explain the Gunshot Victim in the Living Room."

For some reason, it's never come up.

Maybe that's why for a long moment right after Marvin Carrico spoke, I couldn't think of a thing to say to him. I'd, no doubt, been inadequately prepared.

I did get to my feet, of course, as if I were going to answer, but when I opened my mouth, my mind went totally blank.

It didn't help any that Marvin Carrico was a fairly intimidating human being. He may have been in his early sixties, but he was also six feet four inches and at least 250 pounds. A manager of systems design—

whatever *that* is—at General Electric, Marvin always talked with the authoritative tone of someone who never questions for a moment that everybody in the immediate vicinity is hanging on his every word.

"I demand an explanation!" he was now saying. This last statement didn't just rattle the windowpanes—I'd say it rattled me a little, too. I couldn't seem to do anything but stand there, more or less gaping at him, while my mind scrambled for something to say.

Fortunately, as it turned out, I didn't have to say anything right away, because Detective Constello jumped in. Smoothing down his mustache one more time, Constello said in his soft eastern Kentucky accent, "There's been an accident, sir."

I turned to look at Constello. Why is it that the police always call something like this an accident? When as soon as they fully explain what has happened, everyone knows that it was not at all accidental? That, in fact, what was done was clearly done on purpose.

"An accident? I don't understand." Marvin has pink, round cheeks, not just bags under his eyes, but *luggage*, and his face is crisscrossed with more fine lines than a sheet of notebook paper. All these things you'd expect to see on the face of a man his age. What you don't expect to see is what's just above his face—Marvin's hair. Receding though it may be, it's a rich, dark brown.

To the question, "Does he, or doesn't he?" the answer in Marvin's case is clearly, "He does."

If there were any doubt about this, I would offer as Exhibit A the navy blue polo shirt Marvin was wearing. Marvin had left all the buttons at the collar unbuttoned, and quite a few very gray chest hairs were poking out.

Oh yes. He does, all right.

"What kind of an accident?" Marvin's tone was not friendly.

Marvin had probably left all his collar buttons open to show off the heavy gold necklace hanging around his neck. A chain that bulky had to be worth at least several hundred dollars.

Reed had gotten up, too, and his eyes were fixed on the chain when he answered. "Well, sir, there's been a shooting." I think the chain must've been a tip-off that Marvin was somebody who might have considerable standing in the community, because Reed's tone had changed a little. Jack Webb actually sounded apologetic.

"A shooting? Here? In my house? But how could that be?" Marvin looked from Reed to Constello and finally over at me, as if he expected answers from every one of us. Right away. In triplicate.

"You mean, that man they just carried out of here had been *shot*?" Up to this point, Denise Carrico had seemed content to let her husband do the talking, but apparently she could contain herself no longer. She moved forward to stand at her husband's side, her large blue eyes growing larger by the minute.

I stared at her. Denise Carrico is probably the only woman in America trying to look older than she is. As I mentioned before, she's in her early thirties—if indeed, she's that old—but her dark blond hair is so heavily frosted, from a distance it looks as gray as her husband's ought to be. Today she was wearing her hair pulled back from her face into a severe bun, and she was dressed in a long-skirted, sleeveless, floral print dress that would've looked very nice on my mother.

I halfway expected to see orthopedic shoes on her feet, but thank God, the woman had drawn the line somewhere. She was wearing white sandals.

"Oh my dear Lord!" Denise said. "Why, this—this is terrible!"

I was surprised. Up to then, I'd been under the impression that Denise was an uppity sort who had all the warmth of a dead mackerel, but maybe I was wrong. She seemed to be showing real compassion for old Bartlett.

At least, I thought so until Denise hurried on, "This is just awful! What on earth will the neighbors think?"

I blinked. Okay. So maybe I was right about the dead mackerel thing, after all.

Denise pulled at her husband's arm. "Marvin, this is going to be in the papers! Everybody's going to know that somebody was gunned down in our house!"

She made it sound as if the St. Valentine's Day Massacre had just taken place in their living room.

Marvin responded exactly the way I believe a lot of men would under similar circumstances. "Let me handle this," he said.

"But we don't even know that guy!" Denise said. She turned to pin me with an accusing look. "Who was he? What was he doing here? Were you showing him through the house?"

I'd been intending to answer her questions in the order they'd been asked, but Denise's last question gave me pause. Was she actually suggesting that I'd been showing Bartlett through her house *at gun point*?

While that would, no doubt, be an amazingly effective sales technique, surely Denise couldn't be serious.

I found my voice. "Denise, I don't know how he got in here. He was lying on your living room floor when we walked in."

Marvin was the one looking baffled now. "We? What do you mean, *we*?"

I just looked at him. Had he forgotten why I'd come here in the first place? Did the Carricos now believe that I'd just dropped by to wander through their house for the fun of it?

I gestured toward the dining room. "Two prospective buyers are with me," I said. Even from the foyer where the Carricos, the salt and pepper shakers, and

I were all standing, you could see Amy and Jack. There was no door separating the dining room from the living room any more than there was one separating the foyer from the living room. There was just another archway, so you could plainly see Jack and Amy standing over there, side by side. Both of them were looking this way.

Apparently, they'd heard the Carricos' arrival, and had moved to the entrance of the dining room to get a good look at whatever was going on. Both of them, I noticed, were standing as close to the entrance as they possibly could, and yet still be considered *in* the dining room.

In fact, it almost looked as if there were some kind of invisible barrier holding them there. Sort of like that invisible glass wall that mimes are always pretending separates them from their audience.

Apparently, if a policeman told the Bobbsey twins to wait in the dining room, they waited in the dining room. Period. Until either Reed or Constello told them differently, Amy and Jack were going to remain obediently on the other side of the mime wall.

When the Carricos glanced their way, Jack lifted a hand in greeting. "Hi," he said.

Marvin just stared at Jack for a moment, as if trying to figure out why these two young people appeared to be trapped in his dining room. "Hello," he said uncertainly, and then, he turned back to me. "How on earth could anybody get shot here? HOW? We don't even own a gun!"

That little statement seemed to grab both Reed's and Constello's attention. Their eyes were now riveted on Marvin.

"You have no guns at all?" Reed began scribbling away again in his little spiral notebook.

Denise's eyes got even wider when she saw Reed taking notes. "Well, *of course*, we don't have any guns!" She looked horrified that he'd even suggest such a thing.

Marvin gave Reed a withering look. "We're not the *sort* of people who have guns," he said.

From the contemptuous tone he used to say the word *sort*, you could easily get the impression that Marvin here believed that the gun-owning sort of person was a person far, far beneath him on the social ladder.

You had to kind of hand it to Marvin. He'd actually said this to a man who, no doubt, at that very moment had a gun on his person.

Reed didn't even blink. "You don't say," he said flatly.

Constello cleared his throat. "Do *you* own a gun?" he asked. Constello's eyes now rested on me.

So did Marvin's, Denise's, Reed's, Jack's, and Amy's.

All of them seemed to lean forward a little, waiting for my answer. Lord. You might think these people actually believed I was trigger-happy.

"No," I said. And yes, my tone was a little defensive. "I don't own a gun." I did not think it necessary to add that at one time I'd considered buying a little revolver to keep in the nightstand beside my bed. Particularly since I'm a single woman, living alone. Ultimately, I'd decided against it, though. As big a klutz as I am, I'd be a lot more likely to shoot myself accidentally than to shoot an intruder on purpose.

Not to mention, I had been paying attention when a recent news program had reported that, according to statistics, you were three times as likely to get shot yourself if there was a gun in your house. Which, when you think about it, certainly made sense.

I didn't particularly want to go into all this, and yet, everybody was still staring at me. I couldn't tell if they just didn't believe me, or if they were expecting me to elaborate. "I've never owned a gun," I added. "And—and I never intend to buy one."

That seemed to cover the subject nicely. I might've overdone it, though. The salt and pepper shakers seemed to be looking at me with real skepticism.

Marvin Carrico, however, apparently felt we'd covered the gun issue adequately. "So. Who was this guy who was shot?" he asked, looking from me to Reed and Constello and back again. "Does anybody know who he is?"

I guess I don't have to mention how much I hated to answer that question. "Well," I said, "as a matter of fact, I do know him."

Reed seemed delighted to put in his two cents at this point. He actually came close to smiling as he said, in his best Jack Webb, "The victim's name was Edward Bartlett, sir. He was an acquaintance of Mrs. Ridgway here."

Denise's eyes swiveled in my direction. "An *acquaintance*?"

I tried for an offhand shrug. "I barely knew him. I handled the sale of Bartlett's house a few months ago, and I sold him a new house."

"He was suing her," Constello put in.

I glared at him. Thanks so much, Constello. Wasn't there supposed to be some kind of rule about confidentiality in cases like this? Or did that only apply to dealings with people and their lawyers?

"*Suing?*" Denise said the word as if it were obscene. Her hand went to her throat, and she gave her husband a nervous glance.

Marvin, however, missed his wife's look. Mainly because he was glaring at me. "Suing you? The guy who was found shot in our living room was suing you?"

"Coincidentally enough," I said.

Marvin's eyes did not waver. Apparently he didn't believe in coincidences any more than Reed and Constello. "The guy who was found shot in *our* living room was suing *you*," he said again.

Marvin might've watched too many instant replays last winter, just like Jarvis.

I took a deep breath. There didn't seem any way to get around it. I had to go into the entire thing again right there, in front of everybody, while the salt and pepper shakers actually began to look a little bored. Before I'd finished explaining exactly why it was that Bartlett had seen fit to take legal action against me, Denise had started looking a little bored, too. In fact, just as I got to the part where Bartlett was obviously just doing this as part of a scam, Denise gave out with an impatient little sigh, stepped deftly around me, and started to move toward her living room.

"The whole thing will be cleared up in court," I said, more or less winding things up in a hurry.

Marvin was not looking nearly as upset as before, but he did look as if he wanted to ask me something more. At that moment, however, everybody's attention was abruptly diverted by Denise's high-pitched scream.

Apparently, the paramedics had not been anywhere near as careful with Bartlett as I had been. When they'd lifted Bartlett's body onto the stretcher and carried him out, they'd left a little memento of Bartlett's visit.

On the expanse of like-new, beige wool carpeting, you couldn't miss the crimson stain. The stain wasn't large, only about the size of a silver dollar, but it was right in the middle of the carpet so that it was very visible from the entrance of the living room.

I know this for a fact, because that's exactly where Denise was standing when she started to yell, "Oh my dear Lord in heaven, look what they've done to my beautiful carpet!"

Have I mentioned that Denise Carrico is one of the

Perfect People? There are not very many of these Perfect People around, but you run into one every once in a while. In my opinion, these People are the equivalent of aliens from outer space.

I've seen Denise Carrico at least ten different times now, and on every occasion she has never had so much as a strand of hair out of place. Her makeup is always perfectly applied, her clothes are always perfectly pressed, and her nails are always perfectly polished.

Denise, of course, makes me want to see lipstick smeared on her teeth.

Even now, as upset as she was, she stood with perfect posture and screamed in perfectly modulated tones, "It's ruined! My beautiful, beautiful carpet is completely ruined!"

This appeared to be my cue. I moved to her side. "Now, Denise, don't you worry. That stain'll come right out," I said. "Just put a little warm water on it, spray it with some stain remover like Resolve, rub it with a sponge, and it'll be gone just like that." I snapped my fingers.

Lord. I couldn't make up my mind which I sounded most like: Heloise, or a television commercial. In another moment, I'd be saying in an unnaturally enthusiastic voice, "*Yes!* The next time a gunshot victim bleeds into *your* carpet, reach for *Resolve!* One quick spray, and you'll never even know the victim was *there!*"

Denise apparently did not appreciate my unsolicited testimonial. She stared at me as if I were talking nonsense. "Me? You actually expect *me* to touch some total stranger's *blood*? You've *got* to be kidding."

Oh, for heaven's sake. The woman acted as if I'd suggested she lick it up.

"Well, of course, Denise, you'd wear rubber gloves," I said. "You certainly wouldn't—"

Denise interrupted, fixing me with an icy stare. "I

think the person responsible for this mess should be the one who cleans it up."

I blinked. There didn't seem to be any doubt as to exactly who Denise felt was the person responsible.

I cleared my throat. "You know, Denise, I don't think *Mr. Bartlett* will be in any condition to do house-cleaning for quite some time," I said.

Oh yes, I was being deliberately obtuse again. Believe it or not, there are not only men, but also some women in the world who, if you act incredibly stupid, will actually believe you're really that dumb.

Denise was obviously one of these women. She stared at me, apparently trying to decide whether I was intelligent enough to understand anything else she might want to say on the subject of carpet cleaning.

Denise didn't get a chance to say anything more, though, because in back of us, Marvin let out a muttered exclamation.

"Oh good Lord," he said. I turned to look, and found Marvin was now standing in his front door, staring out into his yard, an appalled look on his face.

I moved back into the foyer to see what it was that was making Marvin look suddenly almost as unwell as Bartlett. Over Marvin's shoulder, I watched a uniformed officer string a bright yellow tape all around the front yard. The tape had the words DO NOT CROSS—POLICE LINE printed on it in all capitals. The words repeated for the entire length of the tape.

Denise, unfortunately, had moved, too. She was now standing right behind Marvin, too. "Oh my God!" she yelled. "How long is that thing going to have to stay up?" She started out yelling her question at Reed and Constello, but she finished by yelling at me, "Oh, this is too much. We can't possibly show the house with the police *crawling* all over the place!"

The way she said the word *police* did not sound complimentary. In fact, you might've gotten the idea, particularly since she'd emphasized the word *crawling*, that Denise considered the police in the same category as roaches.

A quick glance at Reed and Constello told me they'd taken Denise's comments in the spirit in which they'd been offered. Jack Webb did not look pleased. Reed was now opening his mouth to speak, but I beat him to it.

Soothing frayed nerves, dealing with various conflicts that arise, and reassuring clients is part and parcel of a real estate agent's job. For the first time since I'd discovered Bartlett in the living room, I actually felt as if I were back on familiar territory.

"Denise," I put in quickly, "I don't think you have anything to worry about. I'm sure that caution tape won't be up a second longer than absolutely necessary."

I was, of course, lying through my teeth. I had no idea how long things like that stayed up. Judging from the looks on Reed's and Constello's faces, however, I'd say that if Denise didn't shut her mouth in a hurry, there was every chance that the yellow caution tape might still be up in the Carricos' yard when the first snow fell.

Denise might have to tell her neighbors it was part of her Christmas decorations.

"I'm *sure*," I went on, "that you want the police to have all the time they need to look into this, so that they can find out who did this terrible thing."

Denise's eyes were still like blue Frisbees, but she said, "Well, *of course*, I want them to catch who did this."

While I was calming Denise down, I decided that there was one other little thing that I probably shouldn't mention to either of the Carricos. I was not about to tell them that, in my considered opinion, Bartlett had not looked as if he were going to make it. Of course, my considered opinion was just that—

an opinion. I certainly didn't have a medical degree or anything. I could easily be wrong.

I *was* fairly certain, however, that I'd seen people laid out in funeral homes who'd looked a lot healthier than Bartlett when he left here.

I also wasn't about to tell the Carricos something else. I wasn't going to even *mention* the last house I'd listed that had had a murder committed there. This particular house was located out in Crestwood, in a subdivision called Eastridge, which was an even more desirable neighborhood than this one.

Unfortunately, the house itself became considerably less desirable after some woman apparently snapped there one night and shot her husband as he slept. After the woman was convicted, her family had put the place up for sale.

I'd taken the listing before I'd even realized that this was the house that had been on the news for months. The house had apparently been shown on all four local television stations several times, but dumb me, I had not made the connection.

Of course, in my defense, I must admit that wondering if a murder has recently been committed on the premises is not generally the first question that pops into my head when somebody wants to list their house. Usually, I'm too busy indicating just which dotted line they need to sign on.

I'd taken the Eastridge listing two years ago.

It was still on the market.

I cleared my throat, and purposely did not look in Marvin's or Denise's direction.

Oh no, I wasn't about to tell either one of them about the Eastridge house. There *was* such a thing as killing the messenger. The Carricos might try to strangle me with that yellow caution tape outside.

Chapter 6

Reed and Constello let me leave first. I was pretty sure that this was not a good sign. In fact, it made me feel the way you did back in high school, when you never wanted to be the first one to leave a party. Because you knew, the second you left, you'd be the one all the others were talking about.

Reed and Constello wouldn't even let me wait around to drive Amy and Jack back to Arndoerfer Realty.

"We'll drive them back," Constello said in his soft eastern Kentucky accent. That soft accent was beginning to sound ominous.

"But I'm heading right back there," I protested. "I'll be glad to wait around and drive them. *After* you've talked to them, of course."

Reed was already shaking his white-blond head before I'd even finished. "That won't be necessary, Mrs. Ridgway," he said. Jack Webb sounded as if the subject was closed.

"We wouldn't want to inconvenience you," Constello said, smoothing his dark mustache again. "In fact, we'd be pleased as punch to drive them back ourselves. Don't you worry about it."

Actually, making sure that Jack and Amy got back to their car was the least of my worries. Particularly after Reed added, "By the way, Mrs. Ridgway, you're not planning on leaving town any time soon, are you?"

Oh yes, after that, I'd say Jack and Amy's transportation problems were way down on the old worry list. In fact, as I stepped over the yellow caution tape encircling the Carricos' front yard, and headed toward my Tercel parked in their driveway, Jack and Amy didn't even enter my mind. I was too busy trying not to panic.

All the way back to Arndoerfer Realty, I tried to tell myself reassuring things, like: Okay, Schuyler, there's no use getting all upset. After all, just because you were the *only* person in the house who seems to have any connection whatsoever to Bartlett, and just because you publicly threatened the guy on the very day he was shot, and just because you have this terrific reason to be very angry with Bartlett—all of this is certainly no reason whatsoever to even *think* that the police could possibly suspect that you were the one who'd shot him.

Uh-huh.

This line of thinking, oddly enough, was not a bit reassuring. By the time I was pulling into the Arndoerfer Realty parking lot, my stomach felt as if I'd swallowed burning rocks.

It occurred to me then that I hadn't had anything to eat since breakfast, hours ago, but I didn't think it would be a good idea to put anything solid on top of burning rocks. Besides, I didn't feel the least bit hungry.

Thank God Jarvis was not still in the office when I returned. I wasn't sure what I would've done if, as soon as I walked through the front door, Jarvis had been there, all ready to continue our earlier conversation. All ready to insist once again that I settle Bartlett's lawsuit out of court.

I was so rattled, I might've actually blurted out,

"Look, Jarvis, I don't think suing us is the top thing on Bartlett's mind right now."

Lord knows, everybody, no doubt, was going to read all about what had happened at the Carricos' in tomorrow's papers. Surely, tomorrow would be soon enough to be pumped for details.

As it happened, only Barbi Lundergan was still there when I walked in, and she didn't even look up as I headed straight toward my desk and dropped my purse on top.

Barbi ignoring me was not exactly a surprise. The woman has not been overly friendly ever since I started dating Matthias. Overly *un*friendly, in fact, is what Barbi has been.

Matthia's full name, you see, is Matthias Cross. That's right, *Cross*, as in Ephraim Cross, the man I'd never met who'd left me over a hundred thousand dollars in his will and whose death had first brought the salt and pepper shakers into my life.

His death had also brought Matthias into my life. As Ephraim Cross's only son, Matthias had showed up here in my office shortly after his father's death all ready to make sure I got a front-row seat in the electric chair. It had taken a little while to convince Matthias that I'd had nothing whatsoever to do with what had happened to his dad.

Lord. Back then, if you'd told me that Matthias and I would end up romantically involved, I wouldn't have believed you.

Barbi Lundergan wouldn't have believed you, either. In fact, she'd done just about everything to attract Matthias's attention except dance naked in front of him.

And I think Barbi probably would've done that if she'd thought of it.

It is probably less than kind of me to say—because Matthias is, without a doubt, a very attractive man—

but in my opinion, Barbi has always been a lot more attracted by Matthias's very wealthy family than she was by Matthias himself. One reason I feel this way is something Barbi herself said just before Matthias turned up on the Arndoerfer Realty doorstep. "The man for me has got to have oodles of money," she'd told me.

That was sort of a tip-off.

I've tried to tell Barbi that Matthias is not the wealthy man a lot of people seem to think he is. His family's money is now completely in the hands of his mother, and Matthias prides himself on being self-supporting. In fact, I believe his exact words were, "I've never taken one thin dime from my parents, and I never intend to."

Barbi, however, won't listen. The only part she's ever heard is the wealthy-family part.

Come to think of it, I guess she's also heard the part where Matthias and I started dating. In fact, when it became obvious that Matthias and I were going out, Barbi immediately started giving me the silent treatment.

I feel kind of bad about it. Before Matthias showed up, Barbi and I had been pretty good friends. I suppose it had been almost inevitable that she and I would get to be friends. We did have quite a lot in common. Barbi and I were both real estate agents, we were both divorced, we were even close to the same age—even though Barbi would be quick to tell you that she's a mere thirty-nine to my all-but-elderly forty-two. She and I both have children about the same age, and she and I both liked to do a lot of the same things. Like have dinner together and share horror stories about our ex's.

Barbi also always used to do the cutest thing. She always referred to Ed, my ex-husband, as "Mr. Ed."

What she called *her* ex-husband isn't printable, but I did enjoy hearing what she called mine.

When you come right down to it, I suppose there's nothing that can bring two women together faster than getting together and discussing what jerks their ex-husbands happen to be. It's a warm, bonding kind of thing.

The minute Matthias came into the picture, however, all that became a thing of the past. Suddenly Barbi no longer viewed me as a friend, but as a competitor.

And once Matthias began to concentrate all his attention in my direction, Barbi actually seemed to view me as an enemy.

Isn't it a shame that this kind of thing happens so often? That men so often come between women? And that, in situations like this, where the man ends up choosing one woman over another, it's always the woman chosen who gets blamed?

I don't get it. It's as if everybody just assumes that a man can't help himself. Apparently, the poor baby is totally at the mercy of his hormones and *must* act accordingly—a condition I believe I've often heard several of my friends describe as "thinking with the little head."

I suppose then it naturally follows that—since all these poor, hormone-ridden men can't be held responsible—it's the women who are left to take the blame. I've finally concluded that this must be how things work, and yet, for the life of me, I still don't understand it. Why on earth isn't Barbi mad at Matthias? *He's* the one who decided against her, not me.

Barbi obviously does not look at it this way. She's made it abundantly clear that I've poached on her territory, and that it is without a doubt *all* my fault that Matthias ended up attracted to me, instead of to her.

Usually Barbi's sullen silence gets on my nerves, but after spending a majority of the day so far with the Carricos, the Bobbsey twins, and the salt and pepper shakers, I was actually glad Barbi was in no mood to chat.

For once, neither was I.

What I was in a mood for, more than anything else, was a drink. Not the kind you might think. I didn't want one with alcohol. I wanted one with the Three Cs: calories, caffeine, and carbonation. I wanted a Coke. Bad. A long, tall Coke heavy on the ice.

I walked straight past Barbi and into the tiny kitchen in the back. There I opened the refrigerator, took out one of the plastic two-liter bottles of Coke I always keep in there for just such an emergency, and I poured myself a tall one.

It made me feel better just listening to the thing fizz.

I guess you could say I'm a Coke-a-holic. I start off my day with a couple glasses of Coke instead of a couple cups of coffee, and any time I'm upset or nervous, the first thing I reach for is a long, tall glass of brown bubbly. Coke, for me, is sort of like a liquid pacifier.

I almost downed the entire glass in one, long gulp. Then I refilled it and carried it out to my desk. Where I found a fairly good-sized stack of pink "While You Were Out" messages waiting for me.

A couple of the messages were from people calling for information on houses I had listed. All the rest, however, were from two particular real estate agents.

These were the agents who'd listed the two other houses I'd intended to show Amy and Jack this morning after we finished with the Carrico house.

I read those messages, and I immediately took another long, long sip of Coke.

Oops. After what had happened, I'd completely forgotten to call these people and cancel.

When I'd made the other two appointments, I'd allowed an hour to look through the Carrico house. So the messages from the first real estate agent started at about 10:15, repeating every fifteen minutes or so until she'd finally given up a little over an hour later.

Her final note had an accusatory tone: WE'VE BEEN WAITING MORE THAN AN HOUR. PLEASE CALL US!

The second agent's first note started out with an irritated tone: WE ARE WAITING! His second note said simply: WE ARE STILL WAITING!! This guy apparently hadn't been anywhere near as long-suffering as the first. He'd given up after only forty-five minutes. His last note had been succinct: WHERE THE HELL ARE YOU?!!

I just stared at the notes for a long moment. Getting stood up happens to a real estate agent all the time. Prospects change their mind, or they fall in love with the house they're shown just before yours, or sometimes, you just get dates and times confused. It happens.

Evidently, however, it had never happened to either of these two agents. Both of them fairly frosted up the phone line when I called to apologize.

Of course, I suppose I did sound rather lame. I didn't want to tell either of them the truth—which was, I would've called but I was too busy trying to convince the police that I hadn't shot anybody lately—so all I said was that I'd gotten the dates mixed up. The guy who'd left me the "Where the hell—?" note actually had the nerve to mumble something about how "we all needed to be more professional."

In my opinion, I sounded extremely professional as I said, "We certainly do." I didn't add the terribly *un*professional "You asshole" until after I'd hung up. And, even then, I only said it under my breath.

After making those two phone calls, and with the kind of morning I'd had, the rest of the afternoon was a breeze. I returned the other calls, took care of all the paperwork that had accumulated on my desk, updated listings, went over loan applications, all the while sipping on my carbonated pacifier.

The entire time I was working, Barbi didn't so much as glance in my direction. Even when Reed and Constello pulled up outside, Jack and Amy got out, and they headed across the parking lot toward their car, Barbi didn't say a word to me.

Barbi must've seen Jack and Amy, too. With the front door standing wide open as always, you couldn't miss the two of them. I myself noticed that Jack and Amy didn't even glance in the direction of Arndoerfer Realty. What they did was practically run toward their car as soon as the salt and pepper shakers released them.

You might've thought that Barbi would've been curious as to why this couple who'd left early this morning with *me* had returned hours later with the police.

Reed and Constello were driving an unmarked car, but Barbi had met the two of them before. When they'd investigated the murder of Matthias's father, the salt and pepper shakers had questioned everybody in the office.

Of course, Barbi *was* sitting clear across the room. Maybe she hadn't gotten a good look at Reed and Constello before they pulled away.

Still, she *had* to have seen Jack and Amy.

Apparently, even if she did think something was odd, though, Barbi wasn't going to stoop to asking me about it.

Break my heart, I might add.

From where I was sitting at my own desk just to the left of the front door, I watched the Bobbsey twins all but peal out of the parking lot.

I took a deep breath. And got up to refill my Coke.

Oh well. It looked to me as if there was an excellent chance that I'd never hear from Jack and Amy again.

Not that I blamed them. If being shown a gunshot victim and ending up having to talk at length to the police wasn't enough to make you want to start shopping for a new real estate agent, I'd say nothing was.

I returned to the paperwork on my desk, grateful all over again that I didn't have to talk to anybody. I could just concentrate on working—and moping.

By the time my desk was clear, though, I was feeling somewhat different. By then, with Barbi long gone, I was ready to talk to somebody about what had happened.

Maybe that somebody would even tell me I was worrying needlessly.

The somebody I had in mind, of course, was Matthias. As I mentioned earlier, we'd already planned a quiet evening together at my place. Matthias doing the cooking, of course.

I'm the first to admit I'm the world's worst cook. I blame it on my mother. When everybody else's mom was teaching them how to cook, mine was teaching me how to open and heat.

I'm hell with a can opener.

My house is on Harvard Drive, usually about a fifteen-minute drive this time of day. Today I made it in ten. Matthias was just pulling up in front of my house when I drove up. Matthias drives this ancient, beat-up green MGB that he's supposed to be restoring. In my opinion, restoring is not the word for what this car needs. *Reviving* would be more accurate.

The thing was giving off death rattles as Matthias coasted to a stop.

What on earth Matthias sees in that car is beyond me, but then again I'm not sure what he sees in me, either. As he got out of the Death Mobile, carrying an armful of groceries, Matthias gave me a quick wink and said, "Hi, Beautiful."

I am not beautiful. While small children do not run screaming at the sight of me, I would never describe myself as anywhere even close to beautiful. My brown hair is too blah, my brown eyes too big, and even though—as I also mentioned earlier—I weigh a mere 128 these days, I really could stand to lose five pounds or more.

If Matthias, however, wanted to call me "Beautiful," I wasn't about to argue with him.

Just looking at him made me think that maybe earlier I'd been wrong about Barbi. Maybe it wasn't just his money she was after. Dressed in a blue chambray shirt, faded jeans, and scuffed boots, Matthias at that moment didn't look at all like the college professor he was. He looked like the Marlboro Man.

A Marlboro Man who doesn't smoke.

And who's six three, with very broad shoulders, very green eyes, and shaggy brown hair that almost touches his shoulders. Matthias also has the distinction of being the only man I've ever gone out with who had a beard. A thick, neatly clipped one that I love running my fingers through.

Matthias, at forty-one, also has another distinction—that of being almost exactly a year younger than me. I might've actually considered myself a cradle-robber, except, let's face it, Marvin Carrico could show me how it's done.

My heart speeded up a little when Matthias smiled at me. "Ready for dinner, sweetheart?" he said. Like I mentioned earlier, Matthias has never said he loves me, but he does call me all these endearing names.

I can't say I mind hearing them.

I also can't say I mind the way he always gives me a long, long kiss the second he sees me.

By the time he and I got inside my front door, I'd

almost forgotten whatever that silly thing was that I'd been so worried about.

Matthias sure can kiss.

He also sure can cook. Being the culinary expert that I am, I had no idea what in the world he was making. I did know that it involved strips of round steak, and garlic butter, and extra wide noodles. And a lot of other things that Matthias found in my kitchen cupboards.

Matthias has done wonders for my kitchen. Before Matthias came into my life, I referred to my kitchen as The-Room-I-Never-Use. For me, my kitchen mainly consisted of a microwave, a stack of discount coupons for every restaurant within a ten-mile radius, and a list of the phone numbers of take-out places in the immediate neighborhood.

Now, wonder of wonders, there's actually food in there. And spices. And things like spatulas. And colanders. And utensils I'd previously only seen in magazines.

Matthias seemed to have used every one of these utensils by the time he'd finished getting Whatever-It-Was to bubble merrily on my stove. While he was using utensils, I was making what I make best. The specialty of my house.

That's right. Two large Cokes heavy on the ice.

Once we'd both finished making our specialties, Matthias and I headed into my dining room.

I think, up to that moment, I'd showed real restraint. In fact, I waited until Matthias and I were both seated at my dining-room table, ready to dig into the Whatever-It-Was steaming in front of us, before I blurted out what had happened.

Matthias's reaction, at first, was exactly what I wanted to hear. *"Wha-a-at?"* he said. He'd been about to put a heavily laden fork of Whatever into his mouth, but he put it back down on his plate with a clatter. "*You* witnessed a shooting? Oh my God! How terrible! Are you okay?"

I almost smiled, that's how much I was enjoying being fussed over. I decided, however, that smiling while I was telling such an awful tale would probably hurt my credibility. Not to mention, it might make Matthias stop fussing. "Well," I said, "I didn't exactly witness the shooting itself." I went on then, explaining in detail how I'd discovered poor Bartlett, and what Bartlett had said to me.

It was at this point that Matthias's reaction took a definite downturn. For a long moment he just looked at me. Finally, he said, "You really think that guy said 'groan,' and then he groaned?"

I nodded. "That's what he said, Matthias. I heard him."

Matthias shook his shaggy head. "Well, you must've heard him wrong." Matthias was now almost talking to himself. "And if you misunderstood that part, then you might've possibly misunderstood the part where the guy said it had been Porter Meredith's girlfriend who'd shot him."

I cleared my throat. "Matthias, I heard what I heard."

Matthias had gone ahead now and taken a bite, so his mouth was full when he answered. "Hmmm," he said.

That "hmmm" sounded skeptical to me.

The rest of what Matthias said after that sounded skeptical, too. Would you believe, Matthias actually began to go over every single thing I'd said, bit by bit, methodically analyzing it? "Maybe Bartlett didn't say 'groan' at all," Matthias said, scratching his beard speculatively. "Maybe what he said was 'groin.' Maybe he was trying to tell you that he was experiencing severe pain in his groin. That would explain why Bartlett groaned right after he said it, too."

It was now my turn to stare at Matthias. "Matthias, do you really believe that a man I hardly knew would use his last ounce of strength to tell me about his groin?"

If this was so, what should I expect next? Strangers on the street stopping me to discuss their prostates?

Matthias shrugged. "Well, it makes about as much sense as him saying 'groan' and then groaning." His tone was defensive.

I cleared my throat again. I couldn't believe my own boyfriend was having doubts about what I'd just told him. Hell, he wasn't any better than the salt and pepper shakers.

I leaned forward. "Matthias,"—and yes, my voice here might've been a bit testy—"I've just spent a good part of this day trying to convince the police that I heard what I heard. And, I'm telling you, *I heard what I heard.*"

Matthias is no dummy. He blinked once, swallowed what he had in his mouth, and then said, "You know, you haven't eaten a bite." He sounded as if it had just occurred to him. More or less, out of the blue. He gestured toward my plate. "Here, try some, and tell me if you like it."

I, of course, am no dummy, either. I refused to have the subject changed on me that easily. "Matthias," I said, "Edward Bartlett told me that it was—"

At that moment, my telephone started ringing. Matthias, oddly enough, actually looked relieved that our little chat had been interrupted.

My answering machine is on a table in my living room. My living room is connected to my dining room by an archway much like the Carricos', so from where I was sitting, I could hear every word the caller spoke. I'd fully intended letting my answering machine just take a message, but when I recognized the near-hysterical voice, I took a deep breath, put my napkin beside my plate, and headed into the living room.

Denise Carrico was in mid-yell when I picked up. "Schuyler, it's terrible! It's just terrible!"

"Denise," I said, interrupting her, "how nice to hear from you."

I was, of course, lying through every one of my teeth.

There was a series of clicking sounds while my answering machine turned itself off, and then I heard Denise again. Her voice had escalated into a near-shriek. "Have you heard? It was just on the evening news!"

When somebody sounds near hysteria, I try to stay ultracalm. To sort of defuse the situation. "What are you talking about?" I said. I believe I sounded almost relaxed. "What was on the news?"

The defusing hadn't worked. Denise sounded, if anything, even more upset. "Why, that—that Edward Bartlett person! He *died* in the emergency room!"

My stomach wrenched.

Staying ultracalm might be out of the question.

Chapter 7

Edward Bartlett was dead? I know I'd already told myself that he probably was not going to make it, but still, hearing that he really had died was a shock. I had to swallow once before I could answer. "No," I told Denise, "I hadn't heard."

"Well, I just don't see how this could've happened!" Denise went on. For one of the Perfect People, she sounded absolutely frazzled.

I, of course, assumed that she was talking about poor Bartlett's demise, so I said, "Well, Denise, sometimes there isn't anything they can do to save—"

Denise interrupted me. "I don't see how on earth that guy could've gotten shot in *our* house," she said. "We always lock our doors. *Always*." She paused for a moment, and her tone changed. "The only way it could've happened, the *only* way, is that *some*body must've gotten careless and left the door unlocked."

It was obvious exactly who Denise thought that somebody was. "Denise," I said, "I didn't leave any of your doors unlocked. In fact, I remember very clearly getting the key out from under your cat, and unlocking your front door. Or else I myself wouldn't have been able to get in."

Denise's voice was now a whine. "Well, I don't see how in the world that guy could possibly have gotten into our house!"

I was fairly certain it was now Denise who was

being deliberately obtuse. After all, she *did* keep a door key under a ceramic cat on her front porch. Where anybody could get to it.

And her house *was* a Multiple Listing. Meaning that, although the Carricos had signed an exclusive contract with me to list their home for sale, the Carrico residence could be shown by any real estate agent in this area who subscribed to the Multiple Listing service. If, indeed, it turned out that one of these other agents actually made the sale, I—as the listing agent—and this other agent would split the commission 50/50.

This was pretty much how Multiple Listings worked. Having explained how they worked to both her and her husband at some length, I was pretty sure Denise was well aware of this.

So, it certainly wouldn't be a *stretch* for her to figure out that Bartlett could've hidden somewhere, watched either me or one of the other real estate agents go into her house, and easily found out where her house key was hidden.

Once Bartlett had located the key, he could've unlocked the front door, opened it, and then returned the key exactly where he'd found it. Under the cat once again. So that it would still be there when I arrived later with Jack and Amy.

What's more, as I mentioned earlier, the Carrico house *had* been on the market for almost a week now. There had already been quite a bit of interest in the property. So the Carricos' neighbors must have gotten used to seeing strangers going in and out of the house by now. Probably nobody would even have noticed Bartlett entering the house. What's more, if anybody *had* noticed, they would've just assumed that Bartlett was one more real estate agent getting ready to show the house.

Oh yes, Bartlett's getting into the house would've been a cakewalk.

And yet, even if you accepted that Bartlett really had done such a thing, there was still the question of why? Why on earth would Bartlett have wanted to get into the Carrico house in the first place? Particularly if, as both Carricos insisted, Bartlett didn't even know either one of them?

What could Bartlett have been up to?

Knowing the little weasel—not to be talking ill of the dead, God rest his soul, but let's be honest here—I wouldn't put anything past him. Hell, Bartlett could even have been *burglarizing* the Carrico house, for all I knew.

Now that was a thought. Could Bartlett have broken in and been interrupted by the Carricos themselves? Could the Carricos have shot him *before* they'd left their home earlier today?

And yet, if that had happened, wouldn't Denise and Marvin have just come forward and told the police the truth? Surely, a justifiable homicide would be better to have in your living room than an unsolved murder.

"Denise," I began, "leaving your key under the cat was probably not the best "

Denise must've known where I was going with this, because suddenly, she seemed anxious to cut our conversation shut. "My dear, I just wanted to let you know Mr. Bartlett died—that's the only reason I called." With that, Denise abruptly hung up.

I stared at the receiver. At that moment I decided I really hate being referred to as "my dear" by somebody nearly young enough to be my daughter.

I hung up the phone and sighed. It seemed obvious that if the Carricos could, they would be going the way I suspected Amy and Jack had already gone.

Denise certainly sounded as if she were of the opinion that if she ever laid eyes on me again, it would be too soon.

Unlike Jack and Amy, however, the Carricos *had* signed the aforementioned contract with me—a contract not due to expire for another three months. So the Carricos were stuck with me for a while. I had no doubt, however, that I could kiss a renewal goodbye.

Matthias must've decided from the look on my face that the phone call was something I didn't want to discuss. "Here," he said, as I resumed my seat at the table, "eat your dinner." He gave my plate a little push in my direction. "It's getting cold."

I didn't have the chance to even take so much as one bite, though. I'd just lifted my fork and aimed it toward my mouth when the ringing began.

This time it wasn't my phone ringing. It was my doorbell. It sounded as if somebody were standing on my front porch, leaning on the button.

I pushed back from the table so fast, my chair almost tipped over. "All right!" I yelled, "I'm coming!" This getting interrupted in the middle of dinner was getting old fast.

Either the doorbell-abuser couldn't hear me over the noise the bell was making, or else he was enjoying too much annoying the hell out of me. The bell kept chiming until I turned on my porch light and opened my front door.

Standing there, her face illuminated by the light, was a very tall, very thin, very angry woman.

Who, incidentally, was a total stranger.

"Yes?" I said.

The woman was dressed in a coral-colored Ellen Tracy silk suit that I remembered seeing in the designer section of Bacon's, a local clothing store. I'd loved the entire outfit right up until the moment I saw the price tag. Then, of course, having never paid that much for anything that didn't have a motor, I'd blanched.

The second I spoke, the woman crossed her arms across her chest and shifted her weight from one foot to another. "I'm Virginia Kenyon," she said.

From the way she said her name—and from the way she was giving me a level, blue-eyed look—I knew her name was supposed to mean something to me.

It didn't.

I continued to stare at her. Her copper-colored hair was done in a cut that a lot of women are wearing these days—neo-Kathie Lee. Parted on one side, with wispy bangs ending at her brows, it ruffled flatteringly back from her face. Even in the less than ideal light, I could tell that Virginia's makeup was perfectly applied, her lipstick perfectly matched her nails, and not so much as a wrinkle marred the perfect drape of her suit.

Good Lord. It was another one of the Perfect People. Counting Denise, I'd seen two in one day. What was this, an invasion?

"I'm *Virginia Kenyon*," the woman repeated. She put a little extra emphasis on her name this time.

I continued to stare at her blankly.

"Look, Schuyler, you can drop the act," Virginia said. "You know perfectly well who I am."

Having not been in all that good a mood before I opened my front door, I believe I was being more than patient. "And who exactly is that?" I said.

Virginia, on the other hand, was not being the least bit patient. She made an ugly sound in the back of her throat. "I'm Porter Meredith's girlfriend!" she snapped.

Well, now, *that* certainly cleared things up.

I immediately nodded, peering at her even more closely. Why, of course, I thought, *you're* the woman who murdered Edward Bartlett.

Fortunately, I stopped myself before I said this aloud. Something must've shown on my face, though, because Virginia Kenyon's eyes blazed. "That's right. I'm the girlfriend who replaced you!"

I supposed that was one way of looking at it.

Virginia's tone was getting angrier and angrier. "Do you have any idea what I've been doing for the last two hours?"

I blinked. If this was a guessing game, I was pretty sure I didn't want to play.

"I've been talking to the police!" Virginia said the last word much like Denise Carrico had said it. With considerable distaste. Evidently, the Perfect People are not all that appreciative of our boys in blue. A thing like this could probably really hurt the salt and pepper shakers' feelings. "And do you know *why* the police wanted to talk to me?"

I decided it wasn't any more necessary for me to answer this question than it had been for me to answer the first one. I continued to stare.

"Because *you* told them," Virginia said, "that I shot Edward Bartlett!"

I held up my hand. "Now wait a minute," I said. "I didn't tell them anything. All I did was repeat what *I* was told. That's all."

This was, no doubt, a subtle distinction, but I thought a valid one.

Virginia evidently was not one for subtleties. "You accused me of being a murderer!"

I shook my head. "Oh, no, you're wrong. *I* wasn't making any accusations. It was *Bartlett* who accused you. Not me."

Virginia made that ugly sound in her throat again. "Sez you!" she said.

Can you believe it? A woman in a suit that expensive actually said, "Sez you."

I went from shaking my head no to nodding my head yes. "That's right," I said. "That *is* exactly what I say."

I hoped I was making sense. When I get angry, sometimes I don't. And old Virginia here was beginning to make me angry. She'd interrupted my dinner for *this*?

"I told the police what Bartlett told me," I said. "I just repeated what I heard, nothing more."

Two bright spots of color made Virginia's cheeks close to the color of her suit. "Well then, you must've heard wrong!" For a moment, apparently, Virginia herself was so overcome with anger, she couldn't speak. Her eyes bulged. Then, unfortunately, she found her voice again. "I came over here to tell you that if you persist in spreading these vicious lies about me, I'm going to sue you for slander! I am!"

I couldn't believe it. Here I'd just gotten rid of one lawsuit—in a manner of speaking—and now I was being threatened with another. Lord. I was getting to be a lawyer's dream. A walking caseload. I took a deep breath and tried to swallow my own temper. "Look, Miss Kenyon," I said, "I'm sure you don't have anything to worry about. Surely the police wouldn't suspect you of Bartlett's murder unless you actually had a motive."

I said this to be reassuring, and to more or less pour oil on troubled waters.

Virginia's waters, however, remained terribly troubled. If anything, she looked as if I'd slapped her.

Drawing her arms even tighter to her body, as if she were giving herself a hug, she lifted her chin. "I'll have you know that Edward Bartlett is *not* the sort of person that *I* associate with." Her perfect mouth twisted with distaste. "He was a seedy, smarmy little man who handled legal cases for the lowest of the low—the scum of the earth."

I blinked again. I certainly hoped that nobody called on Virginia here to give Bartlett's eulogy.

"The fact was," Virginia was going on, "I barely even knew Edward." She paused and then thought to add, "*And* he was only a very distant acquaintance of

Porter's." She gave her Kathie Lee hair a toss, and then sniffed, "Porter and I move in more—shall we say?—*patrician* circles."

Patrician? Where did Virginia think she was? Ancient Rome?

Somehow, I couldn't quite picture her at a toga party.

I also couldn't help wondering if Virginia was lying. For somebody who moved in other circles, Virginia did seem to know an awful lot about Bartlett.

It also didn't escape my notice that she referred to him by his first name.

Matthias must've decided that I was not ever coming back to the table unless he came and got me. At that moment he appeared right in back of me. "Is there a problem?" he said, looking first at me and then at Virginia.

I wasn't sure if he was directing his question to me or Miss Perfect on my porch, but apparently, Virginia didn't care. She jumped right in. "I'll say there's a problem," she said. "It's your girlfriend here!"

I blinked once again at that one. While I did refer to Matthias in my thoughts as my boyfriend, I had never called him that to his face. In fact, I'd say that Matthias and I had gone to some lengths not to define our relationship just yet, and now here was Virginia thoughtfully doing it for us.

How kind of her.

At least Matthias didn't flinch when she called me his girlfriend. In fact, what he did was to put his hand rather comfortingly on my shoulder. "What," he said, "has *my girlfriend* been doing?"

I did notice that Matthias seemed to put a little extra emphasis on the words *my girlfriend*. Or was I imagining this?

"She's been spreading vicious, hateful lies about me, *that's* what she's been doing!" Virginia said, staring at Matthias over my shoulder. "And you know why? Because *I'm* the one who's got Porter now!"

"What?" I said. It was all I could do to keep my mouth from dropping open.

Virginia was nodding emphatically. "That's right, *I'm* the one Porter chose over you, and you just can't stand it, can you?"

Good Lord. Porter and I had only dated two months, for God's sake. Virginia was making it sound as if we'd been married. It was my turn now to fold my arms across my chest. "Virginia," I said, "I don't give a damn who Porter is dating."

Virginia smirked. "Oh *sure*, that's what you say now in front of your *new* boyfriend!"

This time I didn't blink when she said the word.

"I've already told Porter how spiteful you've been," Virginia was hurrying on, "and exactly what you said about me to the police. I have! I phoned Porter from the police station, and I phoned him again just before I came here. I told him everything! Don't you think I haven't!"

I just looked at her. The woman was talking nonsense. "Virginia, I don't care what you've told Porter—"

Virginia was clearly not listening. Leaning forward, she said, "That's right, Schuyler, I am *very* well aware what your relationship with Porter once was." She nodded her head again, her Kathie Lee curls bouncing energetically. "Porter has told me all about it. He's also told me just how vindictive you've been acting ever since he broke up with you!"

This time I couldn't help it. My mouth did drop open. "Wha-a-at? What do you mean, how vindictive I've—" In the middle of saying this, however, something else Virginia had just said struck me. "Wait a minute, Porter broke up with *me*?" I took a deep breath. "Virginia, I don't know what you've been told, but I haven't spoken to Porter in months. And it was the other way around. *I* broke up with him."

Virginia's reaction was not what I might've hoped. She snickered.

"Uh-huh. *Right*," she said sarcastically, just before she went back to staring at Matthias over my shoulder. "Are you listening to this shit?" she asked him. "Have you ever heard such shit in your life?"

For a woman in such high-class clothes, she certainly had a low-class mouth. Maybe she wasn't one of the Perfect People, after all.

Matthias evidently thought Virginia expected him to answer her last two questions, because he started to say, "Look, there's no call to—"

Matthias sounded as if he, too, was beginning to lose his temper.

Before Matthias could finish what he was saying, though, Virginia interrupted him. "Do you really know the woman you've been dating?" Virginia took a step forward, jabbing a manicured finger in the direction of my nose. "Are you aware how this woman treats ex-boyfriends? *And* their new girlfriends?"

The woman was talking nonsense again. "Virginia," I said, "I don't have any idea what you're talking about."

"Okay, I'll make myself extremely clear." Looking straight at Matthias, Virginia said loudly, "Schuyler here is a real psycho."

I just looked at her. Gosh, thanks, Virginia, for clarifying things. That *was* a big help.

One thing that wasn't clarified, however, was *why* she was doing this. Did Virginia have some kind of vendetta against me simply because I'd dated Porter once? If that were true, she was going to end up having a vendetta against half the city of Louisville.

Lord. The ex-girlfriends of Porter Meredith could form a support group.

That might explain Virginia's actions, but what

about Porter's? If Virginia was telling the truth, then Porter had lied to her about me. Why? Was he paying me back for breaking up with him? He certainly hadn't acted upset at the time. Our parting had, in fact, just seemed like an idea whose time had come.

And, even if Porter *had* been bothered by our breaking up more than he'd let on, now he had Virginia. Why would he still be angry with me at this late date?

Virginia was now pointing a manicured finger at Matthias's nose. "You know what they say—Love is blind?" Virginia paused, and when she spoke again, her voice was shaking with emotion. "Well, all I can say is, you'd better get your eyes checked!"

With that, Virginia wheeled on her coral-colored designer heels and stomped off.

Leaving me, of course, standing there in my doorway, with Matthias right in back of me. I sort of hated to turn around and face him.

I had to ask myself, if I were in his place, would I believe what Virginia had just said? Or would I just put it all down to the ravings of a clearly upset and obviously misinformed female?

I couldn't help but wonder.

After all, as I mentioned earlier, Matthias and I had only been dating three months. If I thought this wasn't enough time to decide if you were really in love with a person, it probably also wasn't enough time to be totally sure what another person could be capable of either.

Once Virginia had gotten into her shiny blue Mercedes and pealed off down the street, I did turn around, only to find Matthias looking just like he always seemed to look. Warm, and sweet, and definitely handsome.

"Well," he said, "it's easy to see how a woman with a temper like *that* could be capable of committing murder."

That's all he said. Which should've made me feel better.

Matthias also didn't question me at all about any of the things Virginia had said. In fact, if I'd wanted to, I could've believed that he'd immediately dismissed everything Virginia had said as patently untrue.

And yet, I continued to wonder. All through dinner. The Whatever-It-Was still tasted awfully good, even if it had gotten a little cold. After we polished almost all of it off, Matthias started cleaning up. Just like he always does.

Matthias collected our dirty dishes, went into my kitchen, and loaded up the dishwasher. Then he filled the sink, added detergent, and started scrubbing off my stove and cabinets. Just, as I said, like always. Matthias actually cleans as if it were the most natural thing to do in the world.

If my ex-husband Ed had ever cleaned up after dinner, he'd have made a big production of it. "Do you see what I'm doing here?" he would've said. "Do you? *I'm cleaning.* I'm *actually helping you out* right this minute. That's the kind of guy I am. *Helpful.* That's me, all right."

Ed probably would've insisted that I phone both our mothers and tell *them* how wonderful he was.

Matthias actually acts as if he doesn't even realize he's cleaning. I mean it. He keeps right on talking to you about one thing and another the entire time he's scrubbing and polishing and putting things away.

Can you believe this man is *divorced*? I certainly can't imagine how a thing like that could've happened, but Matthias and his ex-wife Barbara have actually been divorced for over eight years now. Right after everything was final, according to Matthias, Barbara took their daughter, Emily, and moved back to Boston to be near Barbara's parents.

Matthias doesn't talk about it a lot, but I know that,

for him, losing daily contact with his daughter was the worst part about the divorce. This year his daughter will be twenty, and a sophomore at Boston College. Matthias gets to see her on holidays and during summer vacations, but I know he feels as if he never sees her enough.

I myself wouldn't mind seeing either Emily or Barbara. In person, of course. I've seen pictures of them both, but I've never actually met either one.

I suppose I might as well confess that the one I'm most anxious to meet is Barbara. I can't help wondering, of course, if she is totally insane.

As a matter of fact, I was wondering it one more time as I stood there in my kitchen, watching Matthias at the sink, his sleeves rolled up to reveal tanned, muscular arms.

Believe it or not, Barbara married another man two days after she divorced Matthias. It appears, then, that old Barbara—unlike myself—must indeed believe in love at first sight. Or else, my goodness, could it possibly be, that she had actually been running around on Matthias?

I, of course, will never understand this, either. I mean, Matthias can kiss, he can cook, and he can clean. *And* he's wonderful in bed. What else could a woman want?

He also seems to know when to keep his mouth shut. All the time Matthias and I were cleaning up after the Whatever-It-Was, he didn't mention Virginia's little visit once. He kept up a running conversation, too, but that particular subject never came up.

Oddly enough.

After we finally finished cleaning, we both moved outside to my screened porch, and we just sat out there for a while, looking at the autumn skies.

Everything certainly seemed normal.

We talked about the new fall semester just beginning at the Kentucky School of Art where Matthias teaches. Matthias told me about the printmaking class he'd just started teaching, and he talked a little about which students he thought showed promise. He also talked about Emily, and how she'd just changed her major for what seemed like the millionth time.

If you could've eavesdropped on our conversation, you might've actually thought that some woman had not just called me a psycho to my face.

Matthias even kissed me right before he left. Just like always. The closest, in fact, that he came to even mentioning what had happened earlier was when he said, right after he kissed me, "Don't worry, Schuyler, everything's going to get straightened out."

Matthias was obviously trying to be comforting, but I couldn't help noticing that he had not suggested staying the night.

I also couldn't help noticing that it was only a little after ten.

Of course, it wasn't as if Matthias always stayed. We weren't teenagers, after all. Our every date did not end with the windows steamed up in my car.

And, with regard to it being so early, it could very well be that Matthias was just tired. After all, the new semester had just begun, and his first class of the day *was* at eight o'clock in the morning.

Still, as I watched Matthias walk down my sidewalk and get into the Death Mobile, I couldn't make up my mind whether his not staying longer was significant or not.

I also couldn't decide if his kiss hadn't been just a bit cool. Right before Matthias pulled away, he blew me another kiss. I smiled, and blew one back.

For some reason, though, I felt strangely depressed.

Isn't it a shame you can't just ask people straight out? It would've been so much simpler if I could've just said, Matthias, are you leaving now because you're tired and you're just not really interested in a roll in the hay right this minute?

Or, is it because you think that I could've possibly killed somebody recently, and that doesn't exactly do wonders for the old libido?

I would've also liked to ask: Oh, and while we're at it, Matthias, would you say that you're feeling a lot like all those male spiders must feel—once they get wind of the rumors circulating about that black widow they've been dating?

Oh, yes, I was depressed, all right.

I probably would've stood there in my doorway, staring forlornly after Matthias for, oh, maybe the next couple of hours or so, if my phone hadn't started ringing. I closed my front door, and suppressing a sigh, I hurried into my living room to answer it.

"Schuyler?" the voice on the line said. "Look, I think you and I need to talk."

I hadn't spoken to the man in months, and yet, typically, he assumed I'd immediately recognize his voice.

What arrogance.

On the other hand, I *did* know immediately who it was. That's why I said, "Who is this, please?"

I knew it would irritate him.

What can I say? I have a mean streak.

There was a short silence, during which, no doubt, he was mentally counting to ten, and then he said, "It's Porter, Schuyler. From what I hear, there's been some kind of misunderstanding—"

Misunderstanding? His girlfriend had dropped by to call me a psycho, and he thought that was a *misunderstanding*?

"—but I think we can clear things up," Porter finished.

I shifted my weight from one foot to the other, and gripped the receiver a little tighter.

This ought to be good.

Chapter 8

Porter's voice over the phone was as cool and soothing as lotion. "I just talked to Virginia, and frankly, Schuyler, when she told me the terrible things she'd said to you, I felt sick. She was way out of line. *Way* out of line. I told her so, too."

I had to hand it to him. He'd caught me off guard. I'd been expecting Porter to start defending Virginia's behavior, and yet, here he was, throwing *her* under the bus. It was such an unexpected turn of events that for a moment, I hardly knew what to say.

It was just as well, because Porter wasn't exactly waiting for my input. "I hope that you don't think I had any idea that Virginia was going to come by your house and say those things, because believe me, if I'd known, I would've stopped her." Porter took a long breath at this point. "Schuyler," he said, "I can't tell you how sorry I am."

Uh-oh.

Up to then, he'd had me going. I'd actually started to wonder if maybe I hadn't misjudged Porter a little. That last sentence, though, was a red flag.

Back when we were dating, I'd become quite accustomed to hearing Porter's apologies. He never did alter his behavior in the slightest, but he did say "I'm sorry" at the drop of a hat.

Porter had even apologized to me the day I'd met him.

That had been almost six months ago when he'd handled the closing of an apartment building I'd sold. All through the closing itself, Porter had been all business, but the second the meeting was over and everyone else had left, Porter had moved to my side.

"Look, I want to apologize," he'd said.

I'd been putting papers in my briefcase, and I'd just looked at him.

He'd been something to look at, all right. Very tall and lean, in a designer pin-striped suit that was almost the exact shade of gray as his temples, Porter had given me an intense, searching stare. Have I mentioned that Porter, not incidentally, has startlingly blue eyes that could give Paul Newman a run for his money? Needless to say, that first day my silly heart had actually skipped a beat. "Apologize?" I'd said. "Whatever for?"

Porter had run his hand through his thick, black hair. "I was afraid it was obvious. I could hardly keep my mind on what I was doing with *you* sitting right next to me." He'd given me another dose of that unrelenting Paul Newman stare. "My God, you're mesmerizing. What's more, you don't even seem to realize the effect you have on the men around you."

Porter had said this last with just the right mixture of schoolboy bashfulness and frank admiration. I remember thinking at the time: Surely, no one could pull that off unless he was truly sincere.

What I hadn't known then, of course, was that Porter had had a lot of practice.

So, naturally, I fell for it. Like the proverbial ton of bricks. My only excuse is that back then it had been a very long time since I'd met anybody I'd found even the least bit attractive.

As I've mentioned earlier, I became lucid again after about eight weeks. By that time, of course, I'd overheard Porter give his mesmerizing speech to two other women.

The first mesmerizer had been a waitress. After excusing myself to go to the ladies' room, I'd evidently returned a bit sooner than Porter expected. He was just saying the word, "mesmerizing," when I got back to our table.

That first time Porter had laughed it off. "Why, you're jealous," he'd said, giving me a quick kiss. "How adorable!" Then, of course, he'd gone on and on about how I didn't have a thing to be jealous about, and how he'd just been doing a little harmless flirting. I believe his actual words had been, "Just because you're not buying doesn't mean you can't window shop."

Uh-huh.

Porter had also said, his Paul Newman eyes filled with concern, "Schuyler, if I've caused you even a split second of discomfort, I am *so* sorry."

Oh yes, Porter could give lessons on apologizing.

Porter's next mesmerizer turned out to be a teenager going door to door, selling magazine subscriptions to raise funds for her high school sorority. Porter had apparently not realized that, from my upstairs landing where I happened to be standing at the time, you could hear every word said in my foyer. He'd actually asked the girl for her phone number.

From the suggestive comments he was making with regard to the girl's figure, I was fairly certain that he was not getting the girl's number to make sure his subscriptions arrived on time.

After this little episode, Porter had told me, his eyes filled with concern once again, "I am so sorry. *Really.* I wouldn't hurt you for the world. And, if my doing a little flirting bothers you, why, I'll never do it again. I mean it, Schuyler. I'm really sorry."

What can I say? The man has a gift.

By the end of the two months or so that Porter and I had dated, I'd not only heard his mesmerizing speech and his apologies too many times, I'd also had a few long, long weeks of Porter telling me what to do.

Much like, oddly enough, my ex-husband Ed.

I don't know what it is that makes some men believe that they've got to be totally in charge of the women in their life, but some men seem convinced, all right. It's as if they actually believe that, at birth, everybody on earth—men and women alike—draws straws for Who's-Going-to-Be-Boss. These men apparently look into their pants one day, and realize, by God, they've been given the long straw.

It must go to their heads or something.

If anything, Porter was even more of a boss than my ex had been. Which, believe me, took some doing.

Porter seemed to know the right way to do everything. It was as if I'd been searching for Mr. Right all my life, and unfortunately, I'd finally run into him. Porter knew the right way to wash your car, the right way to cut your nails, the right way to hold your fork.

After weeks of Porter's endless lectures, I finally realized that it wasn't Mr. Right that I should've been looking for all those years. The man I really wanted was Mr. I-Could-Be-Mistaken.

Porter told me what time I ought to be in bed at night, what time I ought to be getting up, and what I should be doing in between. He told me what haircut would look best on me, what colors I should wear, and what dresses he preferred to see me in. The man even told me how many Cokes I should drink in a day.

A subject, I might add, Porter should've known not to mess with.

When I finally broke up with him, I didn't think of it as breaking up, so much as cutting class.

Now, over the phone, Porter was laying it on thick as ever. "There are no words, Schuyler, to tell you

how truly sorry I am about the way Virginia behaved tonight."

"Really," I said. My tone was flat.

Porter either didn't notice my tone, or else he chose
to ignore it. "Really," Porter said. "Of course, after talking all this over with Virginia, I realized that Virginia
had badly misinterpreted some of the things I'd told
her."

"No kidding," I said.

Let me see now. Hadn't Virginia mentioned something about how *Porter* had broken up with me, instead of the other way around? And hadn't she also
said something about how vindictive I'd been since
he'd dumped me?

I wasn't sure, but these two things didn't seem subject to a whole lot of interpretation.

Porter, apparently, felt otherwise. "I'm not sure how
in the world Virginia could've gotten things so mixed
up, but Virginia seems to be under the impression that
you and I are enemies, or something." Porter now lowered his voice to a tone of intimacy. "And, Schuyler,
while it's true we're not dating anymore, I would like to
think that you and I will always remain good friends."

He'd done it again. Once more, I was caught off
guard. I couldn't exactly tell him that I considered him
a good friend. Mostly because, let's face it, lying and
cheating were not exactly attributes that I sought out
in friends. And yet, I didn't consider him an enemy,
either. "Well, uh, Porter, uh—" That, I'm less than
proud to admit, was exactly what I said in return.

Porter didn't seem to notice that my reply was not
what you'd call a complete thought. "Virginia must've
also misinterpreted what you said about her," Porter
went on. "Because, can you believe, she actually told
me that you accused her of *murder*?" Porter's tone
was incredulous.

"Look, *I* didn't accuse her of anything," I said. I

was about to point out once again the subtle distinction between Bartlett making an accusation and *my* making one, but Porter didn't let me finish.

"Well, now," he said, "that's *exactly* what I told Virginia. I told her she must've misunderstood you just like she'd misunderstood me. And that if all three of us could get together for a few minutes and just talk face to face, why, I'm sure we could clear the air in no time."

I swallowed once before I spoke. "Are you suggesting—"

Porter finished my sentence. "That we meet over here at my apartment? I certainly am. In fact, before things get completely out of hand, I think we should get together right away." Porter paused and then finished in a rush of words. "Hey, I know it's a bit of an imposition, but Virginia told me that if you're willing, *she's* certainly willing."

I took a deep breath, and thought this one over.

Did Porter really expect me to believe that Virginia had said what she'd said earlier tonight—in front of Matthias, mind you—solely because she thought Porter had said a few things that he hadn't really said?

Or was there so many *saids* in this last sentence, that even *I* didn't know what I was saying?

My head was beginning to hurt.

As I rubbed my left temple with the hand not holding the phone, it occurred to me that it *would* be nice not to be sued for slander. It would also be nice if Virginia was not running around suggesting to anybody who'd listen that I was a living example of that old saying, *Hell hath no fury like a woman dumped.*

Come to think of it, under the present circumstances—with Reed and Constello hovering around, apparently just waiting to hear some really terrible things about yours truly, to confirm their own suspicions—if there was even the slightest chance of clearing the air, I supposed I should probably take it.

Besides, there seemed to be only one way to find out who had been telling the truth tonight. Virginia? Or Porter?

I looked at my watch. It was only a little after ten-thirty.

"Okay, Porter," I said, "I'll be right over."

"Wonderful," Porter said. "I'll call Virginia, and we'll see you in about a half hour, okay?"

I said a quick "Okay," and started to hang up, but Porter added, "Oh, Schuyler? There *is* one thing— I've got a big case in court this week, and until you and Virginia get here, I'm going to be going over some paperwork in my study. You remember, it's in the back of my apartment?"

I remembered, all right. In fact, as I recalled, Porter and I had made love once in that study. On the oriental rug in front of his desk.

It was not the sort of mental picture I particularly wanted to dwell on.

Porter had paused at this point. I wondered uneasily if he, too, was remembering the Oriental rug incident. I also wondered if my going over to his apartment was such a good idea, after all.

Even if Virginia *was* supposed to be there, too.

And yet, I did happen to have a little cylinder of Mace hanging on my key chain, if things got out of hand. I'd been carrying Mace ever since I'd first started in the real estate business, when one day it had dawned on me that this job would entail meeting total strangers after dark in unfamiliar houses.

The Mace had seemed like an excellent idea.

It seemed like an excellent idea right this minute, too. Believe me, I wouldn't hesitate in the slightest to use it on Porter, it I had to.

Although, it really didn't seem likely that I'd have to. Porter certainly didn't sound the least bit threatening.

"Wouldn't you know," he was now saying, "my doorbell hasn't been working all this week, and my landlord hasn't fixed it yet. So if I don't come to my door right away, just knock real loud. To make sure I hear you, okay?"

I hesitated. I wasn't sure what, but there *was* something about this that bothered me.

Porter immediately picked up on my uneasiness. "Hey, I wouldn't want to leave a beautiful girl like you standing outside in the dark all alone, now would I?"

Oh, yes, this was the Porter I'd known and not loved. "I guess not," I told him. What I was thinking, however, was: Don't worry, you won't have the chance to leave me standing out in the dark, because if you don't come pretty soon, I'm leaving.

Porter's apartment was in a ritzy complex across town, a couple of blocks off Hurstbourne Lane, in one of Louisville's pricier neighborhoods. It took me just under twenty minutes to get there. As I drove, traveling a path that had become familiar during the weeks Porter and I had dated, I started feeling more and more uneasy.

I put it down, however, to having déjà vu. After all, it felt almost as if I were dating Porter again.

What a horrible thought.

I parked outside his apartment, and with my right hand in my coat pocket, gripping the Mace—just in case, that's all, *just in case*—I headed up the sidewalk.

Sure enough, when I knocked on Porter's door, he didn't show up. Wouldn't you have thought that, since he knew I was on my way—and he knew exactly how long it took to make the trip between his apartment and my house—Porter would've been looking for me just about this time?

This was just like Porter, though. Totally self-absorbed. He was the only man I'd ever met who couldn't pass a mirror without glancing at his own reflection—and stopping to admire the view.

Hell, that was probably what had happened now. There was probably a mirror on one of the walls somewhere in there, and Porter had been distracted on his way to the door.

I knocked on his door even louder.

Still no answer.

After the fourth knock, I decided to try calling to him, "Porter! *Porter!*"

Where the hell was he? I knew he had to be in there, I'd practically just talked to him on the phone, for God's sake.

It wasn't until my banging on his door and my yelling his name had brought a couple of Porter's neighbors to their windows that Porter finally appeared.

"Where in the world were you?" was the first thing I said to him.

Porter leaned out his front door, and took a self-satisfied look around. "Everybody in the complex has heard you by now, don't you think?"

I didn't know what he was getting at, but I instantly felt cold. It was—as I said earlier—September, so the nights were already beginning to get cool. That, however, did not seem to be the only reason I suddenly began to shiver. "What do you mean?" I asked.

Porter just looked at me for a long moment. He actually looked as if he wanted to grin at me very badly, but was fighting it. Maybe because his neighbors were still looking out way. "What I mean," Porter said, lowering his voice, "is that my neighbors will now testify that you came by to see me tonight. And that you were very loud, pounding on my door and yelling for me. That, in fact, you kept it up until finally I had to come out to shut you up."

Porter said these last three words with undisguised venom.

My mouth went dry.

I had to clear my throat before I could trust my voice to speak. "I take it that there's nothing actually wrong with your doorbell?"

Porter took a step back, so that no one but me could see him. "Why, of course, there's nothing wrong with my doorbell. Whatever gave you that idea?" Porter said. He *was* grinning now. He was standing there, shielded from his neighbors' curious stares, looking at me, and grinning.

I blinked, staring at him.

Porter had set me up. He'd got me out here in the middle of the night, and he'd set me up to look like the psycho Virginia had said I was.

Hell, Virginia could be inside there this very minute, laughing at how easily I'd walked into the trap.

I stood there, shivering even more. And, of course, longing to reach out and slap his smug, handsome face. Or, better still, to let him have it with the Mace I was still concealing in my coat pocket.

But then, there were all those neighbors still looking this way.

I don't believe any of them would testify that I'd Maced Porter in self-defense.

"You damn shit," I said quietly.

Hey, I know I'd said earlier that I thought Virginia was low class for talking this way. I, however, make no bones about it. I *am* low class.

And proud of it.

Porter was now leaning toward me. "If you don't tell the police that you were mistaken in what you thought Bartlett said," he all but hissed, "then I'll tell them that you've been hounding me ever since we stopped dating. I mean it, Schuyler, I'll make the police believe that you and that woman in *Fatal Attraction* are identical twins."

I blinked again. Then, calling upon every ounce of

bravado I had, I gave a quick, careless shrug and said, "Nonsense. They'd never believe you. In fact, why don't you give the police a call right now?"

I was, of course, bluffing my head off. The truth was that *I* seemed to be the only person in Louisville that the salt and pepper shakers consistently had problems believing.

Not to mention, Porter even had *witnesses* now.

While I stood there, trying to look calm, I also couldn't help but wonder if Matthias might also believe Porter. Hell, I had to admit, even I myself might be convinced by what Porter was saying. If, of course, I didn't already know for a fact that it wasn't true.

Porter must've known I was bluffing about calling the police. "Don't tempt me," he said, smirking. "You know very well the police will believe me, all right. For one thing, why on earth would I lie?"

That, of course, was an excellent question. One worth repeating. "Why would you?" I asked. "You and I both know you really *are* lying, so why don't you tell me why you're doing it?"

Was he just protecting Virginia, trying to get me to tell the police that Bartlett had not accused her, after all?

For a long moment, I didn't think Porter was going to answer me. He just stood there, staring at me, an odd half smile curling his mouth.

Finally, he said, "Did it ever occur to you that maybe you really did misunderstand what Edward Bartlett said? That maybe what Bartlett really said to you was, 'It was *Porter Meredith*, Girl.' Porter's eyes didn't look like Paul Newman's, anymore. They actually looked a little more like Freddy Kreuger's as they burned into mine. "You know, if I remember correctly, old Edward called women 'Girl' all the time," Porter went on. "It irritated quite a few of them."

My mouth went dry again.

Lord. Had Porter just confessed?

The night wind must've picked up a little, because now I wasn't just feeling chilled. I was feeling cold.

Porter was actually grinning at me again.

I took a quick step backward.

Offhand I couldn't remember whether Bartlett had ever called me "Girl" or not, but it certainly sounded like something Bartlett would do.

I stared at Porter.

I knew, of course, how Porter could manage to say what he'd just said, and still nonchalantly grin like that. There was no one around but me to hear what had just been said. It would only be my word.

And, even Porter here seemed to know exactly how much weight my word carried these days.

Still staring at him, I decided that this would probably be an excellent time to take my leave.

I turned and almost ran to my Tercel.

On the way home I passed several pay phones. Every time I did, I considered calling the salt and pepper shakers and letting them know on what Porter had just told me. Every time, though, I hesitated.

It really could sound as if I'd come to the conclusion that I was not going to be able to convince the authorities that Porter's girlfriend had killed Bartlett, so now I was going after Porter himself.

My old boyfriend.

The one his current girlfriend and quite a few of his neighbors would say that I'd been hounding ever since he'd broken up with me.

The one I had this fatal attraction for.

Lord. By the time the police and Porter and Virginia were finished with me, I'd have people all over Louisville hiding their pet rabbits the minute they laid eyes on me.

Chapter 9

If I'd thought that Jarvis was upset the day before, it was nothing compared to what he was when I walked into Arndoerfer Realty the next day.

Once again, of course, I spotted him through the storm door when I turned off Taylorsville Road into the parking lot.

And, once again, I spotted the pulsing veins in Jarvis's forehead as I walked through the front door.

Oh my yes. This was déjà vu to the max.

"You've done it again," were Jarvis's first words. "YOU'VE DONE IT AGAIN!"

This time I didn't even try to say "Good morning" to him. I just stood there and looked at him.

I was thinking, of course, *Look, Bub, I don't even have to be here.* Technically, the only two days of the week that I absolutely have to come into the office are Tuesday and Friday. Those are the days I have floor duty.

Floor duty at most real estate agencies involves merely answering the telephone and dealing with walk-ins, either taking them yourself as new clients, or—if you're too busy—passing them on to any other agent who happens to be in the office. At Arndoerfer Realty, however, because our beloved Jarvis is too big a cheapskate to hire a secretary, there's a slight twist. Floor duty here also involves answering Jarvis's personal phone line, doing his filing, and typing his correspondence.

I do wonder if Jarvis's idea of floor duty would continue to hold true if a male real estate agent should ever start working out of this office. So far, however, in the nine years I've been here, only women have consented to work for Jarvis. In fact, I've heard rumors that this real estate firm is referred to on the street as "Jarvis and his All-Girl Band."

I've never actually heard this with my own ears, so it continues to be my hope that this is nothing more than vicious gossip.

Gossip aside, however, it is without a doubt *not* an accident that the only people who can put up with Jarvis on a regular basis are, indeed, those of the XX chromosome persuasion.

XYs, no doubt, would've killed Jarvis long before this.

Not only does Jarvis have a peculiar idea of floor duty, Jarvis also has a bad habit of forgetting exactly which day is your day in the bag, so to speak. So that any day you show up, he's likely to start treating you as if you were his secretary.

Strangely enough, all the real estate agents who work out of Arndoerfer Realty try to avoid the office as much as possible on days they don't have floor duty. And, if they must come into the office on a nonfloor-duty day, they try to come in when they know Jarvis is not there.

Today was a Thursday—definitely not one of my floor-duty days—and yet, here I was walking in the door promptly at nine. I think I would've been perfectly within my rights to stay home and hide. Of course, *that* is the main reason I'd decided to come in. It really would've been hiding. A thing which I do believe is unseemly for a grown woman.

Still, wouldn't you think I should've at least gotten

some credit for being here at all? Not to mention, for being here so early? In the past on the nonfloor-duty days when I've shown up, I've almost never gotten in before eleven. Looking at Jarvis's pulsing veins, however, I decided I probably shouldn't hold my breath waiting for Jarvis to compliment me on my work ethic.

"You just can't keep our name out of the paper, can you?" Jarvis said.

No doubt about it, compliments were out of the question.

As Jarvis spoke, he brushed nonexistent hair out of his eyes and waved a section of the *Courier-Journal* in the air.

Talk about déjà vu. Once again I knew, without even looking, exactly which section of the newspaper Jarvis was waving.

Fortunately, unlike yesterday, Jarvis seemed to be the only person here. At least today I wouldn't have Barbi Lundergan or Charlotte Ackersen listening to Jarvis have his fit.

I don't suppose I have to even mention how tired I was. I'd barely slept all night, what with tossing and turning and trying to decide if I should tell the police what Porter had said to me.

I could still hear Porter's words. As clear as if he were standing next to me whispering them in my ear. *"It was Porter Meredith, Girl."*

Lord. Just thinking about it made me feel cold all over again. If Porter really had confessed to me, then he was a *murderer*. A person who killed people. Not exactly the sort you wanted to see running around loose. Wasn't it my duty to tell the authorities?

And yet, would they believe me? Or would I just be wasting my breath?

Not to mention, Porter's threat to accuse me of being a "Fatal Attraction type" was not something I could exactly ignore.

When my alarm had gone off this morning, I'd still been mulling it over. While I'd showered and dressed in the only thing in my closet that didn't require ironing—a black and white print rayon dress with a full skirt—I'd polished off two large glasses of Coke, heavy on the ice.

The Coke hadn't quite done the trick. Now, as I stood in front of Jarvis, my eyes still felt as if they had wet sand beneath the lids.

"This time the article is on the front page of the Metro section!" Jarvis said. Not only were his veins throbbing, his voice was, too. "THE FRONT PAGE OF THE METRO SECTION!"

Like I said, I already knew what section the news item was in. I also knew that today's headline was quite a bit larger than yesterday's had been. ATTORNEY MURDERED, was all it said, but it fairly leaped at you from the page. There was even a small photo of Bartlett to the left of the article.

So what was Jarvis's point? That I was moving up in the world of media attention? Did he think that was *my* doing? Was he under the impression that I sent out press releases?

I, of course, had been mentioned in the article as someone who, along with Amy Hollander and Jack Lockwood, had found Bartlett at the home of Marvin and Denise Carrico. No doubt, the Carricos were every bit as thrilled to see their name in print as I was to see mine.

The article also gave the Carricos' address—21225 Lakeside Drive. A thing which would, unquestionably, do wonders for the sale of the Carricos' house. Since, I'm certain, it goes without saying that there must be *legions* of people in Louisville anxious to live in their very own, personal crime scene.

The news item also mentioned that Bartlett had a lawsuit pending against me. There were no conclusions drawn or anything. The facts were just stated, that's all. Having that fact even *mentioned*, however, in the same article as Bartlett's death seemed ominous to me.

Maybe it was because it did seem so ominous that I was hardly in the mood to placate Jarvis. I moved immediately to my desk, stowing my purse in the side file drawer. "Look," I told Jarvis, "this is not my fault. I don't want to be in the newspaper any more than you want me to be there. Okay?"

When Jarvis can't think of anything to say, he sputters. "But—but—but—" He sounded like a lawn mower running out of gas.

"But what? How was I supposed to avoid all this? Edward Bartlett had already been shot before I even got there. Believe me, if I'd known there was a guy stretched out in the living room with a bullet in his chest, I would *not* have gone in."

Jarvis didn't sputter this time. "Do you realize how this looks?" Jarvis said. "DO YOU REALIZE HOW THIS LOOKS? A guy who was suing you ends up shot, and *you're* right there?"

I took a deep breath. Was he really under the impression that it had not yet occurred to me that this might look bad? Was he *kidding*?

I gave Jarvis a wide-eyed stare. As if this time his point totally escaped me. "No, Jarvis," I said, "how does it look?"

I don't know what Jarvis had been expecting me to say, but that must not have been it. He actually stammered a little as he said, "Well, we—we just can't keep having this kind of adverse publicity. WE JUST CAN'T—" In his excitement Jarvis's nonexistent hair must've fallen into his eyes again, because he swiped at it one more time.

I gave Jarvis a stare this time that was not at all wide-eyed. In fact, my eyes probably looked like slits.

"What do you want me to say, Jarvis?" I said. "That I won't shoot anybody else? Okay, I'm saying it. I WON'T."

I was being sarcastic, but Jarvis didn't look any too sure about it. The veins in his forehead were really going to town now. He took a step backward, staring at me, and then, without saying another word, he turned and headed straight upstairs to his office. All but running up the steps.

I took another deep breath. Good Lord. Next, the man would be frisking me for weapons before he'd let me come into the office.

My day having started on such an upbeat note, it could only, I suppose, get worse. Right after I finished talking to Jarvis, my sons called. Daniel and Nathan share an apartment in a section of town called Old Louisville. If they were still attending college, I believe they would probably still be living with me. Having flunked out at my expense, however, about a year ago, my sons immediately decided to move into their own place.

I've always thought it was mainly because the two of them were suddenly afraid to eat or drink anything I might prepare.

Even Cokes, my specialty.

Daniel, the oldest at twenty-one, was on the phone first. "Mom?" he said. "I tried to get you at home, but when you didn't answer, I knew you must be at work."

My sons seem to be convinced that I have no life other than work. They both know that I am dating Matthias, but it would never enter either of their heads that I could possibly spend the night at Matthias's place. Mothers, apparently, never do such things.

In fact, I'm fairly certain the two of them are convinced that they were the result of Immaculate Conception. No doubt, I'd had an Annunciation just before each of them were born.

"I saw the paper this morning," Daniel was hurrying on. "Quite a bit of excitement, huh?" Daniel actually sounded approving. Of course, Daniel would sound approving if he'd found out I was pursuing a career in international terrorism.

Daniel is a very laid back sort of person. He wears black as a dominant fashion color, his jeans generally sport enough jagged holes to make you believe he'd recently been caught in a crossfire, and he always wears an earring in one ear. Usually, a tarnished earring. "So how many times had that guy been plugged?" Daniel asked. "I mean, was he already dead when you—" At this point, judging from the sound and Daniel's muttered *"Hey!"* the receiver was torn out of his hand.

Nathan, a year younger than Daniel, apparently felt that his own comments were a shade more important than Daniel pumping me for gory details. "Mom, for God's sake, all my friends are calling me." Nathan said this, using the exact same embarrassed tone he'd used back in the seventh grade when he'd told me in no uncertain terms that he didn't want me to kiss him anymore when I dropped him off at school. "Every one of my friends have read the paper."

Now what was I supposed to say to that? What a relief it was to find out that his friends really had mastered this basic skill, when frankly, having met some of them, I'd have bet against it?

"I mean," Nathan went on, "good Lord, Mom, this is really terrible."

Nathan has always had a lot of his father in him. For both Nathan and his dad, there are things you simply do not do. Things like kiss your kid in front of his school buddies. Or wear anything that does not have a designer label. Or, above all, run into anybody with a bullet in him.

It's so tacky.

I believe I've already established that I was not in my best mood. "Nathan," I said, "believe me, if it weren't for the thrill of seeing my name in print, I would've just as soon skipped it."

I was being sarcastic, but Nathan didn't get it any more than Jarvis had. There was a long silence on the other end of the phone. "Huh?" Nathan finally said.

"I love you, Nathan," I said. "Tell Daniel I love him, too," I added. And, then, unceremoniously, I got off the phone.

I didn't stay off the phone long. It rang almost immediately with a call that was to become the prototype for the roughly thirty or so calls that I was to receive throughout the rest of the day.

"Is this, uh, Schooler Riggway?" the caller immediately asked.

I should've realized, of course, right then that whoever it was did not know me personally. That, in fact, they must've read my name somewhere and were now mispronouncing it. Ten guesses, mind you, where they might've read my name, and—as they used to say in grade school—the first nine don't count.

"I'm Schuyler Ridgway," I said, putting extra emphasis on the first syllable. *Sky*-ler. "May I help you?"

"Oh. Uh. Yeah. Yeah, you sure can help me, all right. I reckon I'd like to take a look at that there house that's in the paper today."

At first, because I had a couple houses listed in the Classifieds, I'd actually thought the inquiry was about one of them.

Silly woman that I was.

When I began to read off information on the first of these listings, the caller kindly pointed out my error. "Nope, nope, that ain't it. I'm talking about the murder house. That there's the one I wanna see."

In my opinion, not many people refer to the place they're contemplating calling home as "the murder house." I cleared my throat. "Are you interested in purchasing this property?"

The caller's answer to this seemed, oddly enough, lacking in sincerity. "Well, uh, *sure*," he said, "uh, *sure* I'm, uh, interested in, uh, purchasing the, uh—"

"Murder house," I finished for him. After which, of course, I hung up.

Only to have the phone ring again almost as soon as I put the receiver down.

Several times that morning the caller actually beat me, hanging up right after I asked him about his intentions to purchase the property.

By the time the morning was over, I was sure I'd talked to every wacko in Louisville. I was wrong, though. I had yet to talk to the two who walked in my door about ten minutes to noon.

Detectives Reed and Constello.

By then, as luck would have it, the population of the front room of the Arndoerfer Realty office had grown considerably. Jarvis was over at the coffee machine, getting what had to be his millionth cup. Charlotte Ackersen was at her desk across the room, helping a prospect look through the Multiple Listings book. Even Barbi was in. She'd just returned from showing a house, and was at her desk in the far corner, going through her messages.

Just having to talk to the salt and pepper shakers in front of all these witnesses would've been bad enough, but Reed and Constello walked in right behind—who else?—Matthias, of course.

I saw Matthias at almost the exact same moment that I spotted Reed and Constello right in back of him. I blinked.

The way my luck had been going lately, I probably should've known that the likelihood of Matthias appearing in my office at any given time was directly proportional to the probability of the salt and pepper shakers being there, too.

Matthias didn't look any happier to see Reed and Constello than I was. "I knew you were probably having a bad day," Matthias said to me, "so I thought I'd come by and take you to lunch." He glanced over at Reed and Constello. "It looks like you might be busy, though."

I didn't even get a chance to answer before Reed and Constello started in.

"This won't take long," Reed said.

"We just need to ask you a few follow-up questions," Constello added. "That's all."

In no time at all, I found out that it's a *lot* more uncomfortable to be questioned by the police when your boyfriend is standing right there, taking in every word.

Not to mention, Jarvis, Barbi, Charlotte, and some prospect I didn't even know.

I would've liked to have fooled myself into believing that, since Reed and Constello were in plain clothes, nobody knew they were police, but the truth was, as I mentioned before, Reed and Constello had been here only a few months ago. You remember, they'd questioned everybody here regarding the death of Matthias's father.

In fact, I'd say that the only person in the room who might not know that these guys were cops was Charlotte's prospect. A plump matron with hair the exact shade of the water in my upstairs toilet bowl, the woman had stopped looking through the Multiple Listings and was now staring fixedly in my direction. Over her wire rims.

Of course, maybe she was just looking in my direction because that's what everybody else in the office was doing.

The salt and pepper shakers didn't seem at all shy

about talking in front of an audience. In fact, I suspected that Reed, for one, enjoyed it. Jack Webb
sounded positively cheerful as he said, "Mrs. Ridgway,
we've talked to Mr. Porter Meredith, and frankly,
what he had to tell us was very interesting."

I raised an eyebrow. I'll bet it was.

Reed didn't elaborate, however. He hurried on.
"We've also talked to"—here Reed took out his spiral
notebook with a little flourish, and consulted it—
"Amy Hollander." Reed seemed now to be reading
verbatim. "According to Miss Hollander, she did not
hear what Edward Bartlett said to you." Reed paused,
and then looked at me. "She said she did hear him
groan."

Reed seemed to expect some kind of reaction from
me. I gave him one. A shrug. "Well," I said, "Amy
was standing in the doorway when Bartlett was talking
to me. It was, I suppose, entirely possible that from
all the way over there she couldn't hear what he said."

I was trying to sound nonchalant as I said this, but
inside, I felt as if the floor had just dropped out of
my stomach. Wouldn't you know it? The one person
who might've backed up my story, and all she could
verify was that Bartlett had indeed groaned.

What a big help.

Matthias had moved so that he was now standing off
to one side while the salt and pepper shakers talked to
me. I gave him a quick glance. Was I imagining it, or
was Matthias beginning to look extremely worried?

I purposely did not look at anybody else in the
room. I was feeling rattled enough already.

All my life whenever I've gotten nervous or upset,
my throat blotches up. Right now I couldn't see it, of
course, but judging solely from how warm my neck
was suddenly feeling, I'd have bet my last dollar that
my throat was beginning to look as if I'd just rubbed
it in poison ivy.

On the bright side, maybe that's why Matthias was looking so worried. Maybe he'd noticed my neck, and was trying to decide if he ought to run out for some calamine lotion.

Having given me the terrific news about Amy, Reed was moving on. "We also talked to the deceased's girlfriend—a Miss Gloria Thurman?"

What could I say? The name was familiar. Lord knows, I'd seen it on enough court documents recently.

"Miss Thurman told us that, as Mr. Bartlett was leaving yesterday," Reed went on, "Mr. Bartlett told *her* he was on his way to see a 'Miss Schuyler Ridgway' " Reed's eyes darted to mine. "We find that very interesting. That a man who ends up shot told his girlfriend that he was going to see you."

My mouth went dry. A quick glance around the room told me that everybody within earshot also found it very interesting.

Even Charlotte's blue-haired prospect was now looking positively fascinated as she leaned a little in my direction.

The look on Matthias's face, however, was the most disturbing.

He looked as if somebody had just punched him in the stomach.

Chapter 10

Reed was moving in for the kill. "That's right, Mrs. Ridgway," he said. "Gloria Thurman said Bartlett was on his way to meet *you* the day he was killed." He paused and took a quick glance around the room.

The man could've been summing up for the jury.

Turning back to me, Reed added, "What do you have to say to that?"

The first thing that flashed into my mind was a word Reed clearly didn't want to hear me say. Two syllables, the first one being *bull*, it was a word that could probably get me into even more trouble with the police than I was already.

Although, let's face it, it would be hard to imagine being in more trouble. What could be worse for them to suspect me of? Being in cahoots with Lee Harvey Oswald?

I looked Reed straight in the eye. My mouth had suddenly gotten so dry, I had to swallow once before I could speak. "Well, I'd say the woman is a liar. Gloria Thurman has lied before, about what I had or hadn't told Bartlett about the house I sold him, and now, obviously, she's lying again."

Reed didn't blink. "You think so?"

"No," I said. "I *know* so."

"What if she isn't lying?" Constello put in, his eastern Kentucky accent thicker than ever.

I wasn't sure what Constello was getting at, but

okay, I'd play along. "If she isn't lying, and Bartlett really did tell her he was on his way to see me, then it isn't exactly surprising that he would use my name. Even though he and I did *not* have an appointment yesterday." I raised my voice and put a little extra emphasis on the word "not" so that everybody in the room would be sure to hear it. "The house in which Bartlett was shot *was* listed in my name. My name, in fact, is on the realty sign right out in the front yard, for God's sake. Bartlett could've just told his girlfriend that he was meeting me, knowing all along that he intended to meet someone else at that house."

I was doing major speculation here, but what else could I do? Maybe if I kicked enough dirt in the air, Reed and Constello would, at least, question whether or not it really had been me Bartlett had intended to meet.

Some more dirt occurred to me. "It would also not have been the least bit difficult for the murderer to come up with my name, you know. Whoever Bartlett arranged to meet could've just told Bartlett that she was me. Maybe Bartlett had *thought* he was meeting me, when in reality, it turned out to be someone else."

By now, even I was getting a little confused.

Reed and Constello were now looking at me as if maybe I was not only confused, I was insane.

I couldn't resist glancing at the others in the room. From the looks on the faces of Jarvis, Barbi, Charlotte, and Charlotte's blue-haired prospect, it was unanimous. They'd all concluded that I needed psychiatric help.

Even Matthias, standing over there by the window, seemed to be staring at me oddly.

Constello started petting his dark mustache again, as if it were a cat. "Mrs. Ridgway, I reckon you know what your old boyfriend, Porter, is saying about you?"

I sighed. I was pretty sure I'd prefer to talk about Gloria.

I nodded. "I certainly do, and Porter is lying about—"

Constello interrupted. "Mrs. Ridgway, there sure seems to be an awful lot of folks lying about you these days, don't you think?"

I just looked at him. He was right. Paranoiacs sounded positively *trusting* compared to me.

I guess it was realizing just how I looked to Reed and Constello—and, incidentally, to everybody else in the room—that made up my mind.

Speaking slowly and distinctly, I told Reed and Constello exactly what Porter had said to me the night before. I finished with, "Porter set me up. What's more, I really can't figure out why on earth he would've done this except that he wanted to muddy the waters for some reason. Obviously, Porter has something to hide."

The salt and pepper shakers did not look exactly blown away by my revelation. Neither did anybody else.

The most sympathetic person in the room seemed to be Matthias. He was no longer looking at me oddly. He was looking at me pityingly.

Reed and Constello exchanged a look that was neither odd nor pitying. It appeared to be skeptical more than anything else. Then, as if he were just making conversation, nothing more, Constello said, "So. You really think that Porter and/or his girlfriend murdered Edward Bartlett? What could possibly be their motive?"

He had me there. "How would I know?" I almost added, *Isn't it your job to find that out?* but somehow, I managed to shut my mouth before that came tumbling out.

For the first time since they'd walked in, Constello nodded his dark head and agreed with something I said. "Well," he drawled, "*we* sure as heck don't know what their motive could be, either. That's pretty much why we're looking in another direction for Bartlett's killer."

Staring into his dark eyes, I didn't have any trouble guessing exactly in whose direction they were now looking.

"You know," Constello went on, in that conversational tone again, "if it happened to be you who shot Bartlett, you'd have killed two birds with one stone when you did it. One, you'd have gotten rid of a guy who was suing you. And, two, by saying that Bartlett told you that it was Porter's girlfriend who'd shot him, you'd be putting the gal who stole your boyfriend behind bars."

I was pretty sure my neck was doing its poison ivy thing again. "Porter Meredith is NOT my boyfriend."

"Not anymore," Reed put in. He gave the words an ominous sound.

Constello, on the other hand, was still talking conversationally. "Mrs. Ridgway, we think you might've been under the impression that just because you were cleared of the murder of Ephraim Cross a while ago, we'd never in a million years suspect you again."

I sort of wished Constello hadn't mentioned Matthias's dad. I'd already decided it was probably best if I didn't look again at the others in the room—it only made my neck get that much hotter—but out of the corner of my eye, I saw that—at the mention of his father's name—Matthias's head turned abruptly in Constello's direction.

"Fact is, we think you might've been *counting* on us never suspecting you again." Reed said, running his hand over his blond head. "But you're wrong."

I stared at both Reed and Constello, appalled. I couldn't believe anybody would actually think *I* could shoot someone. I couldn't even kill ants in my kitchen. I always picked them up very gently with a paper towel, and deposited them outdoors.

I decided, however, I wouldn't mention my aversion to ant homicide. The salt and pepper shakers would probably think that this was just one more indication that I was not any too tightly wrapped.

"Do you really believe," I said, "that I would shoot Bartlett in a house with *my own name*, mind you, on the For Sale sign right outside—and that, after I'd done such a thing, a little while later I'd just blithely show up to discover the body?"

Unbelievably, both Reed and Constello nodded their light and dark heads in unison.

In back of them, I noticed that Charlotte's prospect was nodding her blue head, too. My guess was, the woman was a real fan of *Murder, She Wrote*.

"We think you're one smart cookie," Reed said. "Smart enough to do something like that to try to throw us off."

Somehow, this didn't sound like a compliment.

It also didn't sound like something I wanted Matthias—or anybody else—to overhear.

I couldn't help it. I gave Matthias another quick glance.

He was staring straight at me, his eyes very wide.

It seemed to take Reed and Constello forever to finally call it a day, but in actuality they probably only talked to me for about twenty minutes in all. Constello finally gave me a level look and said, as he petted his dark mustache again, "I don't reckon we have to tell you again not to be leaving town any time soon."

I gave him a level look in return, and said, "You just did."

When the salt and pepper shakers finally left, the eyes of everybody in the room followed them to the door.

And then immediately swiveled back to me.

I felt as if maybe I should stand up, and make an announcement to the room at large. Something on the order of "Thank you so much for your attention. I just wanted to let you know that, in spite of what you might've just overheard to the contrary, I have not killed anyone lately."

I decided against it, though. It probably wouldn't do any good. Besides, when I looked directly at Jarvis, Barbi, Charlotte, and the blue-haired prospect, every one of them immediately looked away.

No use making a speech if your audience wasn't going to listen.

I contented myself with turning to Matthias and saying, "Look, I know all this looks bad, but I want you to know I did *not* shoot Edward Bartlett."

Matthias looked shocked. "Schuyler, I know you didn't shoot him. You certainly don't have to tell *me*."

Uh-huh.

I wanted to believe Matthias. I really did. But if he was so sure I was innocent, why had his eyes been showing the whites all around a few minutes ago? What had he been doing, having trouble with his contact lenses?

I didn't believe that for a minute. For one thing, Matthias didn't wear contact lenses.

"Matthias," I said, "I wouldn't blame you if you did have some doubts."

Now I was the one who was lying. I *would* blame him. I mean, did he really think I was capable of shooting somebody? Who did he think I was? Annie Oakley?

Matthias waved a hand as if sweeping away in that one gesture every possible doubt in the world. "Nonsense. I don't have any doubts. None at all." I couldn't help but notice, however, that he quickly changed the subject. "So. You want to get some lunch?"

I just looked at him. "Yes, I do," I said. "I want you and me to go have lunch with Gloria Thurman."

"Bartlett's girlfriend?" Matthias's voice was almost

a croak, and his eyes started showing the whites all around again. He cleared his throat once before he continued. "You want to have lunch with Bartlett's girlfriend?"

I nodded. Actually, I was not all that interested in having lunch with her. What I was really interested in having with her was a conversation. Regarding why she'd lied about what I had or had not told Bartlett about the home I'd sold him, and even more importantly, why she was now lying to Reed and Constello about Bartlett telling her that he was going to meet me yesterday.

I wanted to hear her explain. What's more, I wanted *Matthias* to hear her.

Matthias, oddly enough, did not look delighted at the prospect. "Schuyler," he said, "didn't you learn your lesson last night when you went to talk to Porter?"

Apparently, I didn't. I was already opening my lower desk drawer and rummaging inside for a Louisville phone book.

It was because I was leaning over, looking for the phone book, that I didn't see Barbi get up from her desk and walk purposely toward Matthias and me. It just seemed as if she were suddenly there when I straightened up.

"Schuyler," Barbi said, twisting a platinum curl around a forefinger, "I couldn't help but overhear a minute ago—"

I just looked at her. Of course, she couldn't help it. She hadn't taken her eyes off any of us since Reed and Constello walked in. Hell, even if she hadn't been able to hear what we were saying, she probably could've read our lips.

"—and, well," Barbi went on, "if there's anything I can do, honey, just let me know."

I might've gotten the impression that old Barbi was

actually trying to bury the hatchet, except for one thing. As Barbi said this, her eyes sort of casually wandered in Matthias's direction.

"Oh, hi," she said. As if she'd just noticed him standing there.

Even Matthias looked a little wary. "Hi," he said.

Barbi leaned toward him. Have I mentioned that she was wearing a low-cut, scarlet red knit dress that looked to be several sizes too small? Matter of fact, I believe *tourniquets* are worn quite a bit looser than Barb's dress. "Schuyler sure does lead an exciting life, doesn't she?" Barbi told Matthias. Her tone implied that she was sharing a confidence. "Not like me. Oh my no. Goodness me, I guess, compared to Schuyler, I'm just as dull as dishwater."

I'd put the phone book on top of my desk and started looking through it, but I took a moment to give Barbi a piercing look. What the woman seemed to be trying to get across to Matthias was that, unlike yours truly, Barbi was not the sort who got interviewed by the police on a regular basis.

"Thanks, Barbi," I said. My tone was flat.

Barbi looked startled. I think for a second there she thought I was being sarcastic about her coming over and making an obvious play for Matthias. "What?" she said. Dragging her eyes reluctantly from Matthias's face to mine.

I gave her a chilly smile. "Thanks so much for offering to help," I said through my teeth. "It's so nice to know that I've got such a good friend."

Barbi blinked heavily mascaraed eyes. "Oh, *that*," she said. "Sure." The woman had no shame. She actually nodded. "Glad to, uh, *help*," she said.

After that, there was nothing else for Barbi to do but wander uncertainly back to her desk.

Giving Matthias a sultry look over her shoulder.

Also, after that, there was nothing else for me to

do except to finish looking up Gloria in the phone book. And, yes, to begin thinking several unkind thoughts about Barbi.

There was only one G. Thurman listed. If this was Gloria, I recognized the address—93005 Cornflower Road. The street was in Vista Gardens, a subdivision located out Dixie Highway in a suburb of Louisville's south end called Valley Station.

I wish I could claim to be the world's greatest real estate agent, having memorized every single street in the Louisville area, and that's why I knew right away exactly where Cornflower Road was. The truth was I recognized the street because thirty-five years ago I'd lived in Vista Gardens myself.

Thirty-five years ago Vista Gardens had offered a dream deal for veterans like my dad. Brand-new houses for $9,000, with no down payment. These days it's hard to build a garage for that little.

Of course, these days that dream deal subdivision doesn't quite look like it did back when the houses were new. The last time I'd showed a listing in Vista Gardens had been a couple months ago, and it had almost broken my heart to see how battered the houses looked. Several of the homes stood vacant, and more than a few had automobiles jacked up in the side yards.

The only things in Vista Gardens that looked better today than when I'd lived there were the trees. Barely twigs when my family had moved in, all the trees had grown into these huge, lush hulks that dwarfed the tiny cracker box houses they shaded.

One thing for sure, if Gloria Thurman lived in Vista Gardens these days, she was not exactly well off.

My own parents had only lived there for five years, and then they'd had the good sense to move on. They had, in fact, moved several times since, each time to a more upscale subdivision, until finally they'd ended up where they are now—in a comfortable, sprawling ranch located in the most affluent subdivision in the Valley Station area.

Somehow, however, I didn't think that my telling Gloria that she and my mom and dad were practically neighbors was going to cut much ice.

Gloria picked up on the first ring, but when she heard who it was on the other end, she didn't sound at all happy that she'd answered her phone. "Why, what—what are you calling me for? I—I don't know nothing."

Gloria sounded as if she might be standing in the middle of an earthquake, her voice was shaking that badly.

There have been occasional tremors, believe it or not, in Valley Station. Recently, too. I know because my mom calls me up every once in a while and tells me how the floor in her garage is moving up and down.

Not many people outside of Kentucky realize it, but this entire area lies on the New Madrid Fault, a thing a lot like the much more famous San Andreas Fault out in California. I myself wouldn't have realized that Kentucky is on the New Madrid Fault except that not too long ago, some so-called expert started predicting a devastating earthquake for this region. Every house I sold around that time, the new owners insisted on buying earthquake insurance.

The earthquake never did happen. And right this minute, I was pretty sure that Gloria's tremors had nothing to do with quakes, either.

"Miss Thurman," I said, "I'd like us to get together and have lunch."

You might've thought I'd told her to meet me at dawn and to bring a gun. "Oh my God," she said. "Oh my *God*."

The woman sounded as if her private earthquake

was rising on the Richter scale, so I hurried to add, "Look, I don't mean you any harm—"

Gloria seemed to be about as impressed with my honesty as I was with hers. "Oh sure, you don't," she said. "*Sure* you don't mean me any harm."

"Miss Thurman, I mean it, I just want to talk to you, that's all."

"And—and if I don't want to talk to *you*?"

"Well, then," I said, "I suppose that would make me think that you have something to hide, and I guess I might have to tell the police that you—"

She interrupted me, her voice going up an octave. "Oh no! There's no call to bring the police into this!"

Evidently, Gloria enjoyed talking to the police every bit as much as I did.

"Then meet me," I said. "Or I'll tell the police you know a lot more than you've told."

I was bluffing, of course, once again. These days I'd probably have trouble convincing Reed and Constello that the sky was blue.

Gloria didn't know it, though.

Gloria's earthquake started again. "Oh God, oh God, oh God," she said. She went on like this for a little while. When her chant finally ended, she sounded as if she might be weakening. "Well," Gloria said, "if I do agree to meet you, I'm not going to do it unless it's in a real public place. I mean, like in a restaurant or a—a bus station. I'm not stupid, you know."

I blinked. Gloria wanted us to have lunch in a bus station? And she didn't want me thinking she was stupid? Was she kidding? I'm not exactly a finicky eater, but the last time I ate in a bus station, I'd been convinced that the food there mainly consisted of leftovers from airplane fights.

"And I ain't meeting you alone. Oh no," Gloria was now saying.

Up until Gloria said this, I'd been under the impression that Gloria was acting nervous because it was awkward for her to talk to the woman she'd helped Bartlett bring a fraudulent lawsuit against.

Now I realized that Gloria wasn't just nervous. Gloria was *afraid*. Of me. Really. The woman truly seemed to believe that I might be going around, bumping off everybody involved in Bartlett's lawsuit against me.

Beginning, of course, with Bartlett himself.

"I ain't going no place with you by ourselves," Gloria added. "Nosirree bob."

Good Lord. Bonnie and Clyde probably hadn't had this much trouble arranging a lunch date.

"Gloria," I said, "I have no intention of meeting you alone. In fact, I was going to ask if you minded if I brought along my, uh, boyfriend."

I glanced over at Matthias. Hey, he'd already referred to me as his girlfriend. I supposed I could return the favor.

Matthias returned my look. He was not looking happy. I rather hoped his discomfort had nothing to do with my referring to him as my boyfriend.

I glanced away.

"Your boyfriend?" Gloria asked. "We'd have lunch with your boyfriend?" There was a moment of silence while apparently Gloria went over in her mind whether or not I might possibly kill her in front of a guy I was dating.

Gloria must not have been able to decide. "I—I don't know," she finally said. Her voice was getting precariously close to a whine.

I took a deep breath. Good Lord. Even if she wasn't sure about me, did the woman actually think that *Matthias* would stand idly by while I murdered her? What kind of people did Gloria generally hang out with, anyway? The Manson family?

"Gloria," I said, "my boyfriend is a college professor. He teaches at the Kentucky School of Art."

"A professor, huh?" Now there was actually relief in Gloria's voice. She apparently was under the impression that, while real estate agents were clearly capable of murder, college professors didn't do that sort of thing.

"Um, all right, that sounds okay, um, I guess," Gloria said. "I'll meet you if the professor comes along. *And* if the restaurant's real crowded."

The closest restaurant I could think of that always seemed to be crowded was Jake Mull's on Bardstown Road.

Jake Mull's is always crowded for two reasons. The food is great, and the restaurant is not very big. In fact, the second you walk into the main dining room, you can take in everybody that's there in a single glance. That makes Jake Mull's a place where you can see and be seen.

Well, I definitely wanted to be seen. That is, I wanted to be seen by Gloria. As soon as possible.

"I'll meet you at Jake Mull's in a half hour," I told Gloria.

"You *and* the professor will meet me, right?" Gloria's voice, unbelievably, was still shaking.

I had to tell her two more times that Matthias would come, too, before she finally hung up.

After I myself hung up the receiver, I took a deep breath. *This* certainly ought to be fun—breaking bread with a person who actually believed I could be a murderer.

As soon as the thought crossed my mind, I couldn't resist giving Matthias another quick glance.

Oh dear. It looked as if Gloria might not be the only person at lunch today who believed me guilty.

I must say, *that* little thought certainly revved up the old appetite.

Chapter 11

I'd never met Gloria Thurman, but over the phone, she'd assured me that she knew who I was and would have no trouble recognizing me. Apparently, this time—for, no doubt, once in her life—Gloria was telling the truth. Matthias and I had just been shown to our table at Jake Mull's when a plump redhead walked in. She took a quick, nervous glance around the room, zeroed in on me and Matthias, and then walked slowly toward us, her high heels making tiny explosions on the black-and-white-tiled floor.

I couldn't help noticing that Gloria had the kind of look on her face you generally wear when you go to the dentist. For a root canal.

"Well, I'm here," was Gloria's opening sentence. Her tone implied that she expected extra credit just for showing up.

Someone must've told Gloria that green is a redhead's best color. She was wearing a grass green coat dress with matching hose and heels. Gloria's purse was grass green, her earrings were grass green, and her eye shadow—which, incidentally, went all the way up to her eyebrows—was, you guessed it, grass green.

I couldn't help staring at her. Gloria Thurman looked like a middle-aged, oversized leprechaun.

Gloria even had a green bow in her hair. Lodged in the middle of a large, red curl, the thing looked like a green butterfly that, having mistaken Gloria's

head for a huge red flower, had lighted just above
Gloria's right ear. Gloria evidently hadn't attached the
bow any too securely, because every time she moved
her head, her green butterfly bobbled.

Matthias had been seated opposite me, but he stood
when Gloria walked over to our table.

Gloria gave him a sidelong glance. "You the professor?" She looked over at me. "He don't look like no
professor I ever seen."

I kept right on staring at her. What was I supposed
to say to that? *Matthias is in disguise?*

In fact, Matthias was wearing what he almost always
wore—scuffed cowboy boots, faded blue jeans, and a
blue chambray shirt with the sleeves rolled up. From
the expression on Gloria's face, though, you might've
thought that Matthias was wearing a black double-
breasted suit, spats, and carrying a violin case.

Matthias stuck out his hand. "I'm Matthias Cross.
Glad to meet you."

Apparently, Matthias just knowing how to introduce
himself was enough to convince Gloria that he was
college material. She actually looked a little impressed
as she shook his hand briefly. "Call me Gloria," she
murmured.

I noticed that when she said this, Gloria was looking
only at Matthias. In fact, throughout most of the ensuing
conversation, Gloria hardly glanced in my direction.

Gloria apparently felt that it was not a good idea
to look a cold-blooded killer in the eye. Maybe she
was afraid I'd hypnotize her, the way a cobra is supposed to hypnotize its victims.

There were two chairs at our table that Gloria could
choose to sit in, one next to Matthias, one next to me.
Guess which one Gloria chose. As she and Matthias
sat down, Gloria scooted her chair even closer to his.
Apparently, if I became violent, Gloria expected great
things out of him.

"I ain't never been here before," Gloria said, glancing around the restaurant. "It's, um, real interesting, ain't it?"

Jake Mull's stark white walls are decorated with framed black-and-white photographs dating back to the thirties and forties. These photographs show downtown Louisville during the infamous 1937 flood, the restaurant's original owner—Jake Mull himself—shaking hands with the likes of Rocky Graciano, and various classes of high school graduates. All the photographs *are* definitely interesting, but Gloria was staring at them as if they were the most intriguing things she'd ever laid eyes on.

She didn't fool me. She may have been trying to look totally fascinated, but she barely glanced at one photograph before her eyes traveled to another.

It was my guess that Gloria wasn't really interested in these little portraits from Louisville's history. They just gave her something else to look at besides me, Old Cobra-Eyes.

Gloria was still staring blankly at a photograph of the graduating class of the long-defunct Girls' School, which happened to be hanging on the wall directly across from her, as she went on. "You was lucky I was home." I was fairly certain her comments were directed at me, but you couldn't tell by looking. Her eyes had not wavered from the photograph. "I'm a permanent office temporary," she went on. "I'm generally working during the day."

A *permanent* office *temporary*? Weren't those mutually exclusive terms? Sort of like, *military intelligence*?

"I've got myself registered with several temporary agencies," Gloria went on, now staring at a photograph of Jake Mull and his wife standing just outside of this very building. "They sends me all over Louisville, you know. A few days here, a few days there."

"You don't say," Matthias said.

I myself didn't say anything, but to tell you the truth, I had no trouble believing that Gloria would only work at any given place a few days. Particularly if the job required a mastery of grammar.

"That's how I met my Eddie, you know," Gloria added. "I worked for Eddie for a week or so, and right away we hit it off."

It had taken me a second to realize that the "Eddie" Gloria was referring to was Edward Bartlett. I didn't really make the connection until I saw the unshed tears suddenly sparkling in Gloria's eyes.

I reached out and touched Gloria's arm. "Gloria, I want you to know that I'm terribly sorry about, uh, Eddie," I said. It felt strange to call Edward Bartlett "Eddie," but I knew—in the interest of good taste— I probably shouldn't refer to him by the name I called him most often. That being, of course, *The Little Weasel.* "I feel awful about what happened," I went on.

I wasn't lying. I really did feel sorry that Bartlett was dead. Even weasels didn't deserve to be murdered.

Frankly, I don't think I could've sounded more sincere, but I probably would've gotten the same reaction if I'd lit a match and pressed it against Gloria's skin. The woman actually flinched and jerked away. "There weren't no need to kill him," she said, her eyes still focused on Jake Mull and the Mrs.

I definitely would've preferred that she hadn't said this in front of Matthias. I took a deep breath. "Gloria, I didn't do anything to Edward Bartlett," I said.

I apparently had as much credibility with Gloria as she had with me. "Uh-huh," she said. Once again to Mr. and Mrs. Mull.

When Gloria had first approached, I'd thought she and I were the same age. Now, sitting this close to her, I realized the woman had to be at least ten years older.

Bartlett's death had obviously been a shock. You could see where Gloria had tried to cover the dark circles under her eyes with concealer.

"If my Eddie hadn't been shot, he'd still be alive," Gloria said. She was still talking to the Mulls, but her tone was now reproachful.

I just looked at her, again without saying a word. Her last statement was one you certainly couldn't argue with.

For a second, I couldn't think of anything to say, but fortunately, Matthias took over. Matthias is one of those people who believe that anything can be made better with a little food. I think he feels this way because he's such a good cook. It has simply never occurred to him that food could possibly make things worse.

Being the kind of cook I am, it has occurred to me. I *never* think of food in times of stress.

Matthias cleared his throat, signaled to a waitress, and immediately ordered a big plate of nachos for us to snack on while we talked.

Another reason Jake Mull's is always so busy is the service. The nachos seemed to appear almost magically within minutes.

As I said, I felt as much like eating as I felt like jumping off the Second Street Bridge downtown, but the food actually seemed to perk Gloria up. The food, that is, and the two frozen Margaritas she ordered right after she started on the nachos.

The Margaritas must've given her a little courage, too, because once she started on them, Gloria started giving me quick, furtive looks. They were the sort of looks you might give a ravenous pit bull, but she *was* actually looking at me. Without flinching or anything. A considerable improvement, if I may say so.

I opened my mouth to start quizzing her about what she'd told the police, but before I could even get a word out, Gloria already had my answer. "You know," she said, swallowing a mouthful of Margarita, "I wasn't lying when I talked to the police. Eddie really did tell me that he was going to meet you." Gloria nodded her head so vigorously, her green butterfly bow looked as if it were flapping its wings. "That's what he said right before he left. *I'm going to meet Schuyler Ridgway.*"

I tried to look as if all I cared about was getting at the truth, but if this was it, I wasn't sure I wanted to hear it. "Are you positive that's what he said?"

Gloria's green butterfly flapped its wings again. "Oh yes," she said, taking another big swig of her Margarita, "I'm absolutely, positively sure." She turned her head and looked over at Matthias. "Eddie told me that he was on his way to meet Schuyler, and then he left, and *I never saw Eddie alive again.*"

I shifted position uneasily in my chair. Gee, thanks, Gloria, for making that little scenario perfectly clear.

If Gloria had done this to get some kind of reaction from Matthias, she was probably disappointed. All Matthias did was rub his beard. In fact, you might've thought he hadn't even heard Gloria if you didn't notice the muscle that started jumping in his right cheek.

I shifted position again. If Gloria was lying this time, she had a real talent in this department. She sounded totally convincing to me. I didn't even want to think about how convincing she must sound to Matthias.

Gloria must not have had all that much tolerance for liquor. Or else her stomach was so used to the stuff that it didn't even bother to digest it. It just shot it full-strength right into her system.

"I had no real intention of testifying against you, neither," Gloria told me, her voice already starting to slur. "About that, um, house you sold Eddie. I was just saying what Eddie told me to say so's your insurance company would settle out of court." Gloria took another even longer sip, and waving her glass in the air for emphasis, added, "That's what Eddie said would happen, you know. He said your insurance company would just fork over the dough." Gloria's tone had become reproachful again. "It wouldn't have been no skin off your nose. All Eddie was doing was trying to make a little money, is all."

Gloria was making it sound as if Eddie had just been doing a little fund-raising for his favorite charity. Which, in a way, was probably the truth. As long as you remembered that Bartlett's favorite charity had been himself.

"He wasn't hurting nobody," Gloria was now mumbling.

I blinked at that one. Apparently, Gloria felt that fraud was just a harmless prank.

She lifted bleary eyes to mine. *"Nobody,"* she said, with an emphatic—if somewhat wobbly—nod of her head. "I mean, *nobody* should have to die over something like that."

I, of course, met her gaze head-on, wondering, What in the world did I have to do to convince this woman that I was innocent? "Gloria," I said evenly, "I did *not* do anything to Edward Bartlett." I know I'd said this once before, but it seemed to bear repeating.

"Uh-huh," Gloria said. She was back to talking to the Mulls again.

It was beginning to get on my nerves. "Gloria—"

Matthias must've picked up something in my tone, because he immediately interrupted. "Are you two ready to order lunch?"

I wasn't, but the two of them certainly seemed to be. Gloria and Matthias both ordered a hamburger and fries. I wasn't even sure I could eat a single lettuce leaf, but I went with the house salad anyway.

While we waited for our food, I scrambled in my mind for something else to discuss other than the likelihood of my having murdered Bartlett—that subject having been discussed all I really wanted it to be. Then I remembered what Virginia Kenyon had said last night. "By the way, Gloria," I said, "do you know if Eddie was acquainted with a Porter Meredith?"

Gloria's head didn't wobble this time. She nodded so vigorously, her green butterfly looked to be about ready to take off. "Oh my yes," she said, waving a plump hand in the air. "Them two were in law practice together. Right after they both got out of law school."

I blinked. Well, now, *this* was news. I leaned forward. "How long did they practice together?"

Gloria shrugged. "Oh, for a while. I don't know exactly how long." Her words were beginning to slur *bad*. " 'Course I knowed all along why it was that Eddie and Porter stopped being partners. It was Eddie's drinking."

I nodded as if I'd suspected as much. " 'At's right," Gloria went on. "Once Eddie started up drinking, his practice fell off. After that, Eddie only defended strippers and—and, you know, people like that." Gloria wrinkled her nose in distaste. "But," she added, "Eddie was still a damn good lawyer, he really was."

I tried to look as if there were not a doubt in my mind that an alcoholic attorney could do a terrific job.

Gloria was now pointing a plump finger in my direction. "Eddie was still a member of the Bar and all, just the same as Porter. So, the way I saw it, Porter had no call to snub him."

I stared at her one more time, wondering, of course, what in the world she was talking about. I also wondered if Gloria herself knew.

Gloria was wiping at her eyes. "It really hurt Eddie's feelings, you know."

I didn't say a word, but frankly, it had been my impression that Edward Bartlett had not had feelings.

Plural. One feeling, at best, was the most he could possibly have had.

(Not to be speaking ill of the dead, God rest his soul, but—as I've said before—let's be honest.)

"What really hurt Eddie's feeling"—I almost left off the "s" on that last word, but I caught myself in time—"s?" I finished.

Gloria looked up at me, her eye shadow beginning to run a little. "Why, Porter ignoring him the way he did. Porter always acted as if he didn't even know Eddie."

I tried to look shocked that anybody would do such a thing. It wasn't easy.

Gloria was warming to her subject. "One time Eddie and I ran into Porter at a real nice restaurant downtown—and Eddie went over to Porter's table to say hi—and, wouldn't you know it, that uppity Porter wouldn't even speak to him. Can you believe that? When Eddie done him a real big favor once." Gloria sounded outraged. Or, at least, as outraged as someone with several sheets to the wind could sound.

If I'd been a German shepherd, my ears would've pricked up.

"A big favor?" I asked. "What do you mean, a big favor?"

Gloria shrugged, and took yet another huge swig before she answered. "Don't know. Eddie never told me."

I believed her. For one thing, I thought she was too soused by then to know to lie.

I leaned back against my chair. What on earth could that favor have been? Could it have given Porter a reason to kill Eddie Bartlett?

I didn't mean to, but while all this was going through my mind, I frowned.

Gloria immediately looked alarmed. She polished off the last of her second Margarita in one huge gulp and said, "It ain't my fault Eddie didn't tell me." Her voice was getting close to a whine. Giving Matthias a quick sideways glance as if making sure he was still close by, she added, "I mean, if I knew, I'd tell you, I really would."

"Gloria," I said, "it's okay." I thought I sounded positively reassuring, but I guess if somebody is convinced you're the sort of person that commits murder, you can never sound quite reassuring enough.

Gloria's face seemed to be growing whiter by the second. In another minute she and the Pillsbury Doughboy were going to have identical complexions.

"I—I mean," she added, "I really want to help you all I can. I really do. It's just that, in this once instance, I—I really don't know." Her voice was no longer getting *close* to a whine. It had made it.

I watched her, and tried not to sigh. But, good grief, was it absolutely necessary for Gloria to talk to me as if she had me confused with Ted Bundy?

In front of Matthias, yet?

It was right after all this went through my mind that another thought occurred to me. Gloria's being afraid of me might not be all that bad a thing. "Gloria, you don't happen to know where Eddie kept his files do you?"

Her butterfly bobbled vigorously. " 'Course I do," Gloria said. "In his office."

"Is there any way I could take a quick look at those files?"

Matthias had evidently not been expecting me to ask such a thing. His shaggy head did this odd little jerk as he turned to stare at me.

Oh yes, that was disapproval on his face.

I ignored him, and purposely directed all my attention toward Gloria.

"Why, uh, sure," Gloria said uncertainly, "I—I

guess. I mean, Eddie gave me a set of his office keys a long time ago—"

"Do you think we could go take a look right after lunch?" I asked.

"Well, uh, I don't know about—" Gloria hedged.

I interrupted her. "Look, Gloria, I realize you think you know what happened to Eddie, but I'm telling you, you're wrong. I didn't do anything to him, and I'm getting very tired of being accused of something I didn't do."

Gloria's eyes widened at that. She swallowed once, and said, in a very small voice, "Oh dear."

"I intend to find out who really shot Eddie," I went on, "but I need your help."

Gloria didn't look any more convinced of my innocence than she'd been when she first walked into the restaurant. She did, however, look significantly more scared. "Oh, dear," she said again. She swallowed once and then went on, "Well, uh, I sure didn't mean nothing by anything that I've said, I mean, I wouldn't want you thinking that I—"

Gloria didn't seem to be folding so I went for my trump card. When she began to speak, I stared straight at her.

And, once again, I frowned.

Gloria's eyes must've increased in size about three times. She broke off in the middle of what she was saying. "Oh, my goodness, *yes*," she said. "I'd be *glad* to show you *all* Eddie's files. I really would. Any of them you want to see. *Right away!*"

Lord. I only wish my frowns had gotten that kind of response when my sons were growing up.

Having agreed to show me Bartlett's office, Gloria must've felt she needed additional fortification to get into a car with me. She put away two more Margaritas while she ate her hamburger and fries.

You know how you've always been told that if you

eat when you drink, you won't get as drunk? Gloria must've been the exception that made the rule.

By the time we were all through with lunch, Gloria was nodding over her plate. At one point, in fact, I was sure her head was about to go right into the ketchup she'd slathered all over her fries, but she caught herself in time.

Gloria's behavior made me wonder if maybe she and Edward Bartlett hadn't had an awful lot in common. An awful lot of alcohol, that is.

It also made me feel sorry for her. I actually had to remind myself that this was the same woman who'd outright lied about me, and that her lies had been printed in the paper for all to see.

Even then, I still felt sorry for her. Not as much, but some.

When Gloria finally did nod off altogether—loudly advertising that fact by sagging forward and beginning to snore—Matthias must've seen it as a chance for him and me to have a little chat. "Schuyler," he said, leaning across the table and lowering his voice to practically a hiss, "do you really think this is a good idea?"

I wasn't sure what he meant. If he was talking about Gloria taking a nap at the table, I'd say no, it wasn't. It looked to me as if Gloria stood a good chance of drowning in a puddle of ketchup.

"What do you mean?" I said. "What's not a good idea?"

Matthias ran a hand over his beard before he answered. "Us breaking and entering Bartlett's office, that's what!"

I just looked at him. "Matthias, we won't be breaking and entering. We'll be *unlocking* and entering. There's a difference."

Matthias evidently didn't see it. His green eyes still looked worried. "Schuyler, maybe we should leave the investigating to the professionals."

I just looked at him again. "Are you kidding? The professionals, as you call them, actually think *I* might've killed a man! Now, I don't know about you, but I don't consider that particular opinion all that professional myself!"

I must've gotten a little too loud, because across the table from me, Gloria stirred in her sleep, breaking off midsnore as she moved her red head restlessly from side to side.

Matthias didn't say anything more until Gloria resumed snoring. It wasn't a long wait. "Schuyler," Matthias said, "now don't take this wrong—"

Uh-oh. The last man who'd said this to me had been my ex-husband. Ed had then proceeded to tell me that he wanted an open marriage.

Meaning Ed wanted to sleep with other women.

And he wanted me to continue to sleep only with him.

As I recall, I hadn't taken that wrong. I'd taken it exactly as Ed had intended it. After which, I'd taken Ed to court.

Matthias was now leaning across the table, giving me an earnest look. "Don't you think that if the police find out about your going through Bartlett's office, it could look as if you were just trying to dig up something to divert suspicion away from yourself?"

I just stared right back at him. That did sum it up nicely. "You're right, it certainly could look like that," I said. "What's your point?"

I guess I sounded a bit testy, because Matthias blinked. "I mean," he hurried on, "aren't you afraid it might look as if you're just scrambling to find evidence to pin Bartlett's murder on somebody else?"

Correct me if I'm wrong, but wasn't that a rehash of what he'd just said? I nodded. "Uh-huh."

Matthias actually looked a little startled.

"Matthias," I went on, and I believe I should get

extra points for patience here, "I don't mind admitting
that the *only* reason I'm trying to find out who killed
Bartlett is because the police think *I* did it. That's my
prime motivation. Believe me."

What did he think? I just happened to love solving
a mystery? Who did Matthias think I was this time?
Nancy Drew?

"Matthias, I intend to go through Bartlett's office
with a fine-toothed comb, if necessary. And, if you
don't want to go, well, then, I suppose I'll understand—"

I was lying yet again. I would not understand. In
fact, I was having a little trouble understanding why
he was questioning whether or not I should go through
Bartlett's office, in the first place.

Matthias, I think, knew it because he reached over
and took my hand. "If you're going, I'm going."

I wish I could say I was pleased. It did, however,
cross my mind that Matthias might've decided to tag
along for his own reasons. Like, oh, say, trying to find
out something that would help him make up his mind
once and for all whether or not I really could be guilty.

I gave him a quick smile, though, just as if none of
this had occurred to me. Then I leaned across the
table so that my mouth was only inches from Gloria's
green butterfly. *"Gloria!"*

"Whumpt?" That, I believe, is an exact quote. Gloria opened her eyes and stared at Matthias dully, as
if for a moment she couldn't quite recall who he was.

Then, of course, her eyes lighted on me.

"A-a-a-argh!" That, I believe, is also an exact quote.
Apparently, even though Gloria might not remember
Matthias, she did—yes, indeedy—recall exactly who *I*
happened to be.

"You were going to show us Edward Bartlett's office?" I said.

Gloria evidently remembered this a bit belatedly,

too. Her plump face fell. "Oh, um, right," she said. "I'd, um, be glad to."

She didn't sound glad.

Sitting next to her, his eyes growing more and more worried, Matthias didn't look any gladder than Gloria.

I guess I made it unanimous. I certainly wasn't *glad* about having to poke around in a dead man's office, but what choice did I have?

I gave Matthias a steady, unrelenting look. It was a look that said, Okay, the very next time I get suspected of murder, I'll sit around and do nothing, and more or less, just wait for the cops to cart me away.

Right now, though, there was an office that needed to be unlocked and entered.

Chapter 12

We took my car to Bartlett's office, but I didn't drive. Matthias did.

Not that I minded, on either count.

I didn't mind taking my car, because Matthias's Death Mobile does not have air-conditioning, and Louisville was having its usual "can't-decide-which-season-it-is" weather.

Kentucky weather never does seem to make up its mind. I suppose this should not exactly come as a surprise in a state that couldn't decide which side it was on during the Civil War.

Today, even though it was September, it had to be over eighty in the shade. There was not a doubt in my mind that if I'd been riding in Matthias's MGB, it would've been a Death Mobile, all right. Only it would've been *my* death we were talking about.

I also didn't mind that Matthias was driving because, frankly, I hate to drive.

I know. I know. It seems like an odd thing for a real estate agent to say, especially when so much of the job is spent driving around in your car. It's probably a lot like a chef saying, "The only thing I hate about my job is the cooking."

Still, I can't help it. I've never liked to drive. I've tried to tell people that in a past life I must've been terribly wealthy and had a chauffeur, just like in the movie *Driving Miss Daisy*. That's, no doubt, why driving has always seemed like such a god-awful chore.

My ex-husband Ed, however, has another theory for why I hate to drive. He's mentioned more than once that, if they ever made a movie about me, it should be called *Driving Miss Lazy*.

The man thinks he's funny.

I myself would've liked to think that Matthias always wanting to drive and my always hating to drive is a sign of our true compatibility. But, let's face it. Matthias is not exactly unusual in this respect. I've never met any man who—if given the choice between doing the driving himself or riding with some woman behind the wheel—would choose the latter.

That's why I'm sure this obsession with driving has got to be some kind of male ego thing. It's the same reason men never let other men cut in front of them in traffic. Every man instinctively knows that letting another man cut in or letting a woman drive directly affects the old testosterone levels.

Oh, sure, men would like us to believe that the reason they won't get into a car with a woman behind the wheel is that they're all convinced we're terrible drivers. The truth is, though, every man is secretly convinced that the moment he starts letting a woman drive, his voice will go up an octave.

Bartlett's office turned out to be only a little over ten minutes away, if you traveled down Bardstown Road toward downtown, took a left onto Broadway, and shortly after that, a right onto Clay Street. After which you traveled toward the Ohio River, stopping several blocks before you got wet.

This put you directly in front of the main entrance of an old office building located at 13201 Clay Street.

I barely paid attention, though. I was too busy trying to get comfortable.

With Matthias driving, and Gloria sitting beside him

giving him directions—albeit slurred—there hadn't been room for me in the front seat.

It was, in fact, the first time I'd ever gone anywhere riding in the backseat of my Tercel.

I can't say it's an experience I want to repeat.

My Tercel is bright red with a gray interior, so it was a lot like riding around in a cave.

A very small cave.

Lord. It was also the first time I'd ever had irrefutable proof that my car was indeed an import. It was obvious that this vehicle had been made by tiny, small-boned, Asian people. Either that, or by the Keebler elves. There just wasn't space for a person my size. I'm not all that big either, I hasten to add. I believe I mentioned earlier that I'm five feet six inches and that I weigh in at 128 pounds these days. Not exactly an Amazon. Nevertheless, my legs felt as if they'd been folded, spindled, and mutilated by the time we pulled up in front of Bartlett's office building.

I had to sit there for a moment after Matthias turned off the ignition. While I waited for the circulation to return to my extremities.

It did occur to me that Amy Hollander had also ridden around in this same backseat, and she hadn't seemed to have suffered any real discomfort. Of course, she was an inch shorter than me, and wouldn't you know it, several pounds tinier. Then, too, maybe Amy *had* been uncomfortable, and she just hadn't mentioned it. Lord knows, if her fiancé Jack didn't make her uncomfortable, it could be that Amy was numb.

While I continued to wait for my circulation to return to normal, I stared up at Bartlett's office building through the small back window of my Tercel.

An ancient five-story brick, painted slate gray, with white gingerbread highlighting long, narrow windows, it was a building that we real estate agents often describe as quaint and charming.

It could also be described as old-fashioned and dilapidated.

Squeezed between a boxy private residence and an equally boxy credit union, Bartlett's office building was right across the street from a low, white frame building that was not the least bit charming or quaint. The white frame building didn't have a name or anything, but you knew right away it was a restaurant. Mainly because above the large picture window facing the street, there stretched a faded wooden sign that said SANDWICHES AND PIE and beneath that, in slightly smaller letters, COFFEE AND HOMEBAKED HAM. On each side of this long white sign were two identical, smaller signs that said *Drink Coca-Cola*. Both of these small signs also displayed a faded drawing of Coke's bottle cap.

Either the restaurant owner had been sent two identical signs by mistake, so he'd decided to use them both, or he'd felt that "Drink Coca-Cola" was a motto so important, it needed repeating.

I could understand that viewpoint.

If, however, you wanted to actually drink Coca-Cola or, for that matter, eat a sandwich any time soon, you were out of luck. The picture window under the long, white sign was boarded up, and the screen door was hanging by a single, extremely rusty hinge.

It appeared, then, that Bartlett's office was in the kind of neighborhood that we real estate agents often say is "in transition." What this generally means is that the neighborhood is going from bad to worse.

Even in a "transition" neighborhood like this one, though, Bartlett's office building would've normally cost a small fortune. For no other reason than it was close to downtown Louisville, where property prices have skyrocketed in recent years.

Bartlett's office building, however, was probably dirt cheap. Not because it was rundown. Not because it was at least a hundred years old. Not even because it looked as if a good wind might claim any remaining window screens.

No, Bartlett's office building was cheap because it was located in this particular area of Louisville: Butchertown. Some parts of Butchertown are trendy and desirable and fetch a pretty penny. This was not one of those parts.

In this part of Butchertown, it's not hard to figure out how this area got its name. Particularly on hot, summery days like this one. You could instantly guess why as soon as you took a deep breath.

There are two large meat packing companies less than a block away, and each of them have slaughterhouses nearby. Just like Kentucky lies on the New Madrid Fault, this part of Butchertown lies within the Slaughterhouse Odor Fault. Only, in this case, it's not *fault* as in a hole in the earth, it's *fault* as in a major defect.

When the wind is blowing in the right direction, the Slaughterhouse Odor Fault is not only enough to cause a prospect to offer much less for any property around here, it's also enough to make the prospect a vegetarian.

I myself was considering going on a strict soybean diet as I finally unfolded my legs and started to haul myself out of the back of my Tercel. Matthias, of course, had already come around, opened the passenger door and helped Gloria out, and now he was just standing there, waiting to give me a hand.

Short of calling 911 and requesting the use of the Jaws of Life, there didn't seem to be a whole lot he could do. I finally decided there was no graceful way to get out of this thing, so I ended up just sticking one leg out, gripping the edge of the door, and propelling myself forward.

The entire experience was probably a lot like being born. Going from an extremely tight place into a bright, sunny place, while some guy stood by, helplessly watching.

Only, hopefully, right after you were born, you actually did want to take a few deep breaths.

I, on the other hand, immediately started doing my best to breathe as shallowly as I could. I was also trying not to gag at the rancid odor hanging thickly in the air, and wondering just how fast we'd all be able to get inside Bartlett's office building.

Getting inside with any kind of speed was not looking good. Gloria was standing, as if frozen, right in the middle of the sidewalk. Holding her nose. Her eyes very round. "Whooo-eeee!" she said. "Gag oh me. Gag OH me!"

Matthias, too, was gasping. I also couldn't help noticing that once I'd gotten my entire body out of the car, Matthias had started moving quite fast. Taking Gloria's elbow and almost hauling her bodily toward the building. "God," Matthias said, "that has got to be the worst smell I've ever smelled in my life."

"Mercy," Gloria said. "Mer-*cee-e-e*!"

Which, I believe, was Gloria's way of saying, "Ditto."

It took Gloria several minutes to get the front door of the office building open. Part of the reason was that the wood of the door was so warped, it didn't fit in the frame anymore.

Another part of the reason was that, by this time, after downing all those Margaritas, Gloria probably couldn't remember exactly what a door key was for.

Once she'd finally unlocked the front door, Matthias ended up having to help Gloria up the stairs. Even with Matthias's assistance, Gloria stumbled several times on the way. She didn't seem to mind it, though. In fact, once the door behind us slammed shut, and some of the smell had lessened a little, Gloria's spirits took a definite upswing. "Whoopsy-daisy!" she started saying gaily every time she missed a step. "*Whoopsy-daisy!*" Gloria appeared to particularly enjoy grabbing Matthias's arm and leaning into him, as he hoisted her up the stairs.

"You know," she said the last time, peering into his face, "your green eyes go great with my suit."

Matthias gave me a look over Gloria's red head that might've been pleading.

I just stared right back at him as if I didn't quite catch his drift.

I believe I've already mentioned that I've got a mean streak.

Bartlett's office turned out to be on the top floor, wouldn't you know it, up five flights of the narrowest stairs I'd ever seen. The stairs, in fact, were so narrow, I wondered how in the world Bartlett had ever gotten a desk up there.

Once inside his office, however, I could see that Bartlett had not only gotten a desk up, he'd also managed to haul in a lot of other stuff. The entire office was crammed full. There was a huge couch covered in the kind of black plastic that furniture salesmen always tell you is leather-look, but looks about as much like leather as Tupperware. There were also several wood veneer end tables, several truly ugly floor lamps—the kind that have multicolored plastic beads dangling from the lamp shades—and several moth-eaten rugs.

There were also rows and rows of gray, shoulder-height, metal filing cabinets. These were all lined up against the wall in the adjoining room, but I spotted them through the open doorway the second we walked in.

Getting up all those flights of stairs had evidently been too much for Gloria. As soon as she'd unlocked Bartlett's office door, and we were all inside, Gloria immediately dropped onto the black Tupperware couch, and just sat there, staring blankly into space.

If I hadn't seen her chest rise and fall, I'd have thought maybe she'd had a stroke.

I actually thought I might be on the verge of one myself. Even Matthias was wheezing a little as we both headed toward the file cabinets.

"Good Lord," Matthias gasped. "If I had this office, I'd need paramedics to meet me up here every damn day."

I would've liked to have told him that I agreed, but I didn't have the breath. All I could do was just nod. And continue to head toward the file cabinets.

I was so winded, the files seemed a mile away. I made it, though. I finally lurched through the door of the adjoining room, switched on the overhead light, and arrived at the first file cabinet a couple steps ahead of Matthias. I immediately reached for the top drawer and gave it a tug.

It came right open.

Bartlett must not have been the least bit afraid of intruders if he hadn't even bothered to lock his file drawers. But, then again, what self-respecting intruder would break in here?

Not to mention, what self-respecting intruder would take anything that he had to lug down five flights of stairs?

I myself would've had to think very hard before I picked up so much as a paper clip.

Bartlett not only didn't keep his file cabinets locked, he *also* didn't label his file drawers. I had to open six drawers before I located the "M's." After that, though, it only took a few minutes to find a ragged folder marked "Meredith, Porter."

"Matthias," I said, as I pulled the folder out of the cabinet, "look."

Matthias was at that moment standing right at my shoulder so I probably didn't have to say anything. His eyes were already riveted to the folder I held in my hands.

Dog-eared, as if it had been handled many times, the manila folder didn't have much in it. Just a single brown envelope. The envelope looked to be six inches by nine inches, and it had a metal clasp holding the flap shut.

I took the envelope out of the folder and turned it over. On the back, in a heavy scrawl of black ink, were the words, "Wanda Faye and Jenny, 1975–77."

"An envelope?" Matthias said, rubbing his beard. "That's all that's in there?" I wasn't sure what he'd been expecting, but Matthias sounded a little disappointed.

At least, he sounded that way up until I undid the metal clasp, opened the envelope, and pulled out what was inside.

It was a handful of photographs. Maybe eight or nine of them. The one on top was an old color snapshot of a curly-headed, dark-haired little girl of about four, sitting on the lap of a thin brunette. The little girl was wearing a blue calico dress, black patent leather Mary Jane shoes, and she was looking off to one side, smiling shyly.

It was the little girl's eyes, though, that really caught your attention. They were large and blue, and they seemed to fill her small face. The brunette must've been the little girl's mother, because she had the same arresting blue eyes.

The snapshot might've, in fact, been a typical mother-daughter picture except for one small detail. The brunette was wearing an outfit that looked as if it had been purchased straight out of a Frederick's catalog—black lace push-up bra and panties, black lace see-through robe, black lace garter belt and black fishnet hose.

I may have been leaping to conclusions here, but it appeared to me as if Ms. Black Lace here was probably not your typical '70s Mrs. Cleaver mom.

At my elbow, Matthias cleared his throat. "Not exactly a Norman Rockwell portrait, is it?" he said.

I looked at him. "Who is this woman? And this little girl? And what do they have to do with Porter?"

Matthias obviously did not have any answers to my questions. His eyes traveled back to the photographs. The back of the first one had the same thick scrawl as the front of the manila folder. "Wanda Faye and Jenny, 10/15/76."

I moved on to the next picture. This one was the brunette alone. She was wearing the same outfit she'd worn in the first picture, and indeed, according to the scrawl on the back, this picture had been taken the same day. It said, "Wanda Faye, 10/15/76."

In this snapshot, Wanda Faye had been caught in the middle of a laugh. Whatever it was that had tickled her funny bone, it must've been hilarious because Wanda Faye's dark head was thrown back, her eyes were almost closed, and her mouth was nearly wide open.

You might've thought she didn't have a care in the world.

The next snapshot showed the little girl and her mom again. The little girl might've been a little older maybe—her brown curls looked longer, and she herself looked a little bigger—but she was still wearing the exact same dress. Once again she was sitting on Wanda Faye's lap, and once again Wanda Faye had apparently selected her own wardrobe out of Frederick's. This time, though, Wanda Faye was all in white—white lace push-up bra, white G-string, white lace stockings and white lace garter belt. She also had a white feather boa looped around her shoulders.

Evidently, Wanda Faye had gone in heavily for the Zsa Zsa Gabor look.

I would've said the Madonna look, except that it occurred to me that Wanda Faye would never have heard of Madonna. Not back in the seventies.

Wanda Faye had pioneered a whole new fashion look, and she hadn't even known it.

I held the photo up to the overhead light to get a better look. Wanda Faye could've been anywhere from twenty to thirty-five. You really couldn't tell. In fact, all you could tell for sure from the photo was that Wanda Faye was beginning to look infinitely weary.

In fact, in this picture she looked as if she'd seen it all, and she hadn't liked any of it.

Looking at the photo this close, I also noticed something else. Her daughter may have been bigger, but Wanda Faye was smaller. The woman looked considerably thinner than she'd been in the earlier pictures. And there were now lines around her mouth that had not been there before.

I swallowed, looking at that photo. The woman did not look well.

The handwriting on the back of this photo was still the same bold scrawl. "Wanda Faye and Jenny, 1/3/77."

I flipped rapidly through the rest of the snapshots. There were only six more, and most of them were variations on the same theme—Wanda Faye and Jenny in various poses.

And various outfits.

Lord. Wanda Faye must've owed Frederick's a bundle. She had red lace outfits, pink lace outfits, and black leather outfits that made her look like the plaything of a motorcycle gang. Jenny, on the other hand, mainly appeared in the same dress or the same shirt and shorts.

Obviously, Wanda Faye had needed help with her clothing budget. Jenny certainly seemed to be getting shortchanged.

The only snapshot that didn't portray the little girl and the brunette alone, had them posing with several other women, all of whom seemed to have the same taste in clothes as Wanda Faye. I couldn't say for sure, having never been in such a place myself, but it looked to me as if this snapshot had been taken in what my mother had always referred to as "a house of ill repute." In fact, this snapshot looked like a still from that Brooke Shields movie, *Pretty Baby*.

The obvious question was, What were these snapshots doing in a folder labeled "Porter Meredith?"

I stared at the photos in my hand as several other questions occurred to me in rapid succession. How exactly did Porter know Wanda Faye and this little girl? Could Wanda Faye and Porter have been intimate, and little Jenny have been the result?

This last was clearly one possibility. Matthias came up with another. "Do you think this woman could've been a relative of Porter's?" he asked. "Like maybe his sister?"

I didn't have an answer for him any more than he'd had for me.

"Maybe," Matthias went on, "Porter Meredith had a sister who was a prostitute, and the 'big favor' Gloria mentioned earlier—the one that Edward Bartlett had done for Porter—was to keep quiet about it. What do you think?"

I didn't know what to think. I did know, however, exactly what I needed to do next. I turned around and headed back toward Gloria, Matthias at my heels.

Chapter 13

Gloria was no longer sitting on the Tupperware couch staring blankly into space, the way Matthias and I had left her. She was, however, still on the couch. That is, if you interpret the word *on* very loosely.

Gloria had done a downhill slide almost all the way off, her lower body suspended between the edge of the couch and the floor. She was just hanging there, more or less defying gravity, head back, legs akimbo, arms thrown wide.

Gloria still looked like a middle-aged leprechaun. Only now she looked like a middle-aged leprechaun who'd been hit by a truck.

When I first caught sight of her, my heart actually did a little jump. My God, maybe that climb up the stairs really had been too much for her. Maybe Gloria had been DOA, and in my hurry to get to the file cabinets in the next room, I hadn't noticed.

I quickened my step. And then, of course, I heard it.

Good Lord. Gloria's snore back at the restaurant had been loud, but this was something else again. I was pretty sure I'd heard locomotives that were *far* quieter than this.

The back of Gloria's red head was resting on the back of the couch, so that if her eyes had been open, she would've been staring at the ceiling.

Gloria's eyes, however, were not open.

Her mouth was.

In fact, Gloria's mouth was open so wide that as soon as I reached her side, I could clearly see that she'd had her tonsils removed.

Either that, or else her snores had simply blown them right out of her throat.

Gloria's current snore was reaching a crescendo. In the next minute, there was every chance she'd be sucking the paint off the ceiling.

"Gloria?" I said.

There was no response. Not even the flicker of an eyelash.

"*Gloria?*" I said.

Still nothing.

It took Matthias grabbing her by both plump shoulders and shaking her until her butterfly bow rattled to get Gloria to finally open her eyes. Even then, she still seemed to have a little trouble focusing. Until her eyes came to rest on Matthias.

"Well, hello-o-o there!" she said, wrapping her arms around his neck. From the look on her face, you might've thought she'd just found Matthias under her Christmas tree.

I hated to spoil Gloria's Christmas, but I was more than a little anxious to get some answers. I thrust the photographs of Wanda Faye and Jenny in front of Gloria's face, as Matthias disentangled himself and took a fast couple of steps away from Gloria's outstretched hands.

From the look on Matthias's face, you might've thought he'd just narrowly escaped one of the dinosaurs in Jurassic Park.

"Gloria," I said, "do you know this woman? Or this little girl?"

The photo I was holding practically under Gloria's nose was one of Wanda Faye's best, I thought. Wanda Faye had on a black bikini trimmed in iridescent pink fringe. To complete the ensemble, she was also wearing long black gloves with pink fringe, a black collar around her neck, and black chaps with pink fringe going down each leg.

No doubt about it. Dale Evans had never looked like this.

Jenny, on the other hand, was once again seated on her mother's lap. Once again the little girl was wearing—you guessed it—the blue calico dress.

It took Gloria a while to answer me. For one thing, she was too busy putting her hands down and looking disappointed that Matthias was no longer within grabbing range. For another thing, she still seemed to be having trouble focusing her eyes.

"What?" she finally said. Her voice was still slurred. "What woman? What girl?"

At this point I believe I exhibited real patience. I took a single, deep breath, and thrust the snapshot even closer to Gloria's face. In another minute, I'd have the thing plastered to her eyelashes.

Fortunately, this last did not prove necessary. Gloria did manage to focus. You could tell the exact moment Gloria accomplished this amazing feat, because that's when her eyes increased in size about three times. "Oh, my," Gloria said. Her mouth pinched itself into a thin line.

"Gloria," I said, "do you—"

Gloria interrupted me. She tried to come up with a sniff, but in her condition, it was too much of a stretch. It came out sounding more like a snort. "Why, look at that," she said, glancing over at Matthias. Who, I might add, showed no signs of moving any closer to her. Oddly enough. "Just look at that." She pointed a plump finger at the snapshot I was holding. "Ain't that icky?"

Gloria was clearly not directing her question to me. Evidently, she was certain that a man of Matthias's educated sensibilities would be instantly offended at this snapshot, whereas someone like *me*—who, every-body knew, killed people in her spare time—might not even realize there was anything unusual about this mother-daughter scene.

Gloria was hurrying on, "Why, that icky woman is sitting right there with that little kid, and she's got on that icky outfit. Why, that's the most icky—"

Gloria sounded as if she might ramble on at length on the subject of *ickiness*. I interrupted. "Gloria, do you know either the woman or the little girl in this picture?"

Gloria lifted her chin. She had trouble keeping it lifted, but I thought she gave it a valiant effort. "Why, of course, I don't know 'em," she said. Gloria's voice was slurring unbelievably bad now, but she still managed to sound affronted. "I certainly don't associate with that sort of-of-of"—it took her a moment to come up with the right words, but even before she said them, I had a pretty good guess what they were going to be—"*icky* person!" Gloria finished.

Oh yes, that would've been my guess, all right.

To drive her point home, Gloria gave her red curls such a vigorous shake that her green butterfly bow finally did fall off. Stooping heavily to retrieve it off the floor, Gloria went on, "Nope. I ain't never seen that poor little girl or that icky woman in my life!" She stuck the green bow back in her hair with a lit-tle flourish.

Having done this, Gloria looked as if she might be inclined toward nodding off again. Her body started slumping again. Watching her was like watching an inflatable doll with a slow leak. Gloria's head began to tilt slowly to one side. Unlike Matthias, *I* moved even closer, and started talking as fast as I could. "Gloria, do you have any idea why this snapshot was in a folder labeled *Porter Meredith*?"

Gloria straightened up and blinked a couple times

before she answered me. "No," she finally said. "Why?"

I guess at this point I must've looked as if I were finally losing what little patience I had left because Matthias stepped in. "That's what we're asking you," Matthias said, moving to stand just in back of my left shoulder. You could tell he wasn't about to get any closer to Gloria than he absolutely had to. You could also tell that he fully intended to keep *me* between them. "Why would this snapshot be in this particular folder?"

Gloria shrugged. "I ain't got no idea," she said. "I ain't never seen that picture before." Gloria pronounced the word "pitcher." She was back to shaking her head again. Her butterfly held on this time, though. "Never before in my life!" Leaning toward Matthias, she gave him a long look through her lashes. "Believe me, hon, I'd tell *you*, if I'd seen it before. *I really would.*"

Oddly enough, Matthias did not looked flattered.

What he looked was long-suffering as he glanced over at me.

I saw his glance heading my way, and turned instead to look at Gloria.

"I mean it," she was saying. "If I knew, I'd tell you."

Well now. The bad thing about knowing for certain that somebody is a liar is that you really can't believe a thing they say.

Gloria could be telling the Gospel truth.

Or she could be outdoing Pinocchio.

The inflatable Gloria was beginning her slow leak again, so I hurried to show her the rest of the snapshots before her eyes completely closed. This time I held the snapshots right up in front of her face. The way you might show flash cards to a preschooler.

"Gloria," I said, "do you recognize *anybody* in these pictures?"

"I already *told* you," she said. With Matthias, she may have been batting her eyes and maintaining her willingness to help, but when I was asking the questions, Gloria actually sounded like a preschooler. Her voice had become a petulant whine. A *slurred* petulant whine. "I don't know nobody in them. I don't know why you keep showing me all these icky pictures when I already done told you that—"

Gloria broke off here as she caught sight of the photo of Wanda Faye and Jenny posing with the other women. Swallowing once, she peered closer at the photo. "Oh, my," she said. Her voice sounded shocked. "Why, that there is Candy! Sure as I'm sitting here! It's her!"

Gloria was not looking exactly super alert as she said this, but her eyes did seem to be glued to the snapshot I was holding in my hand. "I can't believe it!" she went on. "But that's Candy, all right! It really is!"

"Candy?" I said.

Gloria's butterfly was flapping away again. "Candy Cherry. I met her right here in this office. When I was working temporary for Eddie." Gloria dragged her eyes away from the photo, looking first at Matthias and then over at me. "Candy come in for an appointment with Eddie, and we got to talking, and, after no time at all, we got to be friends." At this point, Gloria blinked a couple of times as if trying to clear her head. I could've told her it was hopeless. "Why," she added, looking even more stunned, "Eddie told me that Candy was one of his clients from before!"

"Before?" Matthias asked.

"Before Eddie started, you know, representing strippers and prostitutes—" Gloria pronounced the word "prosh-tee-toots." "—and—and icky people like that," she finished. She was sounding hurt. "I tell you, I had no idea that Candy, of all people, could be a-a-a—"

Once again, I had a good guess for what words Gloria was trying to think of, and once again, she didn't disappoint me. "—an *icky person!*" Gloria finished, shaking her head still again. "I just can't believe my Eddie *lied* to me!"

I didn't say a word, but a few thoughts did flash through my mind. Let me see now. Edward Bartlett had filed a fraudulent lawsuit against me, he had induced Gloria herself to lie under oath, and now she couldn't believe he'd lie to her? What did she think? That even though "her Eddie" had made it a habit to be dishonest with the entire rest of the world, in *her* case, he'd always made a notable exception?

Gloria was hurrying on. "You woulda been fooled, too." She pointed a plump finger in my direction. "You woulda! Candy's a perfect lady. A *perfect* lady!"

I didn't say anything this time, either. Even though, of course, I was now thinking: You mean to tell me that you met a woman in the office of an attorney who you know for a fact represents prostitutes—and the name of the woman you've met happens to be *Candy Cherry*, for God's sake—and you didn't even suspect *once* that she might be a hooker?

Gloria was back to staring at the photograph again. "That's her, though. A lot younger, of course. But it's her, all right. She's still got that widow's peak. I'd recognize that anywhere."

I looked back at the photo. The only woman with a widow's peak was standing right in back of Wanda Faye and Jenny. A tall, shapely woman with very straight, shoulder-length platinum blond hair, she was wearing—believe it or not—what looked to be an upstairs maid outfit. Or rather, the kind of outfit the upstairs maid of a man's dreams might wear. Black fishnet hose, black teddy trimmed in white lace, a tiny frilly white apron, a tiny frilly white hat, and, of course—what no maid should ever be without—a white feather duster.

Cute.

I didn't even want to consider to what uses that feather duster might've been put.

Instead, I peered at the woman's face more closely. Her widow's peak, high cheekbones, and small chin made her face look almost perfectly heart-shaped. She had probably been quite pretty, but you couldn't tell from this photo. You also couldn't tell exactly how old she was.

The reason you couldn't tell, in both instances, was because of all the makeup she was wearing. Candy's large, gray eyes were rimmed in heavy, black eyeliner, her lashes were thick with mascara, and her lips practically glowed under layers of dark red lip gloss.

Goodness. Tammy Faye Baker would've considered this woman's makeup a bit overdone.

"I can't believe I've been feeling so tickled that someone like her would pal around with me," Gloria was now saying. "I mean, I actually thought that Candy was being awful openminded to hang around with the likes of me, since she's so upper crust and all." Gloria's tone was distinctly miffed. "Why, Candy even called me up this morning! Right after she read about Eddie in the paper. Saying how sorry she was and all. She didn't say nothing about being no hooker!"

I blinked at that one. How had Gloria expected that conversation to go? "Hi, Gloria, I just called to say I'm so sorry about Eddie, and, oh, by the way, I'm a prostitute."

Gloria was frowning now. Incidentally, not a pretty sight. Her red eyebrows made almost a solid line across her forehead. It looked as if a red chalk line had been drawn across her face, using a ruler to make sure the line was straight. "I thought Candy was being so sweet and all, but *I* was the one being sweet! Candy shoulda been grateful I had anything at all to do with her!" Gloria now blinked a couple times and then for a long moment, she said absolutely nothing as her eyes got bigger and bigger. "*Oh my God*," she finally gasped out. "I've been going all over town with her! Shopping. And to restaurants. People have seen us together!"

I just looked at her. *So?*

"Oh my Lordy, Lordy, Lordy," Gloria went on. "People might think that we—that we're the same! That we're both—*oh my God*!"

Gloria seemed to be working herself up unnecessarily. Unless Candy was running around town these days in the exact same getup she'd been wearing in the snapshot, I'd say Gloria was being a little oversensitive. "Now, Gloria," I said, "there's no reason to—"

Gloria didn't let me finish. "Candy never even gave me a hint! She just went right on, letting me tag along with her all over town! Right out in public! What a dirty trick!"

Trick was a word I myself would've avoided in this particular discussion, but Gloria didn't even pause. "Why, I've got half a notion to go over to Candy's house right this minute and give her a piece of my mind!"

I blinked. Hey now. Hold the phone. Gloria wanted to have a little chat with her friend Candy? "*What* a good idea," I said. "Would you like us to drive you over there?"

Lord. From the reaction my words immediately got from Matthias, you might've thought I'd suggested a drive-by shooting. Matthias took a step away this time from both me and Gloria. Once he'd put some distance between us, he turned to stare, however, only at me.

I wouldn't have believed his eyes could get that round.

Gloria, for her part, was still frowning. "That's what I ought to do, all right," she grumbled, her voice as slurred as ever. "I ought to tell her to her face just how mean it was to be so nice!"

I wasn't sure I was following Gloria completely here, but I nodded anyway. "You're absolutely right, Gloria," I said. "Why, it's awful the way Candy took advantage of you. She should've told you about her past right away. I think you owe it to yourself to tell her exactly how you feel about it. *Right now.*"

At this point Matthias's eyes were beginning to bear a distinct resemblance to white sidewalls. "Schuyler?" he said, putting a forefinger in the air. "*Schuyler?* Could I speak with you for a second?"

I gave him a quick nod, said, "Sure, just a minute," and then I leaned closer to Gloria. So that I was more or less towering over her. "Listen, Gloria, Matthias and I would be happy to drive you over to Candy's house. So that you can talk to her. And get all this off your chest."

It's amazing what you can talk a drunk into. Gloria didn't even hesitate. She nodded and started trying to get to her feet. She only got about halfway, though, and began to sway as badly as if a stiff wind had just started blowing through Bartlett's office.

It looked to me as if getting Gloria to her feet might end up being a group project.

"That's what I'm going to do, all right." She was now mumbling, as much to herself as anybody else. "Yessirree, I'm going right over to the Willowcrest, and I'm telling her—"

"The Willowcrest?" I said.

Gloria's butterfly flapped again. "That's where Candy lives."

It was here that Matthias not only did his white sidewalls impression, he added a sharp intake of breath.

It wasn't difficult, of course, to guess what had caused Matthias's little fit of apoplexy. The Willowcrest does happen to be one of the most luxurious high-rise condominiums in all of Louisville. It also happens to be one of the most prestigious addresses in the area. And, also one of the most expensive.

Apparently, then, old Candy had left her past far behind her.

Either that, or else her occupation was a *lot* more profitable that I'd ever suspected.

Heavens. This could possibly explain why it was the world's oldest profession.

Hell. It might even beat out becoming an anesthesiologist.

"You're absolutely right," Gloria was going on. "I should just tell her. Candy needs to know what a dirty trick—"

Matthias was now tugging at my arm. "Schuyler, could I speak to you? Right *now*?" His voice was urgent.

I turned to look at him, but evidently, Matthias was intent on getting me out of Gloria's earshot. He took my elbow and more or less steered me back into the adjoining room. There, standing in front of Bartlett's file cabinets, Matthias hissed, "Schuyler, Gloria is *drunk*!"

The man actually said this as if it were news. What did he think? That I thought she just had a speech impediment?

"Well of course, she's drunk," I said. I reached out and patted him on the arm. "Don't worry, Matthias. We won't let her drive."

Matthias can get so excited. He actually threw his hands in the air. "Schuyler, Gloria is drunk, and she doesn't know what she's saying! Hell, she might not even really know that woman in the snapshot! I'm not even sure, in the condition she's in, that she'd recognize her own mother!"

I didn't even blink. "Now, Matthias, she would, too, know her own mom—"

Matthias didn't let me finish. "Schuyler, for crying out loud!"

Matthias says this a lot when he gets upset. He also rubs his beard. Right now he was all but clawing at it. He could've been digging furrows for planting.

"Do you really think," he hurried on, "that it's a good idea to barge into the *Willowcrest*, of all places, and accuse some woman who lives there of being a prostitute?"

I didn't blink this time, either. "Matthias, I have no intention of making any accusations. All I want is some information about the woman and the little girl in the photographs. That's all."

It was Matthias's turn to take a deep breath. "But, Schuyler," he said, obviously making a concentrated effort to talk calmly, "to get that information, don't you intend to ask some woman you've never met before if she'd like to discuss the good old days when she was sleeping with strangers for a living?"

I cleared my throat. That did, I suppose, sum up the pertinent facts, but I certainly wouldn't have put it like that. Moreover, I wished Matthias had not put it like that, either. Mainly, because up to that moment it hadn't completely dawned on me that this was what I was about to do.

And yet, what choice did I have?

"Matthias," I said, "how else am I going to find out what Wanda Faye and Jenny had to do with Porter Meredith? I mean, either Gloria really doesn't know either one of them, or else she's refusing to tell us what she does know. Either way, she's a dead end."

Matthias didn't say a word. He just stood there, staring at me.

"Our only lead," I went on, "is that we know for a fact that this Candy Cherry person knew both the woman and the little girl. What's more, she can't deny it. She's right there in the picture with them!"

Matthias took a deep breath, and dug a few more furrows in his beard. "Schuyler, this woman could call the police on you. For harassing her. Or, for God knows what."

I shrugged. "Well, that's why I think we should bring Gloria along. Surely, Candy wouldn't call the police on her own friend. And while Candy might not be willing to talk to us—people she doesn't even know—she'll surely talk to Gloria."

I believe I was making perfect sense here, but to look at Matthias's troubled face, you'd have thought I was talking gibberish. "Schuyler," he said, his tone beleaguered, "I just don't want to see you getting into any more trouble than—"

"—I already am?" I finished for him. I'll admit it, by this time I was getting irritated. So far, Matthias had objected to my talking to Gloria, he'd objected to my looking through Bartlett's files, and now he was objecting to my speaking with a woman who might know something that would help me find out who really killed Bartlett.

"Look, Matthias," I said, and yes, my own tone now was a bit clipped. "I'm trying to get myself *out* of trouble, understand? That's the only reason I want to talk to this Candy Cherry person."

Matthias rolled his eyes. "For crying out loud," he said.

Didn't I tell you? He can get to be a broken record.

"Schuyler," Matthias went on, "do you really think

a woman who's obviously done very well for herself would now want to dredge up something sordid she did more than fifteen years ago?"

"I don't know," I said. "Why don't we go ask her?" I turned to do just that, but Matthias reached out and grabbed my arm.

"Schuyler, this woman might not like to talk about her past."

I just looked at him. "Matthias, I don't *like* to be accused of murder."

I shook off his hand, brushed past him and once again headed into the outer office.

Chapter 14

As I had expected, getting Gloria to her feet did turn out to be a group project. Matthias had to take one plump arm, and I had to take the other, in order to haul her off the couch. Even so, it took us two tries before we got her upright.

If I had been the one so drunk that I could no longer stand on my own, I believe I would've been embarrassed. Gloria, however, apparently felt that getting this intoxicated was some kind of achievement. "Oh boy, I've really got a buzz on now!" she said, slurring every word. She actually sounded proud.

"Man, oh, man," she went on cheerily as Matthias and I grunted and groaned, pulling her to her feet, "I am *totally* sloshed!"

As Gloria was saying this, Matthias was giving me a pointed look. It was a look that said, *See? Gloria herself is backing up what I just told you.*

I gave Matthias a pointed look of my own. One that said: So? I don't care if Gloria is *comatose*, I still intend to have a little chat with her friend, Candy.

Comatose or not, once she was standing, Gloria did seem to be able to propel herself forward on her own steam. She looked like a broken wheel, wobbling across the office toward the stairs, and she grabbed Matthias's arm every other minute. Still, she did keep right on putting one foot in front of the other all by herself, and she actually reached the landing without falling down once.

No minor accomplishment in her present condition.

On the way, Gloria made no move whatsoever to take *my* arm. As a matter of fact, the second she was on her feet, Gloria shrugged my hand off. Much the way you might've shrugged off Lizzie Borden, if Lizzie had been giving you a little help.

It was just as well. I was holding onto the envelope with the photographs inside, and if Gloria kept grabbing onto me the way she kept grabbing onto Matthias, she probably would've wrinkled that envelope pretty bad.

Once we all started down the narrow stairs, Gloria stopped her grabbing. After that, she just had Matthias's arm in a death grip.

Even with her grip on Matthias, Gloria still scared me a couple of times. She was so unsteady on her feet, I was sure she was about to do a half gainer over the banister. Taking Matthias with her.

That old saying must be true, though. The one about how the Lord watches over children and drunks? Gloria made it all the way to the bottom without incident.

The little trouper.

She became even more trouperlike about five steps from the door. That was where she burst into song.

In my opinion, you've never really lived until you've heard an intoxicated, middle-aged leprechaun belt out the first few lines of "People Who Need People."

Of course, after hearing such a thing, you might not want to *continue* living, but that's something else again.

What possessed Gloria to suddenly begin warbling at the top of her lungs was beyond me, but maybe she was so drunk, she didn't need a reason. She moved on to "I Wanna Hold Your Hand"—a particularly appropriate tune, I thought, under the circumstances—and then on to "Dancing in the Streets."

This last was particularly inappropriate. While we *had* gotten out of the building by then, and were indeed on the street, Gloria could barely walk, let alone dance.

She continued singing after she'd settled herself into the front seat of my Tercel, after I'd gone around to the driver's side, pulled the seat forward, and squeezed myself into the backseat, and even after Matthias had started the motor and pulled away.

The woman would not shut up. If anything, once the car started moving, Gloria sang even louder. Apparently just to make sure everybody could hear her over the engine.

She needn't have concerned herself. You could've heard her over a plane crash.

The only time Gloria called a halt to her little serenade was some ten minutes later, when we were about half way to the Willowcrest condominiums. She stopped right in the middle of "Love Me Tender," and abruptly turned toward Matthias to ask, "You two really *are* taking me to see Candy, aren't you?"

I gave Gloria a long look. Evidently, she'd come out of her alcoholic fog just long enough to realize that she'd actually agreed to get into a car with me. Again.

So now what did she think? That Matthias and I could be taking her on a "ride?" At least, I think that's what it was called in the gangster movies I'd watched when I was little. I had not realized at the time that people like James Cagney and Edward G. Robinson were one day going to be role models for me so I hadn't paid all that close attention.

Matthias was giving Gloria a look that was even longer than the one he'd given me earlier. "That's right," he finally said, "we're on our way to see your friend, Candy." His tone implied that he was speaking to a psychiatric patient.

Matthias's word must not have been good enough, because Gloria went on as if he hadn't even spoken. "Because if you two ain't really taking me to see Candy—and, well, I turn up missing—I want you to know right now that I told a lot of people who I was having lunch with today."

This was too much. "Gloria," I said, "we're going to see Candy. We really are."

Like Matthias, I was wasting my breath. Gloria didn't even glance in my direction. "I've written letters, too," Gloria said, still looking over at Matthias. "Tons of them. I've already mailed them, too. I've told everybody I know exactly *who* they should talk to if something happens to me." As Gloria said the word *who*, her eyes sort of wandered toward the backseat. In my direction.

What a surprise.

I rather doubted Gloria had written anybody, but I decided not to go into it with her. Having a little chat about whether or not Gloria had notified her friends that she intended to lunch with a murderer was not exactly something I wanted to do while Matthias was listening.

Call me sensitive.

"Gloria," I said, biting out each word, "we *are* on our way to the Willowcrest to talk to your friend, Candy. Really."

Gloria's response was to start singing "Love Me Tender" again.

While I listened to her do the worst impression of Elvis I'd ever heard, it hit me why Gloria was singing. For her, it was probably like whistling in the dark. It gave her something else to think about other than homicidal old me.

What it gave *me* to think about was something else

again. Was it possible that Gloria intended to continue her medley of old favorites even after we got to the Willowcrest? If so, we'd be lucky if the doorman there even let us get out of the car.

In Louisville, there are not many buildings that have doormen. Wouldn't you know, the Willowcrest would be one of the few that did?

In fact, the only other building with a doorman that immediately comes to mind is the Seelbach Hotel downtown. I suppose this notable lack of doormen is because Louisville doesn't have the crime rate that a lot of the larger cities do. In Chicago or New York, you might actually need a doorman for security purposes. In Louisville, the thing you mainly need a doorman for is status. It's a not-so-subtle way of reminding passersby that, yes, the people who pass through these particular portals do have a *lot* of money.

Indeed, these people have so much money, they don't have to see just anybody.

They particularly don't have to see some drunk leprechaun bellowing hits from the sixties.

"Gloria," I said when we were only a few blocks away, "let's not sing anymore, okay?"

I don't think she even heard me.

She abruptly left the sixties, and began to sing what was, no doubt, a favorite of hers. It's the sort of song, I'm sure, that's most often heard in truly plush, high-society type surroundings. Like, for example, that of the Willowcrest.

Gloria began to sing, "Ninety-nine Bottles of Beer on the Wall."

She'd gotten to ninety-seven bottles when I couldn't stand it any longer. I tapped her on the shoulder. "Gloria?"

My touch actually made her jump. She jumped even worse this time than she had back at Jake Mull's. She also stopped singing. Which, if I'd had any idea that just touching her would do, I'd have touched her a *lot* sooner.

"Gloria," I said, "how long did you say you've known Candy?"

I didn't much care, but my thinking here was to keep her talking so that any singing in the near future would be impossible.

Gloria was still in the process of recoiling from my touch, but she did answer me. "Awhile." That's all she said.

She immediately resumed singing "Nine-*tee-sev-en*—," and then Matthias interrupted her. Apparently, he'd caught on to what I was trying to do.

Or else by this time his eardrums were aching so bad, he was ready to try anything to shut her up.

"So, *Gloria*," he practically shouted—a thing he had to do in order to be heard over Gloria's "*bott-tulls of be-eee-er*"— "You say you've been friends with Candy for awhile?"

Not exactly sparkling repartee, but it did the trick. Gloria broke off her song. "Friends?" she said. "Why, I wouldn't call that woman a friend of mine." She shook her red curls. "Not anymore. Nossirreebob."

I heard her say this, but to tell you the truth, I wasn't really listening. All that really hit me for a long moment was that Gloria was no longer singing.

It was sort of like listening to the odd silence right after a jackhammer has stopped.

"You don't say," Matthias was saying.

"I *do* say!" Gloria said. "What's more, I shoulda known long before this that Candy was no friend of mine. The way she kept carrying on about Eddie. She said terrible things about him!"

"Terrible things?" Matthias, bless his heart, apparently intended to keep feeding her questions until, oh, maybe, next July.

"That's right," Gloria said. "Why, to hear Candy talk, you'da thought Eddie was a common criminal!"

Matthias seemed to be doing very well all by himself so I certainly wasn't about to put in my two cents. Particularly since my interrupting might put Gloria right back into singing mode.

However, at this point, the words, *Tell me something I don't know*, did cross my mind.

"Candy wanted me to dump him! Really! Can you believe it?"

Actually, what I had trouble believing was that anybody would ever date Bartlett in the first place.

Matthias was shaking his shaggy head. "No kidding."

"*Now* I realize," Gloria was saying, "that Candy was just being spiteful! She didn't want me to have a man of my own, because she didn't have one." Gloria was flapping her green butterfly bow again. "And, of course, she wasn't *ever* going to have a man of *her* own, because no man would have her, after what she's been up to!"

I was waiting for the word "icky" to show up in the conversation. I didn't have to wait long.

"I mean, of all the icky ways to make a living, that has got to take the cake!"

I couldn't help myself. Before Gloria got completely sidetracked, I leaned forward. "What terrible things did Candy say about Eddie?"

I probably shouldn't have said anything, because Gloria did a quick intake of breath. As if maybe Charles Manson had leaned forward and whispered a few things in her ear. "Well, now that you ask," Gloria said, without turning around to face me, "*some people* might not think it was so bad of Candy to say—"

I believe the implication here was that the person who'd killed Bartlett probably wouldn't think it all that terrible. We murderers have been known to be singularly lacking in empathy.

"—but, well," Gloria went on, "*I* thought it was real mean!"

I took a deep breath. This being confused with murderers was getting old. "Gloria," I said, "I am sure whatever Candy said was just awful."

Gloria did not look the least bit impressed by my rush of warmth. "Well, it WAS awful!" she said with a sniff. "Candy actually told me that Eddie would sell his own grandmother if he could get five dollars for her!"

I blinked. Well, now. The way I saw it, Candy was an astute judge of character. This did put a different slant on things. It looked as if I could add Candy's name to the ever-growing list of People Who Wouldn't Be Shedding Too Many Tears Now That Edward Bartlett Was Dearly Departed.

Of course, just having your name on that list didn't exactly make you a prime suspect in his murder.

Or did it?

My own name was on that list, and everybody seemed to think *I* could've done it.

I was definitely getting more and more eager to have a few words with Candy Cherry.

By now I could see the imposing stone and brick facade of the Willowcrest towering up ahead. I'd been to the Willowcrest several times before this, showing condos that came up for sale, so I knew that the Willowcrest not only had a doorman, it also had a security guard.

A bit redundant, you might think, but I believe this is yet another way that the Willowcrest proclaims to the world that it's the home sweet home of those with megabucks. If the winding driveway doesn't convince you, or if the huge oak double-door entrance with the stained glass windows on either side doesn't, then the uniformed security guard housed in her very own building diligently checking every single person who goes in or out should do the trick.

Getting permission to walk barefoot through the gold bullions at Fort Knox would probably be easier than getting into the Willowcrest.

Knowing all this, I had no intention of letting the guard get a good look at Gloria. Matthias apparently concurred. He'd no sooner put on the brakes, than he was opening the car door on his side and bringing the driver's seat forward so that I could get out. He made no move to go around to open Gloria's door.

She noticed it right away, too. From inside the car, we heard Gloria say, "Hey! You want me to come, too, or what?"

Matthias and I answered in unison. "*Oh no, that's okay.*"

I tried to soften it a little. "You don't have to bother," I said, leaning down and looking in at her. "You just sit right there, and I'll go check in with the guard."

I made it sound as if I were doing her a monumental favor.

I quickly headed for the security building, walking very fast, just in case Gloria decided she didn't need any favors. Particularly from me.

As I moved away from the car, I could hear Matthias. He was getting back into the car and asking, "So, Gloria, have you come here often?"

The man was obviously scraping the bottom of the barrel for conversation material.

I gave the security guard Gloria's name first because this would be the name that Candy Cherry recognized, then I gave her mine, and then Matthias's. While the woman phoned Candy to see if it was all right to let us drop by, I looked around. The Willowcrest grounds seemed to have been planted with an inordinate number of magnolias. There was a huge magnolia tree on either side of the front entrance, two more in the narrow courtyard around the back, and three more on the side lawn. Evidently, the Willowcrest is not only intent on convincing people just how rich its occupants are, it's also intent on convincing people that Louisville is indeed a part of the South.

This is hardly a new idea. I've lived here all my life, and I've never heard anyone even question whether or not this is the South. It's just taken for granted. Even though, if you look up Louisville on any U.S. map, you'll find that it's neither particularly north, nor particularly south, but in fact, looks to be in the exact middle.

I suspect, however, that the reason Louisvillians keep on insisting that we're in the South is, no doubt, the exact same reason that the Willowcrest wants to encourage that kind of thinking, too.

The South sounds a *lot* classier than the Middle.

Candy Cherry must've given her permission because the security guard was now extending a clipboard in my direction. "You need to sign in."

There was a tense moment during which I was afraid that the guard was also going to insist that Matthias and Gloria sign in, too. I wasn't the least bit sure that Gloria could even make an X, let alone sign her entire name. Fortunately, however, right after I signed my name, the guard said, "Oh, you can just sign the other guests' names for them. Everybody does that."

This seemed to be a notable breakdown in security, but I wasn't about to argue. I did as I was told, and headed back toward my car.

There was one other tense moment. After Matthias reached into the backseat, retrieved the manila envelope out from where I'd left it, and handed it to me, he got out, went around, and started helping Gloria out of the car. She immediately began wobbling so badly, I was sure she wasn't going to make it to the front door. But, no, leaning heavily on Matthias's arm, she negotiated the trip like the little trouper she was.

Or rather like the little trouper she was no longer. Amazingly enough, Gloria wasn't even humming as all three of us headed inside.

Of course, it was probably taking all her concentration just to figure out which foot to put in front of the other.

Apparently, getting the okay from the security guard put you among elite company. The doorman not only opened one of the front doors for us, he tipped his hat with the sort of flourish you might expect him to give Lady Di.

Gloria certainly seemed to appreciate the attention. As we went through the huge double doors and stepped into the lobby, she gave the doorman a huge grin and tapped her green butterfly bow at him in reply.

The lobby of the Willowcrest was one of those places that immediately make you want to whisper. By the time we'd made our way past the beveled glass mirrors in the ornate gold leaf frames, the huge potted philodendrons, and the antique settee over in the corner, Matthias and I were conversing in the hushed tones of funeral directors.

"What floor is she on?"

"The guard outside said the third."

The opulence of the Willowcrest lobby may have reduced Matthias and me to whispering, but Gloria seemed singularly unaffected. "Boy, oh *boy*," she bellowed, "is this class or what?"

I counted at least four heads in the lobby that swiveled in our direction when Gloria spoke. All of these heads were silver-haired, and none of them looked approving.

I gave Gloria the curtest of nods to acknowledge

that I had indeed heard what she'd said—so she didn't have to repeat it—and then I immediately looked away so she wouldn't say anything else.

With subdued lighting from brass wall sconces, real marble floors, and wallcovering in muted tones of blue, the Willowcrest lobby gave you the same feeling you get when you walk into a cathedral.

If, of course, the cathedral happened to have a huge crystal chandelier overhead, a gurgling water fountain in the center, and a floor the size of a football field.

The irony of a prostitute living in such surroundings did not escape me.

It didn't escape Matthias, either. "Are you sure about this?" he whispered to me. "Because this certainly doesn't look like the kind of place that—"

He didn't finish his sentence, because Gloria interrupted him. Matthias was still holding her arm—more or less guarding against the possibility of her falling down before we made it to the elevator and the two of us having to drag her limp body inside—and she must've thought that Matthias was talking to her. "Oh, this is the right place, all right," she said. "Like I said, I've been here before, and I know."

As we made our way through the football-field lobby, the man behind the ornately curved antique desk near what was just about the fifty-yard line indicated the walnut-paneled elevator about ten feet away with a discreet wave of his hand.

As I mentioned earlier, I—like Gloria—had been here before. Several times. In all those times I'd never once seen this guy do anything other than this. I finally concluded that this must be this guy's entire job. Waving at the elevator. Soundlessly, of course.

Even the elevator in this place knew not to make any noise. Its doors opened without so much as a squeak.

What the elevator knew about silence, however, was

obviously lost on Gloria. When the elevator doors opened, she let out a whistle that not only turned the four heads in our direction again, but could also probably be heard by the guard outside. "Oh, yeah, this is really, *really* posh." She turned to glance at me. "*Now*, do ya unnerstan why I'd of never guessed in a million years that Candy was a *hooker*?"

I may have been wrong, but that last word sounded louder than all the rest. It actually seemed to echo around us.

Gloria's voice continued to be slurred, to be sure, but it wasn't quite as bad as before. I was pretty sure everyone within earshot could understand her perfectly.

Matthias, for one, certainly understood her. As soon as the words were out of Gloria's mouth, he made a sort of strangling noise.

It seemed too much to hope that Gloria's voice had not carried across the lobby. As Matthias and I yanked Gloria onto the elevator, I couldn't help giving the four heads and the Elevator-waver a quick peek.

The mouths of every one of them were hanging open.

Oh God. I mentally weighed the chances of there being anybody else in this building with the name Candy, and decided that they were slim to none.

I certainly didn't want to be responsible for ruining the new life Candy had built for herself.

Thinking fast, I tried to make my own voice every bit as loud as Gloria's had been. "*Yes, yes*," I said. "*Candy sure does hook beautiful rugs*, doesn't she? Why, I do believe she's the best hooker I've ever seen! My goodness, yes, her rugs are gorgeous!"

I wasn't sure the Elevator-waver and the four heads bought any of this, but it was all I could think of off the top of my head. Frankly, I thought I'd done pretty well, particularly on such short notice, but Matthias evidently didn't agree.

He was now staring at me as if I'd lost my mind.

Gloria made it unanimous. "Why, Candy don't make no rugs," she said just as the elevator doors were closing. "What the hell are you talking about?"

I decided it was probably useless to try to explain it to her.

Gloria must not have expected an answer, because she didn't even look my way as the elevator began to climb.

As soon as the doors opened, Gloria lurched through them toward condo #302. Fortunately, that particular condo was only a couple steps away. Gloria was still actually standing close to upright as she pressed the doorbell.

Which, of course, in this place you couldn't hear at all.

The doorbell must've sounded inside, though, because right away, the door opened.

I blinked. Standing there in the doorway was a woman who looked to be in her middle fifties. About my height, she was a good thirty pounds heavier. Her hair was a drab brown, streaked heavily with gray, and pulled back from her face into a ponytail. A ponytail held in place by a thick rubber band.

Wearing a heather gray sweatsuit that made her look completely shapeless, the woman was somebody you might've passed a thousand times on the street and never noticed. Except for one thing. On her feet were large furry, gray slippers. Each slipper had two paws in front, a long tail in the back, button eyes, and felt triangle ears.

The woman was wearing cat slippers.

In fact, she looked for all the world as if she were standing on the backs of two very large, very fluffy Persians.

When, with some effort, I lifted my eyes from her feet, I noticed that the cat slippers were just about the only distinctive thing she had on. She wore no nail polish, no jewelry, no makeup of any kind. Not even lipstick.

I couldn't keep from staring. If anything, this woman looked more like an ex-nun than an ex-prostitute.

And yet, without a shadow of a doubt, this *was* the woman in the snapshot I'd found in Bartlett's office.

Gloria had been absolutely right. It was still easy to see the young woman Candy Cherry had been. With her hair pulled back like that, you could plainly see her widow's peak. And there was no disguising those high cheekbones.

"Gloria!" Candy said, opening the door to her condo even wider. "I am so glad you came by! Honey, I've been thinking about you ever since I read about Eddie in the paper!"

"Yeah?" Gloria said. "Well, I've been thinking about *you*, too." Her tone was belligerent. "Ever since I seen a certain picture."

Candy stared at her, clearly puzzled. "Picture?"

That appeared to be my cue.

I stepped forward, gripping the envelope a little tighter.

Lord. Matthias had been right. This wasn't going to be easy.

Chapter 15

Standing in the hallway of the Willowcrest with Gloria, Matthias, and Candy Cherry all looking at me expectantly, I took a deep breath.

"Miss Cherry," I said, "we just found some pictures in Eddie's office, and we'd like to talk to you about them."

I was using my best no-nonsense professional voice—the one I generally reserve for telling people that their loan application has been rejected. This voice has helped me ward off quite a few ugly scenes—mostly ones featuring my getting yelled at—but Candy Cherry was clearly not intimidated. She turned cool gray eyes to mine, shifted her weight from one cat foot to another, and said, without missing a beat. "It's *Ms*. Cherry. Not Miss."

I blinked. A liberated prostitute. You don't run into too many of those.

"And who are you, honey?" Candy asked.

I really hate being called *honey*, but this didn't seem like a good time to make an issue of it. Besides, in her line of work, Candy had probably gotten accustomed to calling everybody *honey* a long time ago. A habit that ingrained could be hard to break.

I gave her my best saleswoman smile. "I'm Schuyler Ridgway," I said, extending my hand, "and this is Matthias Cross. We're trying to find out—"

I was going to ask her right off about Wanda Faye

and Jenny, because—unless I missed my guess—
Candy was about a half minute from shutting her front
door right in our faces.

As a real estate agent who's done quite a bit of
neighborhood canvassing in my time, I've developed
a second sense about these things. Would you believe,
as soon as somebody answers the door, I can predict
almost to the split second exactly how long I've got
to say my pitch? There's nothing mysterious about it.
It's just reading body language. Picking up on signals.
For example, in this instance, shaking Candy's hand
was a lot like taking hold of a dead fish. That's a tip-
off, all right.

Like I said, I intended to quiz her right off, but
Candy didn't give me the chance. She'd no sooner
finished giving me the fish-hand when she said,
"Schuyler Ridgway? You know, your name sounds familiar, honey." She frowned and, reaching into the
right side pocket of her sweatsuit, she pulled out a
pair of wire-rimmed glasses. As she put them on, the
glasses instantly made her eyes look four sizes bigger.
Now she not only shook hands like a fish, she bore a
remarkable resemblance to one. "Schuyler Ridgway,
hmm, Schuyler Ridgway," she said, leaning closer and
squinting at me. "Honey, haven't we met—"

This time it was Gloria who didn't let Candy finish.
"No, you ain't met her! And you should be glad! On
accounta she kilt Eddie. *That's* who she is!"

I believe, at this point, I made a strangling noise
almost identical to the one Matthias had made earlier.

Matthias, for his part, did a quick intake of breath.

Candy, on the other hand, did neither. She just
stood there, flat on her cat feet, in the middle of her
doorway, and looked stunned.

I tried for a little laugh. As if what Gloria had just
said was simply too, too ridiculous. Even to my own
ears, though, my laugh sounded pretty weak. "Gloria's

a little confused," I told Candy. "What she means is that *I* was the one who discovered Eddie's body. In fact, that's probably why my name sounds familiar to you. It was mentioned in the article about Eddie in this morning's paper."

Candy was already nodding. "Why, that's right. That *is* exactly where—"

Gloria, Lord love her, was now shaking her head emphatically from side to side. Her butterfly appeared to be hanging on for dear life. "Nope, nope, *nope*," she said. "I'm telling you, Candy, she shot poor Eddie *dead!*"

Gloria probably would've made more impact if she hadn't been speaking with such a thick slur.

Candy stared at her skeptically.

I jumped in again. "Ms. Cherry, I not only did *not* shoot Mr. Bartlett, I am very interested in finding out who did." At this point I didn't think it necessary to mention that the main reason I was very interested is that practically everybody in the world seemed to agree with Gloria. "In fact, that's why I wanted to ask—"

Gloria interrupted me. "Why, I had to make her bring her boyfriend along with us to keep her from killing me, too," Gloria said, indicating Matthias with a nod of her head. "I mean it. If he weren't here, I'd be dead for sure! Stone-cold *dead!*"

The last word seemed to echo, much like that other word Gloria had spoken downstairs. It actually seemed to bounce off the pristine, ivory-colored walls around us.

Gloria's echo must've been some kind of signal for Candy. She took a quick glance up and down the hall-way, and immediately began to move very fast, herding us all inside.

While she all but shoved us through her front door, she said, "Well, now, why don't we talk where we can be more comfortable? How about it? Let's just go on into my living room and talk this over, shall we?"

The idea of sitting down and chatting about whether or not I'd killed Bartlett did not exactly appeal to me, but I let Candy herd me inside, anyway. The object was to talk to her, wasn't it? Once we started talking, *I'd* pick the subject.

I noticed that the second we'd all cleared her front door, Candy shut it with a resounding click.

Evidently, Candy did not feel that murder was an appropriate topic to discuss in Willowcrest halls.

If she didn't think that was a good topic, she no doubt would've loved to have heard what Gloria had had to say downstairs.

Candy's front door opened onto a small foyer, which led into an equally small, tastefully furnished living room.

Now it was my turn to look stunned. I wasn't sure what I'd been expecting to see. Bead curtains hanging across every doorway? Gilt-framed oils of nude women reclining on bear rugs? Large posters of porn films?

In reality, Candy's condo was a study in understated elegance. Beige walls were decorated with original watercolor landscapes in simple wood frames, and the expanse of hardwood floor was broken up with wool throw rugs in floral patterns I recognized from the latest Laura Ashley catalogue.

As Gloria more or less lurched in the direction of the living room, Candy immediately pointed her toward a sofa upholstered in a rose chintz. Yet another pattern I remembering seeing in the Laura Ashley catalogue. "Gloria, honey," Candy said, "you just sit right down and make yourself at home, okay?"

Matthias and I followed Gloria into the living room. When I stepped past Candy, she stuck out one cat foot to stop me, leaned forward, and whispered,

"Don't you worry, honey. I realize Gloria doesn't have the foggiest notion what she's saying."

Gloria's head went up at that one. "I do so," she said as she sank back against several throw pillows on the sofa. "I do so have a foggy notion!"

That, I believe, was the absolute truth.

Candy turned to face Gloria, hands on her hips. "Gloria, if you really believe this woman is so dangerous, what in the world are you doing hanging around with her?"

This did seem to be a real flaw in Gloria's argument. Even Gloria herself appeared to be stumped by that one. She cocked her head to one side, and frowned. "Well," she finally said, her voice slurring over every word, "she ain't going to be killing me in front of people!"

That, I thought, was an excellent point.

Gloria was hurrying on. "Besides, I don't feel like driving right now—" This was an understatement and a half. "—and Schuyler offered me a ride so's I could tell you just exactly what I think of you!"

Candy looked puzzled again. "*Me?* Gloria, honey, whatever are you—"

Gloria shook her head again. "I'm talking about that picture! I seen it, you know! I seen it!"

Candy only looked more puzzled as she turned to look first at me and then over at Matthias.

Matthias apparently felt that since this was my bright idea, I was welcome to handle it. All by myself. Looking directly at me, he said, "Schuyler?" and then immediately took a seat in a beige wing-back chair positioned at right angles to the sofa.

That left just me and Candy standing.

Thank you so much, Matthias, for helping me out here.

I cleared my throat, opened the envelope and pulled out the group photograph. "Ms. Cherry," I said, with more than a little reluctance, "all we want to know is if you recognize anybody in this picture. That's *all*."

I was trying to make it absolutely clear that we had no interest whatsoever in discussing her past.

I wasn't sure Candy got it, though. Once again, she had a puzzled expression on her face as she took a long look at the photograph I extended in her direction. As she stared at it, her eyes seemed to enlarge even more behind her reading glasses.

Inwardly I cringed, as I stood there, waiting for her reaction.

It turned out to be even more surprising than the way her condo was furnished.

Candy Cherry laughed.

She looked at the photograph, threw her head back, and laughed out loud. "Oh my goodness, look at that! My, my, my." She looked back up at me, eyes twinkling behind her reading glasses. "I'll say, I recognize somebody in this picture! Matter of fact, I recognize *everybody* in this picture! Honey, that's me right there in the second row!"

I was so shocked she admitted it so readily, that for a second I couldn't seem to make a sound.

Matthias, however, had no such problem. He started making one of those strangling noises again.

Candy now took the photograph right out of my hand, and went over to take a seat in one of two chairs upholstered in a solid rose chintz, positioned in front of a floor-to-ceiling double window. There she held the photograph up so that the light coming through the semisheer curtains shined directly on it, and she squinted at it even closer.

"Oh my Lordy, look at me! Can you believe that getup? *What* a hoot!" Her smile grew wider and wider.

I was taking a seat myself in the chair right next to her, but I gave her an uncertain smile in return.

"That was one of my best outfits, you know," Candy

went on. "It was real silk—even the apron. That one cost me a pretty penny, but it sure paid off in the long run. Oh my yes, honey, I tell you, it certainly did!"

Still struck speechless, I just sat there, trying to look impressed by the shrewdness of her investment.

Gloria was now looking every bit as shocked at Candy's reaction as I and Matthias. Unfortunately, however, old Gloria regained her ability to speak well before I did. Gloria's eyes were still showing the whites all around when she said, "Then you *admit* it?"

The puzzled look was back on Candy's face. "Well, of *course*, Gloria, honey, I admit it."

"You *admit* you lied to me?" Gloria's slurred voice now sounded outraged.

"Lied to you?" Candy now looked more than puzzled. She looked totally bewildered. "Honey, I never lied to you."

"You never told me the truth!"

Candy's response was a shrug. "The only reason I never mentioned it was that I thought you already knew," she said. "I thought everybody who knew Eddie knew. I mean, the guy *was* my lawyer."

"Eddie told me you were one of his regular clients. One of the ones he had from before." Gloria's voice was a petulant whine.

Candy gave Gloria a look. "And you believed *Eddie*?"

Candy's tone implied that anybody who would believe Eddie would also believe in the tooth fairy. Her point seemed well taken to me. However, we'd clearly gotten off on a tangent here. I stepped closer to Candy. "Look, Ms. Cherry, what we wanted to know is—"

Candy was not listening. Her eyes still on Gloria, she gave her ponytail a careless little flip. "Look, Girlie, if I'd had any idea that you didn't know, I would have said something long before this. I would have! Honey, I've *never* done nothing in my whole life that I'm ashamed to admit!"

The size of Gloria's eyes was now rivaling Candy's, only Gloria was not wearing reading glasses. "You're *not* ashamed?" Gloria said. She shifted position on the sofa. "Why, that's—that's the *ickiest* thing I've ever heard!"

Why was I not surprised to hear this word?

Candy's chin lifted. "Icky? *Icky?* I'll tell you what's icky!" Her gray eyes looked as if a fire had just been lit behind them. "Right this minute there's women all over this country staying with their husbands just 'cause he's footing the bills. Not because they love the poor schmuck, but only because he keeps them from having to go out and get a job. Now, I ask you, what's the difference between that and what I was doing? If anything, *I* was being a lot more honest! At least, I told the guy up front that all I was doing it for was the money!"

This was certainly one way of looking at it.

Candy took a deep breath. "Look, I'm not apologizing to nobody. Not now, not ever! My mama was a drunk, and my daddy ran off when I was still a baby, so I never got to finish high school. I did what I had to do, and I saved my money, and I ended up here. I got to retire early, and I don't think I did all that bad!"

Gloria looked as if Candy had slapped her. "Well, of course, you did bad. You did real, real BAD!"

This looked like a good time to change the subject. "Ms. Cherry, do you know this woman and this little girl?" I indicated Wanda Faye and Jenny with an index finger.

Candy looked as if she had a few million more words she wanted to say to Gloria, but she did drag her eyes away from Gloria's outraged face and focus them once again on the photograph. "Do I know who?" She squinted at the snapshot again. "Oh, my yes, will you look at that. Why, I haven't thought of that little girl in years. My, my, how sad."

Gloria jumped in here. "*I'll* say, it's sad! That poor little girl is sitting right there on the lap of that icky woman, and she—"

Candy's jaw tightened. "Gloria," she said, cutting her off, "when I said *little girl*, I was talking about Wanda Faye. She was only twenty-one in that picture. The poor kid."

I tried not to sound too eager. "Then you knew Wanda Faye pretty well?"

Candy nodded and handed the picture back to me. "Sure I did. Hell, I worked with her."

From the couch came an indignant sniff. I chose to ignore it. "Do you know how I could get in touch with either Wanda Faye or Jenny?"

Candy was already shaking her dark head. "I don't know about Jenny, but you're not going to be able to get in touch with Wanda Faye at all."

I swallowed uneasily. I think I already guessed what she was going to say, but I asked, anyway. "What do you mean?"

"Wanda Faye's dead."

My breath caught in my throat.

Candy's eyes were back on the snapshot I was holding. "The poor thing died of a drug overdose just about a year after this picture was taken." Candy blinked a couple times, and hurried on. "It was a waste, that's what it was. She was so young. The poor kid was really hooked bad, though. Fact is, by the time Wanda Faye died, Lordy, I think she was doing everything—uppers, downers, even heroin." Candy looked up at me. "It was a mercy that she finally agreed to give her daughter up for adoption."

I blinked. "The little girl was adopted?"

Candy nodded. "Eddie handled the whole thing

when the kid was around five. Of course, the way I heard it from Wanda Faye, Eddie was supposed to put Jenny up for adoption right after she was born. That's what the father told him to do. But Wanda Faye wouldn't agree to it. Not then, anyway."

"Do you know who Jenny's real father was?" This question came from Matthias. Apparently, since the tough part was over, he'd decided to help me out a little, after all.

Candy looked over at Matthias and shook her head. "All Wanda Faye would tell me was that he'd been a friend of Eddie's from college."

My heart actually seemed to skip a beat. I exchanged a look with Matthias. Obviously, Porter Meredith met this description.

Candy was going on. "As I recall from what Wanda Faye told me, she'd met the guy at a fraternity party at the University of Louisville. Wanda Faye was still in high school back then, and the poor thing actually thought this guy was the love of her life. Wanda Faye truly believed they were going to get married, and settle down in the storybook cottage with the white picket fence, the whole bit." Candy sighed again, and wiggled her feet in her cat slippers. It made the things look as if they were wiggling their noses.

"Then, of course," Candy went on, "one day Wanda Faye told Prince Charming she was pregnant, and after that, he wanted nothing more to do with either her or the baby." Candy shrugged again. "According to Wanda Faye, the guy tried to talk her into getting rid of the kid right then and there, but she wouldn't do it. After that, he just split. He left everything for Eddie to take care of. Eddie was supposed to get the kid adopted privately, and that was supposed to be that."

I stared at Candy. There was something in her tone

now that had not been there before. Something hard and unforgiving. "So what happened?"

Candy took off her glasses, and rubbed her eyes before she answered. "Eddie was Eddie, *that's* what happened. Even though he'd made an agreement with the baby's dad, he had Wanda Faye telling him she didn't want to give her baby up. So Eddie just let Wanda Faye keep it."

Candy was frowning now. "Eddie actually let Wanda Faye keep that baby knowing full well what was happening with her. Her family had thrown her out once they found out about the kid. So she started hooking to support herself and the baby—and, of course, her habit."

Candy was now shaking her head, much like Gloria earlier. "I think the poor kid got started on drugs because she just couldn't stand the way everything had turned out. Whatever the reason, Lord knows, she wasn't any kind of a mom after a while. Eddie knew it, too, but Wanda Faye kept slipping him a fifty here and a twenty there." Candy was frowning again. "You would not believe what Eddie would do to make a few extra bucks."

I stared at her. There was contempt in her voice now. This woman had made a living selling her body, and yet, there were obviously things she wouldn't do for money.

Things that Edward Bartlett, on the other hand, would do.

What a touching testimonial to the man's character.

"Eddie was getting money from the mom *and* money from the dad," Candy went on, "and for a long time, he wasn't doing a thing in the best interest of that little baby. Like I said, she was five years old before he finally got her adopted out of the mess she was living in."

I just looked at Candy. Could this adoption have

been the "favor" that Gloria had mentioned earlier? The one that Eddie was supposed to have done Porter?

I turned toward Gloria, still seated over on the couch, intending to ask her that very question. Apparently, however, the sad history of Wanda Faye and her daughter had not exactly been riveting for old Gloria. Once again, just like in Bartlett's office, Gloria's red head had lolled backward and was now resting on the back cushions of the sofa. Once again, her eyes were shut, her mouth was open—and, of course, once again she was doing her best to suck the paint off the ceiling.

With accompanying sound effects.

The moment Gloria let loose, Candy's head immediately jerked in Gloria's direction, too. "Lordy, she's really got a snootful, doesn't she?" Candy said.

A "snootful" was putting it kindly.

"She did have a few Margaritas at lunch," Matthias admitted.

"Would you believe, she wasn't drinking at all when I first met her," Candy said. "She'd just started working for Eddie, and she'd kicked it. She was going to AA meetings and everything. Then Eddie and she started going out, and he gave her somebody to drink with, I guess. After a couple weeks, she was on the stuff all over again. Hell, Eddie even gave her wine as a birthday present. That was just like him, though, just like him to—"

That hard, unforgiving tone was back again. I turned to stare at Candy.

If you didn't know better, you could almost believe that Candy had despised Eddie.

Candy must've realized that I was looking at her rather intently because she immediately broke off what she was saying. "—of course, I don't mean to be talking bad about old Eddie. Particularly since he's gone now and all. I mean, he was an okay guy, I guess."

Uh-huh. Right. And Jeffrey Dahmer was just badly misunderstood.

Candy now quickly changed the subject. Oddly enough. Moving toward the sofa, she looked down at Gloria. Who was at that moment sawing some pretty gigantic logs.

"I know Eddie's death hit her hard," Candy said. "I'm sure she feels real guilty."

Matthias and I both looked alert at that one. "Guilty?" he said.

Candy shrugged. "Because, you know, Eddie died before they could patch things up."

I blinked. This was news. "Were they fighting?"

"Oh, my, yes, honey, they certainly were," Candy said. She was wiggling the nose of her right cat slipper again. She turned toward me. "It was on account of you."

I blinked again. "*Me?*"

"Gloria really didn't want to lie under oath. Not that I blame her. I mean, that kind of thing can get you put in jail." Candy gave her ponytail another careless little flip. "I've been in jail a couple of times myself, and believe me, honey, it's not the sort of place where you want to spend a whole lot of your time."

I just looked at her. Gloria and Bartlett had been arguing just before he died? If this was so, why hadn't Gloria mentioned it before now? Was it possible that Gloria had omitted this crucial piece of information because she was all too aware that it could make her a suspect in his death?

That line of thinking led me to wonder: *Had Gloria been accusing me all this time just to throw suspicion off herself?* Let's face it, one sure way to keep people from suspecting *you* was to act as if you were convinced someone else had done it.

Not to mention, we had only Gloria's word that Bartlett had said that he was on his way to meet *me* the day he died. What if Gloria had lied?

Lord. Could Gloria really be that smart?

If she was, she was certainly hiding it well.

And yet, if you'd just killed your boyfriend, you'd probably want to get very, very drunk, wouldn't you?

I stared at Gloria, snoring up a storm on the couch.

"Goodness, yes," Candy was saying, "Gloria was plenty mad at Eddie that last day."

Now I stared at Candy. If Gloria could be trying to divert suspicion, so could someone else. Could Candy be telling me about a fight between Gloria and Bartlett just to keep me from suspecting *her*?

Unlike Gloria, Candy appeared to be terribly savvy. What's more, Gloria had to know how she'd sounded a few seconds ago. She also had to know that, if you were making a list of suspects, her name would be on it.

Was it possible that Candy was making up the whole story about Gloria and Bartlett having a fight? I would've liked to have asked Gloria about it, but from the sounds coming out of the woman's mouth, I'd say interviewing *Bartlett* would probably be easier.

Matthias had another question for Candy, however. "Do you, by any chance, know a guy by the name of Porter Meredith? That was the name on the file we found this picture in."

Candy looked over at Matthias and shook her dark head. "Porter Meredith? No, the name doesn't ring a bell, but, then again, I've known a lot of men." Candy merely made the statement. She didn't sound proud of it, but she also certainly didn't sound ashamed. "Can you believe," she added, turning back toward me, "not all of them told me their real names?"

"No kidding," I said.

Candy's smile crinkled the edges of her eyes. "No kidding."

I returned her smile, realizing suddenly that I liked her. Candy Cherry seemed to be honest, and down to earth, and totally without self-pity. What was there not to like?

There was one other question I wanted to ask her. "By the way, at the risk of being rude, I did want to know one more thing—is Candy Cherry your real name?"

Candy didn't even blink. "It sure is," she said, pushing up the sleeves of her sweatshirt. "My full name is Candy Louise Cherry. I guess maybe it was destiny that I ended up doing what I did." She smiled again. "Then again, maybe I would've done it, no matter what. I always sort of liked the idea of selling something and still getting to keep it."

I blinked at that one.

I was also glad Gloria wasn't awake to hear that little comment. Matthias was bad enough. He made another one of his choking sounds, and then noisily cleared his throat.

I didn't even look in his direction.

Candy, however, did. As she glanced once again over at Matthias, she said, "You know, maybe this Porter Meredith person was the little girl's father. Maybe that's why Eddie kept those pictures in his file."

"We've thought of that," I said.

"If he was Jenny's dad, honey, he was a real jerk," she said.

What could I say? Porter should probably have that printed on his business card. Porter Meredith, Jerk at Large.

I took another look at the photo in my hand. "Boy, I'd love to see the expression on old Porter's face when he first gets a good look at these pictures."

I was almost talking to myself, but the second I said the words, it certainly seemed to be an idea whose time had come.

In fact, I'd love to see the expression on Porter's face in, oh, say, the next half hour or so.

I turned toward Matthias.

He must've guessed what I was thinking. His white sidewalls were showing again.

Chapter 16

I was determined to head for Porter's office as soon as possible before I lost my nerve.

I quickly said my goodbyes to Candy, thanked her for her help, and started toward Gloria. To haul her off the sofa.

Matthias got up and started in that direction, too.

I believe by now he and I were getting to be old hands at hauling Gloria around. It was a lot like being one of the stars in that movie, *Weekend at Bernie*'s.

It was Candy who put an end to our next big scene, however. "Look," Candy said, "why don't you just let Gloria sleep it off where she is? I'll see that she gets home when she wakes up."

I didn't know about Matthias, but that was certainly all I needed to hear. Matthias must've concurred, though, because his face all but lit up as soon as Candy spoke.

I thanked Candy all over again, and this time, I believe I was significantly more sincere than I had been earlier.

"So," Matthias said, as we walked out of the Willowcrest and headed toward my Tercel. "I guess you want to head downtown right now? Straight to Porter Meredith's office?"

I believe Matthias's tone would've been exactly the same if he'd been asking me if I wanted to head downtown right now to throw myself in front of a bus.

We were at my car by the time Matthias finished asking his question, and I busied myself, unlocking the doors and settling myself in the front passenger seat. Pretending, of course, that I was so preoccupied with doing all this—Lord knows, getting into a car certainly takes a great deal of concentration—that I didn't quite have time to answer him.

The truth was, you see, that while I *did* intend to head downtown, I did not intend to take Matthias with me.

This wasn't a decision I'd just reached. I had, in fact, decided this while we were still up in Candy's apartment. I'd decided it right about the time that the whites in Matthias's eyes had started to show. For what seemed like the millionth time.

I'd looked at Matthias, and I'd made up my mind then and there that it was going to be bad enough talking to Porter again without Matthias standing at my elbow, doing his personal impression of white sidewalls.

Not to mention, there was no telling what Porter might say. Porter certainly had been full of surprises last night. If he'd been comparing me then to that woman in *Fatal Attraction,* who was next? Kathy Bates in *Misery*?

And, let's face it, Porter could be very convincing. He'd certainly fooled me last night on the phone. I didn't particularly relish Matthias hearing Porter's lies firsthand.

"Actually," I told Matthias as I fastened my seat belt, "I think I'd rather head on back to Arndoerfer Realty."

"Well, thank goodness," Matthias said. He closed the passenger door on my side, went around the front of the car, got in, and as he secured his own seat belt, added, "I can't tell you how glad I am you've decided not to talk to Porter, after all."

I blinked. Obviously, Matthias had misunderstood.

For a moment, I confess, it did cross my mind to just let Matthias continue assuming what he obviously wanted to assume.

But then, almost immediately, I felt guilty.

And cowardly.

I mean, I was a grown woman. If I wanted to do a thing, I didn't have to get anybody's stamp of approval.

Matthias had started the car, and we were now pulling out of the Willowcrest parking lot onto Willow Avenue, heading in the general direction of Cherokee Park and eventually, Bardstown Road. I cleared my throat. "Well, now that you mention it, Matthias," I said, "I do think I might drop by Porter's office. But you don't have to come. In fact, I think we should just drive you back to my office to get your car, so that you—"

"Wha-a-at?" Matthias said. He was doing his white sidewalls impression once again. The man had a real talent.

I took a deep breath. "Matthias," I said, "there's absolutely no reason that you have to come along."

I didn't say anything more than that because Matthias was obviously no longer listening. He was too busy pulling over to the curb, and slamming his foot on the brake so abruptly that we both lurched forward and back.

"Now, just a second," Matthias said, turning to stare at me, "you're not even *considering* going to see Porter alone, are you?"

I smoothed a nonexistent wrinkle in my skirt. "Actually," I said, keeping my voice even, "I'm not considering it. I've already made up my mind."

Matthias now took his own deep breath, put the car into park, switched off the ignition, and turned to face me. "Schuyler," he said, "for crying out loud—" Matthias's tone, for some reason, had gotten angry. "—you've said so yourself that this guy could be a murderer. And *now* you expect me to let you go down there alone?"

I could feel my face freeze. I know I should've been feeling terribly protected and all that, but one word of what Matthias had just said rankled a bit. That word *let*.

"Matthias," I said, and now, I suppose, I sounded a bit angry, too, "if I want to go down to Porter's office by myself, I'll go. There's no *letting* about it."

Okay. Okay. Maybe I was being a bit touchy, but after dating one Mr. Right several months ago, and marrying another Mr. Right several years ago, I wasn't the least bit inclined to let anybody act as if he were my boss.

I already had a daddy, thank you very much. Dad was seventy-three, and *he* didn't tell me what to do anymore, either.

Matthias was now taking another deep breath. Sometimes it's all too clear how very much I try his patience. "Schuyler," he said, "all I meant was that I'm worried about you." He ran a big hand through his shaggy hair. "Far be it from me to try to tell you what to do."

I wasn't sure if he was being sarcastic or sincere. "Good," I said.

Matthias took still another deep breath, and reached for my hand. "Schuyler, for God's sake, you drive me crazy," he said.

Looking at him, I could feel myself softening. The man did have the greenest eyes.

"Surely you can understand that when you love somebody," Matthias went on, "you can't help worrying about them."

I blinked again, and now not only could I feel my face freeze, it was as if I were frozen all over.

What? What was it that he'd just said?

For a long moment, I just stared at Matthias. Then I decided I had to have misunderstood him. Surely Matthias had not said what I thought I had just heard. I actually had to swallow once before I spoke. "Well, of course, you're concerned. I do understand that, but—"

Matthias gripped my hand tighter and leaned toward me a little, his green eyes growing even more intense. "Schuyler," he said, "I mean it. I've been wanting to tell you this for some time now. I love you."

I blinked yet again, and it was all I could do to keep from pulling my hand away. I believe I mentioned earlier that I was sure if Matthias ever did say such a thing to me, I'd look at him as if he were out of his mind.

As it turned out, I was right. That's exactly what I did. I not only looked at Matthias as if he were insane, I also started stammering.

As if *I* were insane.

"Matthias, I, uh, I, uh—"

Matthias reached over to put his index finger gently against my lips. "Look," he said, "I didn't mean to put you on the spot, okay? I don't expect you to say anything."

I stared at him, wondering if he were telling me the truth. I mean, isn't it only natural to expect, when you tell somebody you love her, that she'll say it right back?

And yet, how could I say something I wasn't sure I meant? I stared at Matthias. He really was a wonderful man. I did care about him a lot. But was I in love? I'd thought I was in love with Ed at one time. Hell, I'd even thought I was in love with Porter. For about ten seconds.

So how could you know something like this for sure?

I was beginning to wish I was one of those Hollywood types. The kind that said, "Love ya, babe," every other minute, and really didn't give it a second thought.

"I know how difficult it is for you to say this sort of thing," Matthias was now saying.

I cleared my throat. Now wait a minute, I say *this sort of thing*, as Matthias put it, all the time. Yesterday I'd told Nathan I loved him. And I'd told Nathan to tell Daniel that I loved him, too. And, my goodness, I tell both my parents "I love you" every single time I visit them.

Not to mention, I do believe I've never hesitated to say that I loved rolled oysters. And rainy weather. And UPS packages. Hell, I love a lot of things. And I absolutely *adore* large, icy-cold glasses of Coke.

I knew, however, even as I was going through my mental list of loved ones that this wasn't exactly what Matthias was talking about. That was, no doubt, why I just sat there, like an idiot, saying absolutely nothing.

Matthias, though, was doing enough talking for both of us. "Look, I just wanted to tell you how I felt, that's all," he said. "So you'd understand why I don't want you going down to Porter's all by yourself."

I, of course, babbled some more. "Well, uh, sure, uh—"

What in the world was wrong with my mouth? And my brain? While I seemed to be taking in everything that was going on—Matthias was still holding my hand, he was still giving me an intense, green-eyed look, he was still leaning toward me a little—a running commentary had started going through my mind. Like subtitles in a movie.

Did Matthias really say I love you? I thought we had an understanding about this. That it takes time for love to develop. That love isn't something you fall into, like a hole in the ground.

While all these subtitles were chasing themselves through my mind, Matthias was saying, "You know, I think I've been in love with you from the first day I met you."

I blinked all over again. The day Matthias and I met had been the day his father's will had been read. Leaving me $100,000. Even though I'd never even met Mr. Cross. And, if I recalled correctly, one of the first things Matthias had said to me on that particular day was, "I know who you are. You're the woman who killed my father."

Correct me if I'm wrong, but that doesn't sound particularly loving to me.

Apparently, Matthias had just come down with a bad case of retroactive memory. Meaning that the way he remembered things had happened in the past changed according to what was now happening in the present.

My skepticism must've shown in my face, because Matthias actually smiled and shook his shaggy head. "Okay, Schuyler, you don't have to look like that. I know it's going to take some time for you to be able to trust me. I know it. And I understand. I know you've been treated pretty shabbily by the men in your life, and that's made you very cautious. Hell, I don't blame you."

I would've blinked again, but for some idiotic reason, my eyes had started to fill. If I blinked, it would send tears streaking down my face. Which would definitely be a most embarrassing thing to have happen right in front of Matthias.

So, instead of blinking, I just sat there, holding my eyes as wide open as I possibly could.

I probably looked as if I'd been poleaxed.

"That's also, no doubt, why you've got this problem with commitment," Matthias said.

My chin went up at that one. Matthias was making me sound like some kind of emotional cripple. "Now, just a minute, I don't think I've got a problem with commitment. I really don't think I do."

Even as I said the words, though, I realized that I was not exactly telling the whole truth. While I didn't have any trouble with *commitment*, if you read the word *commitment* as *marriage*, well, then, I had a problem. I had a big problem.

I'd been married before, and I couldn't say that I'd particularly liked it.

In fact, *that* I suddenly realized was the real reason I couldn't bring myself to say, *I love you*, right back to Matthias. Because saying things like that could lead to other things. Things like gold bands, and vows, and somebody singing "Oh Promise Me."

After all, it certainly had in the past.

The plain fact was, I wasn't sure I ever wanted to get married again. I realize that this is contrary to what the popular conception is these days. From what I gather from women's magazines and all the TV talk shows, evidently every one of us single women over forty are supposed to be doing everything but throwing nets over every eligible man within a five-mile radius. We're supposed to be positively desperate to snag ourselves a husband. Somebody, *anybody*, to give meaning to the empty shells of our lives.

Oh brother.

How far wrong can you get? By the time a woman gets to be my age, she's established professionally, and is usually making a fairly good living. Far from having an empty life, she's finally got one that's exactly the way she likes it.

So why on earth would she want to get married, and take the chance of messing all that up?

In fact, I think the conclusions drawn from that survey they did a few years ago were way off base. You know the survey I'm talking about, the one that everybody argued about? The one that said women over forty are more likely to be killed by a terrorist than to get married? As far as I could tell, nobody ever actually asked the women in that survey if they *wanted* to get married. It was just assumed.

In my opinion, the real conclusion that should've been drawn from that survey's results was that women over forty would *rather* be killed by a terrorist than get married.

Matthias was holding up his hand again. "Schuyler, it doesn't matter. I don't care whether you're afraid of commitment or not. I've got time. In fact, I've got all the time in the world. I'll wait until you're ready, okay? I know how this sort of thing frightens you."

My chin went up one more time at that one. My subtitles now were going by as fast as the credits at the end of a movie. *Hold the phone, already. What did Matthias think I was? Some kind of skittish creature who has to be coaxed out from the underbrush? Like Bambi? Or worse—Flower?*

"Matthias," I said, "I wouldn't say I'm *frightened* exactly. I just don't want to rush things, that's all."

Matthias rubbed his hand over his beard, and just looked at me for a long moment. "Schuyler," he said, "I don't want you to ever do anything you're not comfortable with."

If that were true, then he didn't want us having this conversation. Because, believe me, I was uncomfortable. I was very, very uncomfortable.

Particularly when Matthias said it again. "Just don't forget what I said, okay? I do love you." He leaned even closer and kissed me, his lips warm against mine.

When Matthias finally pulled away, I'd been reduced to babbling again. "Matthias, I—uh—I—"

I could've kicked myself. I was, after all, a grown professional woman. Why was it that having a man tell me he loved me turned me into a babbling idiot?

Of course, maybe it could be because it was just a shock. Up to a moment ago, I'd been convinced that Matthias felt exactly as I did about such things.

Obviously, I'd been mistaken. Matthias didn't appear to feel the same way I did at all. In fact, it seemed clear to me now that if Matthias had not told me that he loved me before this, it had not been because he didn't believe love happened that quickly.

It had been because he hadn't wanted to scare me off.

Matthias was still holding my hand. "I don't want anything happening to you, understand? That's why I want to go down to Porter's office with you. Okay?"

I was so relieved not to be talking about whether or not I was in love with him that I found myself nodding. "Okay," my mouth said before I could stop it.

Of course, maybe my mouth was right. Come to think of it, it might be a good idea to have a witness along. That way I'd have someone else to corroborate whatever Porter might say.

Lord knows, I could've used a witness last night.

Matthias was now giving me a gentle smile. "Then you're going to *let* me come along?"

I returned his smile a little uncertainly. Okay. So there's letting, and there's letting. "Sure," I said. "Why not?"

Matthias started up the car again, and pulled out onto Willow Avenue.

While he was accomplishing this little maneuver, I was, of course, sitting right next to him, thinking: *You know, if this had just been a ploy on Matthias's part to make sure I'd let him go with me to Porter's office, it had been a stroke of genius.*

Because, frankly, I probably would've agreed to let Matthias throw me into the lion's den at the Louisville Zoo if it meant that we would no longer be continuing this particular conversation.

On the positive side, however, having this conversation with Matthias made the upcoming discussion with Porter seem like child's play.

I mean, the worst Porter might be was a murderer. That wasn't anywhere near as scary as an extremely attractive man with intense green eyes who said he was in love with me.

Chapter 17

I'd been to Porter's office several times before, so it was nothing new to me. Matthias, however, let out a low whistle when we pulled up in front of the First National Tower at Fifth and Main.

"None too shabby digs," Matthias said.

That was an understatement, if I'd ever heard one.

Porter Meredith's law firm occupied the entire twenty-sixth floor of the First National Tower. I've always thought it was probably no accident that Porter's office happened to be in one of the most visible buildings downtown. In fact, if you look at a photo of Louisville's skyline, the First National Tower is easy to recognize. It's the sleek, black building standing taller than every other building, except for the one with the lighted dome.

The one with the dome is the Providian building, and until it was built, the First National Tower had the distinction of being the tallest building in Louisville. There are those around town who will tell you that the Providian building cheated in the Tallest Building Race because a significant part of its height is derived from its lighted dome rather than genuine floors.

I, of course, would find it difficult to care less.

In addition to being tall, the First National Tower is also one of the few modern buildings in downtown Louisville that isn't a strange color or a weird shape.

It's just your basic black shoe box standing on its end, the ultimate statement of conservative good taste.

Matthias and I were lucky. We actually found a vacant parking space on Main Street, and we only had to circle once before we found it.

During the work day, finding a place to park on Main Street is akin to stumbling upon the Holy Grail. You almost always have to park in a garage or a lot somewhere.

Not today, though. Matthias fed the meter, and we headed inside.

The interior of the First National Tower is every bit as conservative as its exterior. The lobby is all glass and gray marble, with its floor covered in light and dark gray marble tiles arranged in a geometric pattern that has never failed to remind me of the hopscotch squares I used to draw when I was a little girl.

In fact, it has occurred to me more than once, when I've had closings or whatever in this building, that if I ever completely lose my mind, the white coats will probably find me playing hopscotch in the First National Tower lobby.

This was certainly a comforting thought as I walked through one of the revolving doors on my way to have a meaningful chat with Porter.

When you walk into the First National Tower lobby, one of the first things you notice is the massive marble information desk, on the front of which appears the directory. It is here that all the occupants of the building are listed in discreet raised, brass letters.

The raised, brass letters look very chic, I'll admit, but let's face it, this is an awkward place to put the directory. I suppose the thinking here was that, once a visitor has looked and looked and looked, and finally decided that the building does not have a directory posted anywhere on the walls, he'll walk over to the desk to ask for information.

And spot the directory.

This way, I believe, all first-time visitors to the First National Tower can practically be guaranteed to be in a bad mood.

If hiding the directory doesn't do the trick, the First National people have a fall-back plan that should really annoy first-timers. The First National people have divided up their elevators into sets, one set to a corridor. These sets are not even in numerical order. The set of elevators in the corridor on your right goes to floors 16 through 29, the set in the middle corridor to floors LL through 15, and the set in the corridor on the far left to floors 30 through 38. Ostensibly, the elevators have been divided this way in order to more evenly distribute traffic on the things.

You're supposed to be able to tell which elevators go to which floors by checking out the brass numbers hanging just outside each corridor. These numbers are every bit as chic as the ones in the directory. The problem is that these particular numbers are so chic, so discreet—meaning, *tiny*—that anybody unfamiliar with the building never gives them much notice.

That's why I've concluded that the real reason the First National people have divided up their elevators in this way is to provide comic relief for the person manning the information desk. This way, whoever is at that desk gets to sit there and snicker at all the people who hurry into one corridor, disappear into an elevator for a minute or so, only to come right back out and run into another corridor.

That information desk job evidently needed comic relief. Bad. When Matthias and I walked past the guy sitting there, he looked as if he were asleep with his eyes open. As I mentioned earlier, I'd already been to Porter's office a few times before, so I didn't have to ask the guy for any information. I also already knew exactly which corridor of elevators would take us to the twenty-sixth floor so the guy was going to have to look elsewhere for comic relief, too.

Matthias and I hurried into the proper elevator, and waited until it hummed into motion. When the elevator started moving, I tried to act nonchalant.

I tried to act nonchalant in the face of what Matthias had just told me. And I tried to act nonchalant in the face of what, I suppose, is a bad case of elevator phobia.

The fact is, I've always hated elevators. It wasn't so bad back at the Willowcrest when we only had to go up three floors. Now, sailing skyward, knowing we had twenty-five floors to shoot past, my stomach started knotting up the second I walked into the thing.

I guess what I really hate most about elevators is the total lack of control. When I get into an elevator, I feel the exact same sense of helplessness that I feel when I get into an airplane. In both cases, I am very well aware that, if the thing is going to crash, there's absolutely nothing I can do about it.

If I didn't already hate elevators in general, I think I'd still hate the ones in First National Tower. These elevators don't even have music. As the thing hurtles skyward, you can actually hear a kind of whoosh. In all the times I've been in this building, I haven't been able to decide if that whooshing sound is the sound of the elevator itself, or the sound of all the blood in my body rushing to my feet.

I was definitely feeling a little shaken when the elevator doors finally opened. I wanted to put it down entirely to elevator phobia, but it might also have had something to do with the little talk I was about to have with Porter.

Then again, to be absolutely honest, my sudden shakiness might also have a little something to do with the conversation Matthias and I had just had out in the car.

I was trying to put the whole thing out of my mind, and act as if nothing unusual had occurred. As if perhaps I had men coming up to me every day and declaring their love.

I wasn't sure how successful I was at acting nonchalant, though. For one thing, I didn't say so much as one word to Matthias in the elevator. Mainly because I really couldn't think of anything to say.

My guess was that my neck was a paisley mess.

I could've checked to make sure. The hallway leading into Porter's office was mirrored on one side. I purposely did not look in that direction, though. If I was going to have to go into Porter's office with a bad case of Paisley Neck, I didn't want to know about it. Instead, I walked resolutely toward the mahogany double doors at the end of the hall, without so much as a glance one way or the other.

The hallway was so plushly carpeted, it was like walking on a marshmallow floor.

I suppose the floor would've had to have been made out of toasted marshmallows, now that I think of it, because the carpet was a light brown.

As I walked down the hall, I kept my eyes on the gleaming brass letters in the center of both mahogany doors. These letters were not chic. At least a half-inch thick and ten inches tall, so you couldn't miss them even if you wanted to, the letters said BROWNE, CUNDIFF, AND MEREDITH.

Matthias moved ahead of me, and opened the huge door, stepping to one side to let me go in first.

I gave Matthias a quick smile as I went past him.

Fact is, I always smile at Matthias when he opens doors for me. What can I say? I like to have my doors opened. I realize that, as a so-called liberated woman, I'm supposed to be eagerly awaiting the chance to reach out and grab those doorknobs myself, but I can't help it. I like it when the man with me actually acts like a gentleman.

Besides, I've never quite understood what equal opportunity has to do with manners, anyway. I mean, just because we women don't want the old Employment Door slammed in our faces, it doesn't necessarily follow that we would like every other door in the world abruptly shutting within inches of our noses.

Like I said, I always smile at Matthias when he opens a door for me. This time, though, giving him a smile actually felt a little awkward.

I wasn't even sure why it felt so awkward, either. I mean, did I think just smiling at him now meant that we were engaged or something? Lord. Maybe Matthias was right. Maybe, after all this time on my own, I really was terrified of getting tied down.

Inside the double doors of Browne, Cundiff, and Meredith, there's a raised portion of the floor where a receptionist always sits behind what looks to me to be a quite expensive, ornately carved antique desk. When I'd been here before, for a closing on one of my listings or some such, I'd always gotten the feeling, as soon as I walked in, that I was approaching a deity. Sitting up there on her throne.

Today's deity was a woman I didn't recognize—a young brunette wearing a pale blue silk suit that exactly matched her eyes. She was wearing her hair in that frizzy all-over curl that is the height of fashion today, but back in the sixties, we would've cried if our perm had turned out that way. Not a day over twenty-one, Frizz gave us a bright smile as she said, "Good afternoon. May I help you?" Her large blue eyes rested on Matthias.

I don't know why this is but nine times out of ten, if I walk into an office with some guy, the guy will be the one the receptionist talks to. Receptionists seem to always assume that I'm just there to take notes.

I've never been able to decide if this is the receptionist's problem. Or mine.

I took a step forward. "We'd like to see Porter Meredith, please."

My speaking instead of Matthias must've thrown Frizz off a little. Her smile immediately dimmed, and she gave Matthias a quick, uncertain look. Then recovering nicely, she turned to me and said, "Of course." Her hand hovered over the intercom on her desk as she added, looking first at me, then over at Matthias. "May I give Mr. Meredith your names?"

I nodded. "I'm Schuyler Ridgway, and this is Matthias Cross."

Frizz's eyes had returned to me when I began to speak. When I said my name, though, something flickered in those big blue eyes of hers. Her hand was still hovering over the intercom button, but it seemed to freeze in midair. Clearing her throat, Frizz said, "Oh, you know, I'm terribly sorry." She tapped her forehead. "I don't know what I was thinking. Mr. Meredith is not available right now."

I just stared at the young woman. To her credit, she must not lie all that often, because it was obvious she needed more practice.

I glanced at the name plate on Frizz's desk. It said, Lynnda Hutchins, Administrative Assistant.

That's right. *Lynnda.* I had a feeling that this was not how her name appeared on her birth certificate. Or else her parents needed spelling lessons.

I gave her a cool, businesslike smile. "Miss Hutchins, I'm sure if Mr. Meredith knows we're out here, he'll want to see us."

Lynnda's own smile was beginning to harden into concrete. "I *said* Mr. Meredith is not available. I'm *very* sorry. Perhaps you'd like to make an appointment?"

I didn't even blink. "Miss Hutchins," I said, "would

you let Mr. Meredith know that we're out here, and that we'd like to talk to him? Please?"

I am nothing if not polite.

Lynnda was nothing if not alarmed. Her blue eyes were already very big, but now they seemed to increase in size several times. "I'm afraid that won't be possible," she said. "Mr. Meredith, um, told me not to disturb him." Her ability as a liar had not improved. Lynnda couldn't even meet my eyes anymore. Instead, she made an elaborate show of referring to the desk calendar in front of her. "Mr. Meredith has a meeting scheduled in a couple of minutes, and then he's going to be completely tied up for the rest of the day."

Lynnda must've thought I was a total idiot. It was almost three, and even upside down, I could plainly see that there was nothing written next to the three on the calendar she was reading. Unless she'd been recording Porter's appointments in invisible ink, I'd say Lynnda was lying again.

I'd also say that it was obvious that Porter had told her what to say in the event that somebody by the name of Schuyler Ridgway showed up.

"Look, Lynnda—" I said, putting a little extra emphasis on the first syllable of her name. *Lynn*-da. "I know you're just trying to do a good job, but why don't we let Mr. Meredith decide for himself if he wants to see me?" From where I stood, you could see three doors down the hall. I knew the first one to my right was the one that opened into Porter's office. I indicated it with a wave of my hand. "Why don't you just let him know we're here?"

Lynnda swallowed once before she answered. "Perhaps you didn't hear me." Her blue eyes were now shooting sparks. "I *said*, Mr. Meredith is busy."

I met her eyes. Staring at her without blinking, the way you used to back in grade school when the school bully challenged you.

"I'm not leaving until I see him," I said. My voice was very quiet, but you might not have thought so from Lynnda's reaction.

She must've thought I was getting ready to make a break for Porter's office door because she got to her feet and came around the corner of that expensive antique desk. Standing right in front of me, blocking my way, Lynnda said, "Look, Mr. Meredith has told me all about you. He said that you might be coming around to bother him."

Standing, Lynnda was a sizable girl. In fact, she had to be at least five foot nine, a good three inches taller than I was, if you didn't count the inches her frizzy perm added to her height.

Lynnda also looked as if maybe she worked out.

As in, lifted weights.

As in, old Lynnda here could probably beat me to a pulp if she put her mind to it.

The same thing must've occurred to Matthias, because he took a step closer to me. "Look," Matthias said, "all we want is a few minutes of Mr. Meredith's time. We just want to talk to—"

Lynnda interrupted him. "Look, Mr. Meredith is really a very wonderful man. He has been so kind to me ever since I started working here, and—"

I didn't doubt it for a minute. Porter made it a point to be kind to attractive young women.

Lynnda was hurrying on. "—Mr. Meredith certainly doesn't deserve what *she's* been doing to him." Lynnda jerked her frizzy head in my direction, and then turned back to Matthias. "You seem like a very nice man, too. Why don't you just take her out of—"

Since Lynnda seemed to think interrupting was such a good idea, I decided to do it myself. "Look, I don't know what Mr. Meredith has told you, but—"

Lynnda must've liked interrupting even more than

I thought. She did it again. "Porter has told me *everything*," she said.

Porter? It sounded as if Lynnda here might have more than a purely professional interest in her boss. She didn't even seem to realize that she'd called Porter by his first name, she was so intent on telling me off.

"He's told me that you just won't accept the facts. That you just won't believe that he's not interested in you anymore." Lynnda shook her frizzy curls. "I just don't understand women like you. If a man tells you it's over, why don't you just give it up? Don't you have any pride? You really should have more self-esteem than to go running after somebody who doesn't want you."

I couldn't believe I was being lectured about self-esteem by somebody half my age. Lynnda had, no doubt, watched Oprah one too many times.

Lynnda shrugged her pale blue shoulders, and turned back to Matthias. "It really would be better if you'd just take her out of here," she told him. "I'm sure you don't want a scene, and I'll have to call security if—"

Have I ever mentioned that it is very irritating to be talked about as if I were not even in the room? "Now just a minute, *Lynn*-da," I said. "I don't want a scene, either. So why don't you just—"

Before I could finish the sentence, Porter himself walked out of the door to his office. Wearing a monogrammed ivory dress shirt, gray pin-striped slacks, and a burgundy print silk tie with matching burgundy print suspenders, Porter looked as if he did exactly what I knew for a fact that he really did do—he ordered all his clothes straight out of the Spiegel catalog.

"If it's in Spiegel," Porter had once told me, "I know it's real quality." It had been just before he and I had split up. I had looked at him and thought, Well, now, that explains why I've never seen *you* in the Spiegel catalog.

Now Porter said, "Lynnda, what seems to be the problem out here? I'm trying to get some work done, but with all this noise, I—"

Porter's voice shut off, like a water fountain abruptly gone dry, when he caught sight of me. For a long moment, he didn't seem to do anything but blink. Then glancing over at Matthias, he cleared his throat, and turned back to me. "What are you doing here?"

Porter did not sound any friendlier than Lynnda. *What* a shock.

Of course, I guess I didn't sound particularly friendly myself. "I came by because I thought you might be interested in seeing some pictures I found."

Porter shrugged, but he didn't turn around and go back inside his office. Instead, he said, "What pictures?"

I didn't need any further encouragement. I showed him.

I opened the battered manila folder, moved to Porter's side, and held up the first snapshot so that he could take a good look at it.

I did, however, tighten my grip on the thing. Just in case Porter decided to make a grab for it.

Porter didn't try.

He took one long, long look at the photo of Wanda Faye and Jenny, and noticeably paled.

Porter tried to cover it up, glancing away and clearing his throat again, but it was obvious.

Every bit of the blood seemed to have suddenly drained from his face.

Chapter 18

Porter stared at the photo of Wanda Faye and Jenny much like I myself might've looked at a snake. As if he were afraid the thing might bite him.

"Where did you get this picture?" Porter's voice was almost a croak.

I didn't hesitate. "From Edward Bartlett's office."

For a long moment, Porter just looked at me. Squinting his eyes a little. As if he couldn't quite comprehend what I'd just said. Then he cleared his throat and said, "Edward Bartlett's office? What in the world were you doing in Edward Bartlett's office?"

I decided that was one question it was probably best to ignore. "I found this folder in one of Bartlett's file cabinets," I said. "There's quite a few photographs inside just like that one."

I dropped the first snapshot back into the battered manila folder, and pulled out another one. To more or less demonstrate the truth of what I'd just said.

Porter, however, barely glanced at the new photograph I now held in my hand. "So?" he said. "What's all this got to do with me?"

I just stared at him. To paraphrase Humphrey Bogart, Porter was good. Very, very good. He actually sounded annoyed that we were bothering him with this trivia.

"I think you know exactly what all this has to do

with you," I said. "In fact, I think you know exactly who Wanda Faye and Jenny are."

Porter didn't blink this time. "You're mistaken," he said. He stuck his hands in his pockets, and leaned against Lynnda's desk, assuming an attitude of nonchalance. "I don't recognize either one of them."

Porter lifted clear blue eyes to mine—blue eyes a great deal like little Jenny's. Let me see now. If I remembered my high school biology lessons correctly, blue eyes were a recessive characteristic. Meaning that blue-eyed parents almost always produce a blue-eyed child.

So blue-eyed Porter and blue-eyed Wanda Faye could very well be little Jenny's parents.

Matthias was now clearing *his* throat. "Are you actually trying to tell us that you don't have any idea who this little girl or this woman is?"

Porter had the gall then to smile at me and Matthias. "That's what I'm saying, all right," he said. "I have never in my entire life ever seen either that woman or that little girl before."

I don't know what it was, but the moment Porter said the word *girl*, it was as if I were hearing an echo of Bartlett's last words. "*It was Porter Meredith's girl.*"

Good Lord. Could Bartlett have been talking about Porter's *daughter*? I stared at the photograph in my hand. Could the sweet-looking child in this picture have grown up to be a murderer?

But why? What reason would she have *today* to kill Bartlett, a man her father might've known pretty well years ago, but apparently pretty much avoided lately? It didn't make any sense.

I took a deep breath. "Porter," I said, "you may say you don't know either one of them, but the file folder we found these pictures in has *your* name on it." I held up the folder so that Porter could plainly see what was printed on the tab.

Porter now managed to look baffled. "Well, well," he said, "isn't that odd?"

Porter's smug arrogance seemed to be getting on Matthias's nerves as much as it was getting on mine. Matthias took a step toward him. "It's odd, all right," Matthias said. "How do you explain it?"

Porter now turned to look at Matthias, his eyes like slivers of blue ice. "As a matter of fact, I don't have an explanation," Porter said. He gave an elaborate shrug of his Spiegel-clad shoulders. "As a point of fact, however, I don't believe I have to explain it." Porter shifted his weight from one highly polished shoe to another. "If, however, I had to hazard a guess as to why these pictures were in this particular folder," he went on, "I'd say it had to be some kind of clerical error."

Clerical error? Porter actually expected us to believe that these pictures were in a folder labeled "Porter Meredith" because Bartlett had made a filing mistake? Did Porter think we were idiots?

Apparently so. He was giving another insolent shrug. "Clerical error," he repeated. "It happens all the time."

Matthias made a scoffing sound in the back of his throat. "Do you really expect us to believe that?"

Porter glared at him. "I don't give a damn what you believe," Porter said. His tone had taken a turn for the worse.

His voice had risen quite a bit, too. Now, as Porter spoke, I noticed several doors opening down the hall, and an equal number of heads poking out, looking in our direction.

Having an audience did not exactly do wonders for Matthias's mood. A muscle in Matthias's jaw was beginning to jump.

I took a step toward Porter, and raised my own voice. If Porter didn't mind his business associates overhearing, I certainly didn't. "Porter, Bartlett's girl-friend told us that Edward Bartlett had once done you a big favor. What was she talking about?"

Porter actually looked as if he were going to laugh. "A favor? Are you joking?" His tone had become contemptuous. "What kind of *favor* could somebody like Edward Bartlett do for somebody like me?" He glanced over at Lynnda and was rewarded by a quick smile. Turning back to me, Porter added, "I mean, it would be the other way around, wouldn't it?"

So much for humility.

Porter was clearing his throat still again. "Now, are you two through? Because I'm getting sick and tired of this harassment." He glanced down the hall, no doubt, to check to see if his audience was still tuned in.

They were.

Giving me a look that could possibly frost glass, Porter hurried on. "Schuyler, I'm going to say something now, and I want you to listen. Do I have your complete attention?"

What did he think? That I was mentally doing a crossword puzzle, even as he spoke? "I'm listening," I said.

Porter ran his hand through his designer haircut. "You and I are not ever going to get together again. It's *over*. I mean it. I want you to stop coming up with these idiotic excuses to come in and talk to me."

Porter's eyes were riveted on mine the entire time he said this. I actually thought I caught the ghost of a smile flicker across his face, but it was gone as quickly as I thought I'd seen it.

"You've *got* to face facts," Porter went on.

When I get really angry, I can hardly breathe. I was now feeling as if a huge hand were squeezing my chest. A quick glance told me that all those heads down the hall had heard every word Porter had said, and were now staring at me. I raised my own voice even more. "Porter, you know damn well I haven't—"

Porter must've gotten exactly the reaction he'd hoped for because a look of satisfaction now passed quickly over his face. He went right on as if I hadn't even spoken. "If you don't stop stalking me," he said, enunciating every word slowly and distinctly, "I'm going to have to take out a restraining order against you. I'd hate to do that to you, Schuyler, but if you don't quit harassing me, you'll leave me no choice."

Porter was now talking loud enough so that if anyone in the office had missed what he'd said earlier, they had to hear him now.

Hell, people in planes flying overhead could probably hear him.

I had to fight an almost overwhelming impulse to slap his smug, self-satisfied face.

Porter now turned to Matthias. "A word of advice, buddy. Don't ever break up with this lady. She's real nasty when you do."

Matthias now looked almost as angry as I felt. I stared at him. Good heavens. Apparently when Matthias gets mad, his lips turn white. "Now, you look, buddy," Matthias said, jabbing a finger in Porter's face, "if you think I'm buying this little act of yours, you're an even bigger fool than I thought you were."

Porter's mouth curved into an odd half smile. "Oh? What makes you think it's an act? How do you know for sure that I'm not telling you the truth about her? How could you possibly know?"

Matthias didn't hesitate. "Because I know Schuyler."

I turned to look at Matthias. My goodness, did he really think he knew me this well after only three months? If so, then he sure seemed to trust his instincts a lot better than I trusted mine.

"If Schuyler tells me you're lying, then you're

lying," Matthias was going on, his eyes still riveted on Porter. "That's all there is to it. You're lying about those snapshots, and you're lying about her."

If Matthias was hoping to get a rise out of Porter, he was disappointed. Porter just continued to stand there, with that odd half smile on his face.

I glanced over at Lynnda. She, too, was just standing there in front of her desk, watching Matthias and Porter, her eyes bouncing between them as if she were watching a Ping-Pong match.

I couldn't help but notice how Lynnda's face softened considerably whenever her eyes fell on Porter.

I stared at her. Oh yes, Lynnda was hooked, all right. I'd seen fans look at Elvis with less adoration.

If you didn't know better, you might actually think old Lynnda here would do anything for her boss.

I blinked and turned to stare at her all over again, as yet another thought crossed my mind.

"I'm telling you, I've never seen that little girl or that woman before," Porter was now saying to Matthias. "And you can't prove that I ever—"

Porter had begun to repeat himself. I stopped listening, took a step toward Lynnda, and lowered my voice. "You know," I said, "just before Bartlett died, he told me he'd been shot by Porter Meredith's *girl*."

I didn't have to spell it out for her. Obviously, Bartlett's words could be interpreted to mean: Porter Meredith's *secretary*.

Lynnda's eyes seemed to get even bigger as she turned to look at me.

I took a step even closer. "That's what Bartlett said. *Porter Meredith's girl*."

Lynnda didn't even blink. Leaning in my direction again, she lowered her own voice. "Porter told me you might say something like this to me."

I blinked again. "He did?"

My goodness. Had it also occurred to Porter that

Bartlett had been talking about Porter's own secretary?

Lynnda was nodding her frizzy head. "Oh yes, Porter said you might try something like this, and he even told me what I should say if you did."

Uh-oh. This didn't sound good.

Lynnda now moved closer to *me*, and lowered her voice even more. "You're right," she said.

I was so shocked, for a moment all I could do was just look at her. "What?" I finally said.

Lynnda glanced down the hall, and evidently was satisfied that the only person who could hear her was me. "I said, *You're right*," she repeated.

I felt a distinct chill. "What do you mean, I'm right?"

Lynnda was nodding her frizzy dark head. "*I* killed Edward Bartlett," she repeated, her voice barely a whisper. "*I* shot him."

I took a quick step away from her, my stomach clinching like a fist. My God. Had this frizzy-haired young woman really just confessed to murder?

I glanced quickly over at Matthias. Porter and he were now inches away from each other, each talking at the same time, their voices loud and angry.

Wouldn't you know it, once again it looked like I was the only one who'd heard.

I hoped I was wrong. "Matthias," I said, "did you hear her? Did you hear what Lynnda here just said?"

Matthias's eyes had been glued to Porter's face, but now he turned to look at me. "No, what did she say?"

"She said she killed Edward Bartlett!"

Matthias's reaction was something of a disappointment. He stared at me for what seemed like an interminable moment, and then said, "Are you sure?"

I nodded. "I'm sure that's what she said."

Matthias now looked over at Lynnda. "Did you just tell Schuyler that you killed Edward Bartlett?"

I blinked at that one. Wait a minute. Wasn't this the exact same guy who'd just told Porter that he knew me—and that when I told him something, he believed it?

So why was he asking Lynnda to verify what I'd just said?

Unbelievably, Lynnda just shrugged. "Of course, I didn't say any such thing. She, um, must've misunderstood."

This was too much. "What?" I said. "Lynnda, I didn't misunderstand anything. You know you just admitted that you shot Edward Bartlett!"

Lynnda turned cool blue eyes in my direction. "I am terribly sorry, but you must've misunderstood me," she said.

I was beginning to want to slap her face every bit as bad as I'd wanted to slap Porter's moments earlier. I turned back to Matthias. Who, if the truth be known, was beginning to look a little bewildered by all this.

"Matthias," I said, "she did say it. I don't care what she says now, she just told me she killed Bartlett!"

Matthias appeared to be at a complete loss for words. He looked from me to Lynnda and back again, his eyes growing more and more bewildered.

While Matthias was looking bewildered, Lynnda and Porter were looking amused. "Schuyler, let me get this straight," Porter said. He held up a forefinger as if making a crucial point. "Are you now saying that my *secretary* killed Bartlett? Is that what you're saying?"

Porter's voice was so loud, it seemed to thunder down the hall. Toward every one of those heads poking out of every one of those doors.

Of course, it hit me then. Just exactly how it looked. My god, I seemed to be accusing everybody Porter knew. I'd started out accusing Virginia Kenyon, his girlfriend. Then I'd suggested to Detectives Reed and

Constello that Porter himself might be guilty. And *now* I was homing in on Porter's *secretary*, for God's sake.

I mean, who was next? Porter's *mom*?

Porter had clearly won this one, and he knew it. That half smile on his face had stretched into a wide grin. "Okay," he said, "you two have asked your questions and made your ridiculous accusations. So, why don't you run along?"

I didn't budge. I just stood there, fuming.

"And, Schuyler?" Porter added. "I think you ought to go straight to the police and repeat everything you just said. Okay? In fact I'm sure the police will want to hear all about how my *secretary* murdered Edward Bartlett." His smile grew nastier. "In fact, I wish you'd tell them all about it. *Right away.*"

All right, I admit it. I am slow. It wasn't until Porter said this last that I realized that, once again, of course, I'd been set up. Obviously, Porter had put Lynnda up to saying what she'd said. So that if I should decide to repeat all this to the police, I'd sound once again just like the love-crazed psycho Porter had been making me out to be.

Talk about feeling like a fool.

Porter was still smirking when I turned on my heel and left.

It did not help any to have Matthias say, after we'd walked down the toasted marshmallow hall and gotten into one of those damn elevators again, "Schuyler, did Porter's secretary really say she'd killed Bartlett?"

I had to take a deep breath before I could trust myself to answer. "Matthias, I don't know if she really did kill him. I do know, though, that's *exactly* what she said."

I guess I could've told him right then that I'd come to the conclusion that Porter had set me up. Once again. Much like he'd done last night. I didn't, though.

I was suddenly too angry at Matthias to even say a word.

In fact, neither of us said anything until we'd gotten into my car and Matthias had pulled into the bumper-to-bumper traffic on Main Street. That's when he glanced over at me and said, "You know, it does seem strange that you're the only person these things keep getting said to."

I turned to look at him. "What exactly does that mean?"

Matthias shrugged and ran his hand through his shaggy hair. "It means that it just looks odd, that's all."

I may have been mistaken—I'll admit, this being suspected of murder was, no doubt, making me more than a little touchy these days—but it appeared to me as if Matthias—you remember, the man who had only very recently told me that he loved me—was now trying to say either (1) I didn't hear what I thought I heard.

In which case I was a moron.

Or (2) I was making things up.

In which case, I was a liar.

And if I was a liar, then—I believe—it only naturally followed that I had a reason to lie. And the only reason I could possibly come up with for doing such a thing was that I had something pretty awful to hide.

In fact, it seemed clear to me that Matthias could actually be entertaining the notion that *I* really might've murdered Bartlett.

Oh yes, that definitely ended all conversation until we got back to Arndoerfer Realty.

It was about a twenty-minute drive. I believe Matthias might've been under the impression that I was just lost in thought, because when he parked my car—and I got out and slammed the door behind me as hard as I could—he looked surprised.

I don't know. But I really don't think that it's too much to ask of a man who insists that he loves you to also believe that you're not capable of murder.

Call me picky.

Matthias followed me to the Arndoerfer Realty front door. "Schuyler, can we talk about this?" he said.

"What's there to talk about?" I said. I held my hand out for my car keys.

Matthias did not look happy, but he gave me my keys. "Schuyler—" he said.

I have no idea what he was going to say, because I didn't wait around to hear it. By the time Matthias finished saying my name, I had already walked through the front door of the real estate office.

Matthias did not follow me. Instead, he stood there for a long moment, just outside the front door, looking even more bewildered than he had back at Porter's office.

Then he slowly walked across the parking lot to where he'd left his Death Mobile, got in the thing, and drove off.

At my desk I found that I was actually shaking.

What in the world was wrong with me? Matthias had simply made a comment, that's all. And, let's face it, he was right. It *did* seem odd that I was the only one people kept saying things to.

Matthias had not exactly accused me of murder or anything.

And yet, from the way I'd reacted, you'd have thought he'd tried to make a citizen's arrest.

I hated to admit it even to myself, but maybe the reason I'd suddenly gotten so angry with Matthias did not solely concern the mess with Porter. It *was* possible that, subconsciously, I was just doing all this to push him away.

Maybe Matthias was right. Maybe I really was absolutely terrified of getting close to somebody again.

I took a deep breath.

Then I hurried into the kitchen for a large Coke. Extra, extra-heavy on the ice.

Amy interrupted me, "Well, since you just shot For-

Chapter 19

Barbi Lundergan was the only person in the front room of Arndoerfer Realty when I came back in from the kitchen, carrying my Coke.

Barbi had been over at her desk when I'd walked in, and I believe Barbi must've watched my little exchange with Matthias through the open front door. Evidently, Barbi must've immediately realized that all was not well. She looked as if she were dying to ask me what was going on. In fact, Barbi actually got to her feet, looking as if she fully intended to head my way.

No doubt, to ask if Matthias had finally decided to dump me in favor of someone with fewer homicidal tendencies.

Even from across the room, though, it must've only taken one good look at my face to convince Barbi that this was not the best time for a little chat. She immediately sat right back down, and began making phone calls. Without so much as another glance in my direction.

Okay. So I wasn't in that terrific a mood.

My mood did not improve when I noticed the stack of pink "While You Were Out" notes on my desk. Most of them, no surprise, appeared to be requests to see the Carrico house.

One of them, however, was a message from Amy Hollander. I picked that one up and just stared at it

for a long moment. I knew, of course, even before I started dialing the phone number written there, exactly what Amy was going to tell me. You didn't exactly have to be clairvoyant to figure out that Amy and Jack had, no doubt, decided to employ another Realtor to help in the search of their "starter home."

The only surprise about it, in fact, was that Amy had taken the time to phone me to give me the news personally. Usually, if a client decides to dump you, they just fade into the woodwork, and you never hear from them again. What's more, if you try to call them, they don't take your calls. Or return them.

So, this was rather decent of Amy. To take it upon herself to tell me that she would rather not work with someone who'd very recently given her and her fiancé a personal tour of a murder scene.

I was so sure that this was how the conversation was going to go, that as I finished dialing and waited for Amy to answer, I took a deep breath, steeling myself against the inevitable.

I do hate to lose a prospect.

Particularly this way. When it was really through no particular fault of my own.

When Amy answered, though, her voice was oddly cheery. So cheery, in fact, that for a second I thought I might have the wrong number. "Hi there!" Amy said. "Well, I just wanted to let you know that Jack and I are still very interested in seeing those other two houses you were going to show us yesterday—"

Talking about blowing your mind. I was so surprised that for a moment, I hardly knew what to say. I believe, however, considering my track record for the last couple days, I was getting accustomed to being shocked speechless. I recovered a lot faster than I had earlier. In less than a heartbeat, I was saying, "Well, sure, Amy, I'd be glad to show you those other houses."

"Great!" Amy said. "Jack and I would like to see them as soon as possible. We're still very interested in the Highlands area." She paused here, and apparently thought it necessary to add, "But Jack and I don't think that the house we saw yesterday is quite what we were looking for."

I could imagine. I suppose, then, that I should just assume that she and Jack would prefer *not* to have a body in their living room.

I'd certainly make a note of that.

I cleared my throat. "Amy, I'll make appointments for us to see those other two houses right away."

I was trying not to sound overeager, but, to tell you the truth, I was so surprised that Amy and Jack were not dumping me, I was practically stumbling over my words.

Amy went right on as if she didn't even notice. "We'd also like to see some other houses besides just those two."

"Well, of course," I said. "OF COURSE!" Good Lord. Now I was sounding like Jarvis.

"There were a couple of houses that we saw last night in the latest *Homes* magazine that look very promising," Amy was going on. "So, if it isn't too much trouble—"

The *Homes* magazine is a publication put out every two weeks by the Louisville Board of Realtors, featuring photographs and descriptions of houses currently on the market in the area called Kentuckiana. This area includes several counties on both sides of the Ohio River, in both Kentucky and Indiana. Not only does the *Homes* magazine feature houses for sale in Kentuckiana, it also features photographs of quite a few Realtors in this area. In fact, the publication averages about one Realtor photograph per page, and the last *Homes* had over two hundred pages.

If Amy had glanced through the *Homes*, she had to

have seen a great many other people she could've called to help her with her house hunt. Besides yours truly.

I was feeling a rush of warmth toward this sweet girl. What an absolute doll. And how unbelievably openminded of her to overlook a little thing like running into a murder victim.

I was even beginning to feel a little guilty for comparing her earlier to Flossy Bobbsey. My goodness, Amy wasn't anything at all like four-year-old Flossy. It took real maturity to be this tolerant.

I promised to make appointments to tour the other houses she wanted to see, and when I hung up the phone, I was smiling for perhaps the first time in about twenty-four hours.

My good mood, of course, did not last. To start off with, making appointments all over again with the two real estate agents I'd stood up yesterday was not exactly a laugh-fest. The guy who'd left me the "Where-the-Hell" note actually said, "Now, let's get this straight, you WILL be there tomorrow, won't you?"

Oh yes. My mood was definitely on a downward arc. "I'll be there," I said through my teeth. "You can count on it."

"Because," he went on, "unlike *some* people, *I* am a very busy man. While a lot of real estate agents do this part-time—just to more or less get out of the house once in awhile, and maybe to make a little pin money on the side—for me, it's a *real* career. I can't afford to waste my time."

Naturally, after that little speech, the first thing that came to mind was a sentence beginning with the words, "Look, Asshole—" I was now striving, however, to demonstrate every bit as much maturity as Amy. I took a deep, deep breath before I said, with all the calm I could muster, "I'm a full-time agent, too, and believe me, I'll be there. I certainly don't want to waste my time, either."

I hung up on the jerk before he could say another word.

Calling Amy back did not help my mood, either. I intended to make it short and sweet, just to let her know that we were now scheduled to see the two houses we'd missed yesterday, and that she and Jack should meet me at one tomorrow afternoon at Arndoerfer Realty. Amy, however, did not answer the phone.

Jack did, and his tone, to say the least, was clipped. "Oh," he said. "It's you."

I said what I had to say, and Jack's tone, if anything, took a nosedive. "One thing I want to get clear," he said. "There's not going to be any more surprises, is there?"

Apparently, Jack was not nearly so openminded as Amy. In fact, from the way he sounded, you could actually get the idea that old Jack blamed me personally for yesterday's unpleasantness.

I tried to suppress it, but to tell you the truth, I felt a quick surge of anger. What did Jack think? That I'd called ahead to make sure that there would be a body in the Carricos' living room? Did he think I considered a gunshot victim to be the latest decorator touch?

I had to count to five before I spoke. I probably needed to count all the way to ten, but it would've taken too much time. "No, Jack," I said evenly, "there won't be any more surprises."

"Well," Jack said. "I certainly hope not." And he hung up.

Oh yes, my mood was plummeting, all right.

It dropped a little more right after that, when my phone rang almost the second I hung up. With what would become the first in a series of wacko calls. Apparently, all the wackos in Louisville who had not been able to get through yesterday and earlier today were giving it the old college try once again. Several of the people who phoned didn't even know the address of the Carrico home—they simply referred to it once again as "the murder house."

Of course, the ones who referred to the Carrico place as the "murder house" were the easy ones. They were the ones who you knew right off the bat were nut cases, and you could hang up on them without so much as a second thought.

It was the smart ones that gave me trouble. The ones who'd wised up since yesterday and now knew to actually act interested in the house. These were the ones who, just to be on the safe side, I actually had to go ahead and make appointments with.

There were not as many of these, but there were a few. In fact, by the time the day was over, I was not absolutely sure I'd made appointments with any real prospects. And yet, I'd booked five appointments to show the Carrico house during the rest of the week.

Every time I phoned Denise Carrico to make yet another appointment, she sounded progressively more pleased with me. By the time I was making the fifth one, you might've thought that I was one of Denise's favorite people. "Oh, this is wonderful, my dear," she said. "You know, I was really afraid that we'd get no interest at all, after what happened. But, I suppose, when you have a quality property like this one, well, people are still going to be very interested. So, my dear, what do you think? Do you suppose we'll have an offer by the weekend?"

"Well, you never can tell," I said. I tried to sound optimistic, but it was hard to pull that one off. Apparently, it had not yet occurred to Denise that the burgeoning interest in her so-called "quality property" might not be the sort she wanted to encourage. She actually seemed to believe that since the yellow police tape was no longer strung around her front yard—according to Denise, it had come down all of *sixteen* entire hours ago—everybody would simply forget what had occurred there.

Uh-huh.

I had no intention of telling Denise that, of the five appointments I'd made, this last one was really the only one that I was almost completely sure about. Notice that I said *almost*, because I still had a few reservations even about it.

The last call had been from a woman who'd identified herself as a Mrs. Patterson, and over the phone, Mrs. Patterson had sounded as if she were in her sixties at least. She'd told me that she and her husband had just driven by "that lovely Tudor on Lakeside Drive," and she went on to say that she'd gotten my number off the sign in the front yard.

"My husband Alexander and I have been looking for some time for just the right place for us to retire to," Mrs. Patterson told me, "and we think this might be it. Do you suppose we could see it right away?"

When I put the question to Denise, she was not exactly delighted to have so short a notice. "I'd really prefer, my dear," Denise said, "to have a little more time in the future, but if you really think that these people are *that* eager, well, I suppose I'll just have to make do." Her tone was long-suffering.

"I'd certainly appreciate it," I said.

"By the way," Denise added, "Marvin and I will both be home when you get here. We think this would be best, from now on." She cleared her throat and added, "We're doing this to make things easier for you, my dear. This way, you don't have to worry about locating the spare key."

Uh-huh. Lifting that ceramic cat *was* a terrible chore.

Apparently, the Carricos had decided that I could

no longer be trusted alone in their house. There was, of course, no telling what I might do. Lord knows, I could fly into another homicidal rage, and, once again, put a really ugly stain on their like-new beige wool carpet.

On the phone with Denise, however, I didn't act as if any of this crossed my mind. All I said was, "Oh, good. Having you there will be a big help."

In fact, it ought to be almost as big a help as, oh, say, having *Bartlett* there.

I'd told Mrs. Patterson that I would meet her and her husband at the Carrico house at 5:30 p.m. and sure enough, a white late model Cadillac pulled right in back of my Tercel almost the very second I pulled into the driveway.

True to her word, Denise and Marvin Carrico were both standing in the doorway, eyeing us all as I and the Pattersons made our way up the sidewalk.

The Pattersons turned out to be exactly as I'd pictured them over the phone—two gray-haired people in their sixties. The only thing I hadn't pictured was how short the two of them were. Mrs. Patterson couldn't have been more than five feet tall, and her husband was only about an inch taller.

It was like showing a house to Munchkins. Elderly Munchkins. Elderly Munchkins who were almost as wide as they were tall.

"Oh, this is just wonderful," Mrs. Patterson said as she waddled through the front door.

I, of course, made the introductions, and then I went into the same pitch that I'd given Jack and Amy. "If you'll turn to your left, into the living room, you'll notice the hand-rubbed oak mantel, and—"

The Carricos must've decided that this was where they came in, because they immediately made themselves scarce. I believe Denise and Marvin went out to the backyard, but I was trying to remember to point out the antique light sconces on the either side of the fireplace so I didn't pay much attention.

When the Munchkins and I actually walked into the living room, I did feel a certain chill, but I tried to shake it off. I concentrated on telling the Munchkins the exact dimensions of the room, and I made it a point not to look in the direction of the spot where Bartlett had been lying.

Actually, I would've had a hard time picking out the exact spot. Denise had apparently found an extremely effective carpet cleaner, because now there wasn't the slightest trace of crimson marring the beige plush in the middle of the room.

I assumed that once we moved out of the living room, the chill I was feeling would go away.

Oddly enough, it didn't.

In fact, as I was moving down the hallway, with the Pattersons waddling right behind me, the feeling of unease got worse.

A lot worse.

Something was not right.

What was it?

The Pattersons were now moving past me toward the master suite, and for a moment I just stood there in the hallway, glancing around.

In the hallway directly off the living room there were three doors, the one on the right leading to the master suite, the first door on the left opening into a closet, and the door next to that opening into the bathroom. There was yet another door on down the hall, in the other direction, leading into the garage.

Mrs. Patterson was now ooing and ahing over the "genuine brass outlet covers." I nodded. "Those are the originals, too," I said, "the ones that were here when the house was built."

I was saying this out loud, but in the back of my mind, I was thinking, *Something didn't make sense.*

What in the world was it? What should I be remembering?

Now, even though the Pattersons were moving forward, I moved back down the hall a little so that I could once again see into the living room.

Standing there in the arched entranceway, I found myself staring at that immaculate carpet.

And, of course, remembering once again poor Bartlett's closing statement. "It was Porter Meredith's girl."

No matter what anybody else thought, that *was* what he'd said. I was sure of it.

The thing I wasn't so sure about was what he'd meant by the word "girl." Had Bartlett been talking about Porter's girlfriend, or Porter's Girl Friday, or Porter's daughter?

Could Porter really have had a child out of wedlock? A little dark-haired girl, for example, whose mother was pursuing the world's oldest profession?

That could certainly explain why Porter had gone so pale when he'd first seen those photos.

And yet, if all this were true and Porter was indeed little Jenny's father, what could the favor be that Bartlett had done for Porter? The favor that Gloria had talked about? Obviously, if Bartlett had the photographs in his possession in the first place, and had put them in the file he was keeping on Porter, then Bartlett had known about the child. Had the favor been that Bartlett had agreed to keep his mouth shut?

Was that why Bartlett had been killed? After having Porter snub him that time in the restaurant, the way Gloria had described, had Bartlett decided that he would no longer keep quiet?

Or there was another possibility. Could Bartlett have been *blackmailing* Porter?

I was suddenly anxious to talk to Porter all over again. Only this time I wanted to confront him away from all the listening ears at his office. I'd been so rattled at his office by his ridiculous accusations that I hadn't even told him what Candy Cherry had said about Jenny's father being an old college friend of Bartlett's. I would really like to hear what Porter had to say to *that*.

I picked up my pace.

Mr. and Mrs. Patterson, however, did not pick up theirs. They moved through the master bedroom, checked out the garage, and looked into the first-floor bathroom as slowly as if they were trying to memorize the place.

When we'd gone through the entire upstairs, and were finally once again in the downstairs hall, Mrs. Patterson gave me a cherubic smile. "It's a lovely home, sweetie," she said. "A lovely home."

She waddled toward the living room. "This room, though, is my absolute favorite."

I followed her, taking a long, patient breath.

In spite of what Bartlett's lawsuit had said to the contrary, I always make it a point to tell prospective buyers *everything*. Because even if Bartlett and his lawsuit had not recently reminded me just how important doing such a thing was, I was already well aware that real estate agents must be very careful to make as complete a disclosure to prospects as possible.

Meaning, you have to tell a potential buyer anything and everything that they could possibly need to know in order to make a well-informed decision.

Particularly anything and everything *bad*.

Now, watching Mrs. Patterson move happily around the living room—even stepping a couple of times on what I thought had to be either the exact spot where I'd found Bartlett, or very close to it—I tried not to cringe.

"It is a very nice room, all right," Mr. Patterson

was saying, giving his wife what looked to me to be a particularly significant look over his wire-rims.

It was hard to believe, but it actually looked as if the Pattersons had not heard a word about the murder that had occurred here.

Lord. They had to be the only people in Louisville who didn't read the paper. Or, for that matter, listen to television.

I took still another long breath, knowing that I was probably about to kiss a perfectly good sale good-bye. "Mrs. Patterson," I said, "I—"

Mrs. Patterson held up a plump hand. "Shhhh," she said, giving me an uncharacteristic frown. "Please. We need absolute quiet."

I stared at her. Absolute quiet? For what?

Mrs. Patterson then closed her eyes, and heaved a huge sigh.

I, of course, just stood there. Wondering what in the world she was doing.

I glanced over at Mr. Patterson, but he didn't seem to think his wife's behavior was at all odd. He immediately moved to stand right next to his wife, and he, too, closed his eyes.

I wasn't sure what to say. The two of them were just standing there, with their eyes shut. Munchkins at rest.

I hated to interrupt, but enough was enough. "Mr. Patterson?" I said.

Neither Munchkin moved.

I raised my voice a little. "Mrs. Patterson?"

Mrs. Patterson opened just one eye and looked at me over the edges of *her* wire-rims. "I'm sorry, sweetie," she whispered, "but it's particularly strong right now, and I don't want to scare it off."

I blinked. "Scare what off?" I asked.

I was once more getting a chill, but now it had nothing to do with standing out in the Carricos' hall.

Mrs. Patterson opened her eyes, and gave me another cherubic smile. "It's gone now," she said. "But it was definitely here. I'm sure you must have felt it, too."

What, in fact, I felt was irritated. And not a little spooked.

I took an uneasy glance around the room. "Felt it?" I repeated.

Mrs. Patterson smiled so wide, her eyes almost shut all over again. "Why, yes, it's very strong, sweetie, right here in the living room."

I knew I sounded like an echo, but I couldn't help myself. "Living room?"

Mrs. Patterson nodded and beamed at her husband. "Of course. It's the soul of that poor man you found in this room. He's here, you know. He's here, all around us, right this minute."

I blinked again.

After that, strangely enough, I was more than a little eager to hurry the Pattersons through the house. I was also particularly eager that neither of the Munchkins stop for a chat with the Carricos.

That would be a perfect end to a perfect day. Having the Pattersons mention to the Carricos just how strong Bartlett's soul seemed to be in their living room.

The Pattersons actually seemed good-natured about my sudden hurry. In fact, the two of them seemed to expect my reaction. They both kept smiling cherubically the entire time I was hurrying them through the house and right out the front door.

When we were finally standing out in the driveway, and I was all but shoving the two of them bodily into their Cadillac, Mrs. Patterson gave me a quick pat on the arm. "The idea of an afterlife frightens you, doesn't it, sweetie?" she said.

I gave her a tight smile. I didn't want to hurt her

feelings, but I had no intention of discussing the possibility of life after death with a crazy old lady who went into trances in other people's houses. "Oh no," I said. "Not at all."

Mrs. Patterson patted my arm again. "Now, hon, it's nothing to be ashamed of. A lot of people don't like to confront their own mortality."

I gritted my teeth. How do you tell somebody that it's not the afterlife that's your biggest problem? It's the present life. The one in which you've just wasted quite a bit of time taking certifiable loonies through a house in which a tragedy occurred?

"Mrs. Patterson," I said, "are you really interested in buying this property, or—"

Mrs. Patterson held up a plump hand. "Well," she said, twinkling at me, "I will have to think about it, you know. It's an awfully big decision—"

Mr. Patterson was nodding his gray head. "We'll get back to you when we've made up our mind."

Uh-huh.

I said a final good-bye to the Pattersons, and I headed for the backyard to say good-bye to the Carricos.

"Do you think they'll make an offer?" Denise asked the second she saw me. Her voice was eager. "They do seem awfully interested."

I told her the truth. "They're interested, all right—" I chose not to specify exactly what the Pattersons were interested in. "—and if they make an offer, I'll let you know right away."

While I mentally added the words, *Fat chance*, I headed for my car.

And, of course, for Porter's apartment.

It didn't seem to take any time to get there. Of course, my mind was probably going a little faster than my car the entire way.

This time I was determined to make Porter tell me

once and for all why those photographs of Wanda Faye and Jenny were in a folder with his name on it. I also intended to mention the word "blackmail," and see what kind of reaction I got.

I got out of my Tercel, slung my purse over my shoulder, and resolutely headed toward Porter's door. On the way I took the safety cap off the little container of Mace hanging off my key chain.

Just to be on the safe side.

I really didn't expect things to get ugly, but let's face it. Up to now, my track record with regard to the things I expected out of Porter had not been all that good.

I must have rung Porter's doorbell ten times.

Once again, just like before, he didn't answer.

I could see, however, a light inside. Having fallen for the old "Get-Schuyler-To-Wake-The-Neighborhood" trick, I decided this time I'd try the door first.

It was unlocked.

Opening the door all the way, I stuck my head in. "Porter?" I said.

In the living room, I could hear a stereo going. Tina Turner was belting out "What's Love Got to Do With It?"

Ever mindful of Porter's neighbors, I closed the front door behind me, and I started to move toward the sound.

That's when I saw him.

Sprawled in the middle of his living room, Porter was in almost the exact position as I'd found Edward Bartlett.

The hole in the middle of Porter's chest also looked horribly familiar.

As did the dark crimson stain on the front of Porter's monogrammed ivory dress shirt.

Chapter 20

"Porter!" I screamed as I ran to his side.

Once again, just like with Bartlett, it was as if I couldn't move fast enough.

It was, in fact, the worst kind of déjà vu. A nightmare repeating itself.

There was one difference this time, though. When I got to Porter's side, Porter didn't open his eyes.

And—unlike Bartlett—Porter had no closing statement.

I wouldn't have believed that anybody could've looked worse than Edward Bartlett, but Porter had managed it. Porter's face had a distinct yellowish cast, as if it had been molded out of wax.

Oh, God. As angry as I'd been with him back at his office, I would never have wished this on him in a million years. "Porter," I said again, sinking to my knees next to him.

It was then that I realized that I still had the Mace in my hand, and that I was still pointing it directly at Porter. Holding that thing on a man in his condition seemed particularly cruel.

Even for somebody like me, who has already admitted to having a mean streak.

I dropped the Mace into my purse, and reached toward Porter, steeling myself to be able to touch him.

There was no pulse in his wrist. No pulse in his throat. And his eyes were fixed and staring.

Porter's skin, though, was still warm to the touch.

I jerked my hand away, and scrambled to my feet. Frantically searching around the room, I spotted a telephone on an end table.

Maybe, I thought as I dialed 911, just *maybe* Porter isn't really dead. I mean, paramedics work miracles all the time, don't they?

I put the receiver to my ear.

There was no dial tone.

I stared stupidly at the phone, as chilling thoughts flashed through my mind.

Porter was still warm. So if he really *was* dead, then he hadn't been dead long. And, if he hadn't been dead long, then his killer could still be around. In fact, the killer could still be hiding in this apartment somewhere.

Right this minute.

I took another even more frantic glance around, my heart beginning to beat so loud, it sounded like drums in my ears.

Oh my God *Oh My God OH MY GOD*.

I didn't consciously think any further than that. I was too busy grabbing up my purse, turning, and starting to head toward the door.

But where was the door?

I hadn't noticed when I'd first walked in, but there were quite a few doors from which to choose in Porter's spacious apartment. When we'd been dating, we'd almost always ended up at my house, rather than at Porter's apartment. The couple times I'd been here had been an awfully long time ago.

Then, too, I guess I was so rattled at finding Porter's body that I was more than a little disoriented.

The first door I opened turned out to be a closet.

It was like being in some kind of macabre comedy.

I'd just slammed the closet door shut, run over and was reaching for the doorknob of the next door to my right when all of a sudden it dawned on me exactly why I'd been feeling so uneasy at the Carrico house earlier this evening.

As I was yanking open what turned out to be—thank *God*—the front door of Porter's apartment, I remembered very clearly that, when we'd found Edward Bartlett's body, Amy Hollander had not hesitated in the least when she'd run to the bathroom to get the towel I'd yelled for. There had been *four* doors in that hallway, and yet, Amy had run directly to the correct door, opened it, and gone in.

She'd known exactly which door had led to the bathroom.

As if she'd been there before.

But how could she have been? According to what Amy had told me, she and Jack were touring the place for the first time.

Unless, of course, she'd been lying right from the beginning. Unless, oh God, Amy had been the one who'd met Edward Bartlett there earlier.

My mouth went dry. Good Lord, was it really possible that it had been *Amy*?

As it turned out, I didn't have much time to think it over. As soon as I opened Porter's front door, the first thing I saw was Amy herself.

The second thing I saw was the gun in her hand.

It was pointed directly at my chest.

Chapter 21

For a long moment, I just stood there, staring at the terrible thing in Amy's hand.

I was particularly fascinated by that little hole at the end of the gun barrel. When you think a bullet could be coming out of that little hole shortly, headed directly at you, that little hole gets to be positively mesmerizing.

While I stared, several things flashed through my mind. The least of which was: No wonder Amy had insisted on continuing to use me for hers and Jack's house search. She wasn't being extremely tolerant, or demonstrating what an open mind she had. Amy knew full well that, through me, she could continue to keep tabs on the investigation into Bartlett's murder.

Considering, of course, that the police clearly suspected me and seemed to be discussing it with me on a regular basis.

While I was staring at Amy's gun, Amy was staring at me. Neither one of us had said a word so far, and it was almost as if Amy expected *me* to begin our little conversation.

I wasn't quite sure what I should say.

Usually, when I unexpectedly run into somebody I know, no matter who it is, I say, "Well, hello, nice to see you again," or some such, just to be polite. I believe, however, that when there's a gun involved, good manners fly right out the window.

Amy apparently didn't think a polite greeting was necessary, either. When I didn't speak right away she must've decided it was going to be up to her, after all, to start things off. "He deserved it, you know," Amy said.

I believe I immediately asked the obvious question. "Who?"

Amy actually looked annoyed that I didn't already know. "Why, Porter Meredith, of course."

I blinked. She needn't use that tone with me. She could've been talking about Edward Bartlett, for all I knew. It would've been an easy assumption to make.

Of course, Porter *was* lying on the floor right in back of me. It was probably a good guess that Porter would be the subject of any conversation Amy might be interested in having right this minute.

Amy lifted her chin almost defiantly. "Porter Meredith threw me away."

This last, I was certain, needed clarification. "He threw you away? What do you mean, he threw you away?"

Amy's chin went a little higher. "He threw me away right after I was born, like—like I was just so much trash. I mean, who could do a thing like that? *Who* could be such a complete jerk as to just throw away his own flesh and blood?"

I didn't particularly want to admit it out loud, but what could I say? The name *Porter Meredith* did immediately spring to mind.

Not to be speaking ill of the probably dead. God rest his soul.

I stared at Amy, trying now to see the little girl she'd been. The dark-haired, little girl, *Jenny*.

I couldn't see her.

This, I decided, would probably not be a good time, however, to ask Amy if she bleached her hair.

"Come on," Amy said.

"What?" This time I was not being deliberately obtuse. I really didn't quite understand what she meant.

Amy gave the gun a little wiggle sideways. "Turn around and go right back inside."

I just stared at her again. This time, I admit, my obtuseness *was* deliberate. "What?" I said again.

"Move!"

For a woman who looked like a Bobbsey twin, Amy could sound positively threatening.

Of course, the gun helped.

I turned on my heel and headed right back into Porter's apartment. Porter's body lying in the middle of his living room was something of an obstacle, but I stepped around him and moved farther into the room.

In back of me, Amy gave the apartment door a slam, and followed me.

The whole time I was moving back into Porter's apartment, I, of course, was trying to figure out how to get out of this little predicament. Let me see now, I still had that little container of Mace hanging off my key chain. Of course, at this moment that key chain was buried somewhere in my purse.

Talk about hindsight being twenty-twenty. Words can't express how much I now regretted dropping the damn thing back into my purse. Now that I thought about it, it really hadn't been all that mean of me to point the thing at Porter, even if he was quite probably dead. After all, if Porter was no longer alive, it probably didn't matter anymore *what* I pointed at him. He was, no doubt, beyond getting his feelings hurt.

I, on the other hand, was still quite capable of getting a lot more hurt than just my feelings.

As I continued to move, with Amy right behind me, I took a quick glance down at my purse. Have I mentioned that it is a Dooney & Bourke satchel that is not the least bit small? In the space of a single glance, I tried to calculate just how long it would take me to reach down into the thing, fish around in its dark depths, locate and finally come up with that damn Mace.

On the upside, I'd just dropped the Mace in, without bothering to fasten the top flap, so that should certainly shorten my Mace-grabbing time.

On the downside, dropping anything into my purse is like dropping it into a Black Hole.

Still doing mental calculations, I took a quick glance over at Amy.

And, of course, the gun.

Oh yes, there was no doubt about it, Amy would definitely *not* be able to shoot me more than three or four times before I got that Mace out of my Dooney & Bourke.

I immediately discarded the Grab-the-Mace Plan, and started scrambling around in my mind for another.

"Would you like to hear the whole story?" Amy asked.

I blinked again. Was she kidding? I may have been jumping to conclusions here, but it seemed to me to be a very good bet that as soon as Amy stopped talking, she was going to shoot me. Perhaps several times. Perhaps quite dead. Given that as a definite possibility, I'd say I would not only like to hear the whole story, I'd *love* to have her read me the *Encyclopedia Britannica*.

Hell, I was all ears.

"I'd like to hear *everything*," I said. To make sure she understood just how eager I was to listen, I backed up what I was saying by nodding my head. Emphatically.

"I want you to understand," Amy said, "how none of this was my fault."

I kept right on nodding. I tried to look as if I agreed with every single word she was saying. *Of course*, none

of this was Amy's fault. None at all. How could anybody even *think* such a thing?

"Everything that's happened was set into motion
before I was even born," Amy said. *"Everything."* She
gave her fluffy blond hair a toss, and began talking in
a monotone.

As if what she was saying held no real significance
for her.

As if it were just something that had happened.
Nothing more.

According to Amy, back when Porter was still in
law school, he'd gotten her mother pregnant, and then
simply handed the responsibility over to his good
friend at the time, none other than Edward Bartlett.
It had been agreed that Bartlett would immediately
arrange a discreet adoption.

Amy's original birth certificate had not even shown
her real father's name, and in fact, Amy had only
found this out when Edward Bartlett had told it to me.

When Bartlett had said, "It was *Porter Meredith's*
girl," Amy had heard every word. Knowing that she
was indeed the person Bartlett was talking about,
she'd realized that Porter Meredith had to be her father. In fact, she'd heard her natural father's name for
the first time in her life.

As I recalled, it had not been all that touching a
moment.

"That's what kind of man Porter Meredith was,"
Amy said. Her voice was now filled with contempt.
"He thought people were just to be used. He didn't
even bother to talk all this over with the woman he'd
gotten pregnant. He just told Bartlett what to do, and
then walked away."

I believe I've already mentioned what a Mr. Right
Porter had been when we were dating. What Amy was
saying certainly made sense. Porter would have, of
course, simply decided on his own the right way to

handle his little predicament, and that would've been that.

Amy was hurrying on, the words now spilling out as if she'd been waiting a very long time for the chance to tell all this to somebody.

I can't say I felt all that thrilled to be the one she'd decided to tell.

In fact, it crossed my mind that it probably wasn't all that good a sign that Amy had chosen to tell all this to me. It could actually make you think that Amy must be pretty sure there wouldn't be the slightest chance I'd ever be repeating these little revelations.

To keep from dwelling on that cheery thought, I tried to concentrate all my attention on what Amy was now saying. "Porter Meredith didn't even care enough about his own flesh and blood to see that his instructions were carried out. He didn't even stick around long enough to see that I was placed in a decent home somewhere. Oh no, he just went on his merry way, and left everything in the hands of that—that awful Bartlett person!"

Amy was getting so upset now that the hand holding the gun started wavering a little. This is not a terrific thing to notice in a person holding a gun on you.

Particularly since the gun was still pointed unerringly at my chest.

In fact, the main danger right now seemed to be that Amy—in her growing agitation—might accidentally squeeze the trigger.

Lord knows, if that should happen, Amy would no doubt be terribly sorry. Having killed me before she really meant to.

"And you know what? Porter Meredith acted as if his walking away and never looking back was some kind of excuse. He told me today that he'd never had any idea that Bartlett hadn't followed his instructions! That, as a matter of fact, Bartlett had even told him a couple years ago exactly who all had adopted me, and what my new name was, and everything. So Porter Meredith had been convinced that all had been done just as he'd said."

I just looked at Amy. This certainly explained why Porter had gotten so pale all of a sudden when I'd shown him the snapshot I'd found in Bartlett's office.

Porter had immediately recognized Amy's mother, and at that moment, he'd had to have known that the little girl in the photographs had to have been his.

It obviously had not escaped his notice that there had been a little *girl* in those pictures, not a baby. So Porter had known right then and there that his instructions to Bartlett, made so long ago, had not been carried out.

He'd realized that Amy's mother had kept his child.

Or, at least, she'd kept her for a while.

"Porter Meredith actually told me today that if he'd only known what had happened and how I was living, he would've stepped in and tried to get me back." Amy actually snickered a little at this point. "Can you believe he actually expected me to believe that a man who'd abandoned me twenty-two years ago would've changed his mind, and come back for me—if he'd only known?" Amy's eyes were flashing fire. "Porter Meredith thought I was a fool."

It was odd how she kept referring to her natural father by his complete name, never "Porter" or "my father." Always "Porter Meredith." As if he were nothing more than a stranger to her.

Which, in a way, I guess he was.

I tried to make my voice both sympathetic and smooth as silk. "You poor thing," I said. "How awful—"

Apparently, the sympathy bit was not the best idea I ever had. Amy's blue eyes flashed. "Look, bitch, I don't need you slobbering all over me, understand? I can take care of myself. I've done it all my life, and I'll keep on doing it, all right?" Amy's gun was not shaking anymore. If anything, she was gripping it even tighter. "I just wanted you to understand how *none* of this is my fault. That's the only reason I'm telling you. So you'll *understand*."

I stopped the sympathy, and now tried to look understanding.

Let me see now. Amy had shot two people, but it was not her fault. Yes, I'd say I understood that, all right. Hell, it had probably just been a problem with the gun. Some kind of manufacturing defect that caused it to pump bullets into people. That *had* to be it.

As all this went through my mind, I tried to keep my eyes off that little hole at the end of the gun barrel.

Amy now seemed to have lost her train of thought. She was staring past me, her eyes vague. I decided maybe she needed a little prompting. "Of *course*, it wasn't your fault," I said, with a shrug. "Anybody could see—"

"*Shut up and listen*," Amy commanded.

She didn't have to ask me twice.

I shut up.

And I listened.

As Amy's gun began wavering again.

"I had to live with that terrible woman until I was almost six." Amy actually shivered, remembering. "In all those awful places! I'd like to say I don't remember them, but I do! I remember all those other women, too." Her blue eyes were getting wild. "And—and I can still see that woman's face!" Amy's mouth was twisting in disgust. "She always smelled of this awful flowery perfume—and—and booze. All mixed together."

I couldn't help thinking of that one picture of

Wanda Faye, with her head thrown back, looking as if she didn't have a care in the world. Lord. She'd been so young. I cleared my throat. "Amy, I'm sure your mother—"

Talk about saying the wrong thing. I was three for three. "*Don't* you call her that!" Amy said. "Don't you ever call her that!"

I shut my mouth in a hurry.

Maybe the best plan here was not to say a word. While Amy rambled on.

"That woman was not my mother!" Amy was now saying. "She was just this awful person who kept me from my real parents, that's who she was!"

According to Amy, when she was almost six, she'd been privately adopted by the Hollanders, a childless couple who'd paid Bartlett generously to finally have a little girl of their own.

Amy's chin lifted again. "After that, I forgot that I was ever the child of any one else. I really did."

I didn't bat so much as an eyelash, but I knew what she really meant was that she'd spent all the years since her adoption, *trying* to forget.

"And then," Amy hurried on, "from out of the blue, just as I'm getting ready for what should be the happiest day of my life, who should suddenly show up but Edward Bartlett. I hardly even remembered him, but he sure remembered me, didn't he?" Amy's voice was bitter. "That damn slimeball thought that, since I was marrying into a wealthy family, he could bleed me dry!"

Bartlett—having personally arranged her adoption—had, of course, known Amy's adoptive name right from the beginning. According to Amy, when he'd read about her impending marriage in the *Courier-Journal*, Bartlett had shown up on Amy's doorstep, demanding money to keep his mouth shut about her past.

Amy had been all too aware that if her fiancé ever found out that she'd lied to him—if Jack ever discovered her true "pedigree"—he would never marry her. Because sanctimonious Jack insisted on marrying a woman who was truly "nice."

I, of course, was struck speechless when Amy got to this part. She'd done all this for *Jack*? She'd committed murder for *him*?

Good Lord. There really was no accounting for tastes.

Amy was now sounding almost proud of herself. "Edward Bartlett thought he had me over a barrel. Well, I sure showed him!"

Oh yes, she'd showed him, all right.

It suddenly struck me why Amy had not come all the way into the Carricos' living room the day I'd discovered Bartlett but had hung back near the entrance. She'd been afraid that Bartlett would see her over my shoulder, and that he'd tell me that the person who'd shot him was *in the room* with us.

I also suddenly realized what Bartlett had meant when he'd said, "Groan." He'd meant "grown." He'd been trying to tell me that his murderer was Porter's daughter, all grown up.

Listening to Amy now, you might've thought she was bragging. "The whole thing was a lot easier than I thought it would be. I watched you, you know, the day before Jack and I were to see the Carrico house. I was parked right across the street, and you didn't even notice I was there. You were showing some other people through the house, and I saw you get that key out from under that dumb cat. Once I knew how I could let myself in, I called up Bartlett."

Amy was actually grinning now, as she remembered all this. "You'd already told me that the Carricos were going to be out the first half of the day, so I told

Bartlett to meet me there an hour before you and I were to meet."

Amy shrugged. "I thought, of course, that Bartlett would have plenty of time to die before we got there."

I gave a quick nod to show just how understanding I continued to be. I mean, don't you just hate it when your gunshot victims don't die on time? *What* a nuisance.

Amy's grin suddenly faded. "Once Bartlett was out of the picture, I thought everything would be okay. That Jack would never find out. And then that very night my so-called *real* father calls up! I'd never talked to him before in my entire life, and he phones to tell me that he knew what I'd done."

I just stared at Amy. Porter must've called her right after he'd talked to Virginia. After Virginia told him what Bartlett's closing statement had been, Porter must've immediately suspected his own daughter. Since she was the only "girl" in his life who had any kind of real connection to Bartlett.

But he couldn't have been positive. So Porter must've called Amy hoping that she'd tell him that his suspicions were wrong.

Instead, he'd discovered that his daughter was a murderer.

Amy gave her hair another toss. "I still don't know how he figured it out, but once I found out that he knew, I thought, *What the hell*. I told him what I'd done, and I told him why." Amy was grinning again. "You know what he said?

I was game. "What?"

"He said Bartlett deserved it. He really did. He said Bartlett was an asshole."

Now what was I supposed to say to that? How nice it was that father and daughter had found a subject on which they both could agree?

I decided to say nothing instead.

"Then Porter Meredith said a lot of other stuff," Amy went on. Her grin faded once again as her voice became bitter. "Porter Meredith said that he wanted me to know that he was on my side. And that he wanted to help me." Amy was frowning now. "Can you believe it? He really thought I'd buy that load of garbage! He really thought that I'd believe that the man who didn't care any more about me than to just walk away, without looking back, would now help me get away with murder." Amy's pretty face twisted with anger.

I watched her, wondering how on earth I could've ever thought that Amy might've been one of the Bobbseys.

"Porter Meredith told me not to worry, that he was going to take care of everything. *Sure* he was."

Amy may not have believed Porter, but I did. This, of course, was why Porter had immediately started trying to make me believe that I hadn't really heard what I'd thought I heard. It was also why he'd called me last night—probably right after he'd talked to Amy—insisting that I come right over.

Porter was, at long last, trying to protect his daughter.

By, of course, setting *me* up to look like a psycho whose eyewitness testimony could not be trusted.

What a sweet and touching thing for a dad to do.

The sentiment, however, seemed to be pretty much lost on Amy. She looked even more angry. "Right, he was going to help me. *Sure* he was! He was going to help me into a jail cell, *that's* what he was going to do!"

I swallowed, watching her. God, how ironic. Porter had finally tried to act like a father and protect his child, and the only thing Amy had heard Porter say was that he now knew the truth about her and what she'd done.

Which made Porter as much a threat to her as Bartlett had been.

"So, naturally, I had to come over here today and take care of one final loose end."

Naturally.

Amy seemed to have run out of words.

I couldn't help it. My eyes sort of wandered to that hole at the end of her gun again.

I've heard that if you're shot real bad, sometimes it doesn't hurt. That sometimes it's such a horrible wound that you don't even feel it.

Like I said, I've heard that. I have not, however, ever actually talked to anybody who has personally been shot.

"He deserved it, too, you know," Amy now added.

I wasn't about to ask who she was talking about this time.

As it turned out, Amy immediately told me, anyway. "Porter Meredith was as big an asshole as Edward Bartlett. They were both the lowest of the low."

I wasn't about to argue with her, but to my mind, Amy was not exactly one to talk. She did kill people, let us not forget. A murderer, in my opinion, did not rank any higher on the social ladder than your basic asshole. In fact, to my way of thinking, assholes might just beat murderers out.

Amy was now staring at me, an odd half smile on her face.

I felt a sudden chill.

What do you know, the kid actually had her father's smile.

"It's kind of too bad that I had to drag you into this," Amy said, "but after I saw that article about Bartlett suing you in the paper, well, I'd have been a fool to pass up that kind of an opportunity."

Staring back at her, trying to remain calm, it all hit me. Amy had deliberately killed Bartlett in the Car-

rico house in order to implicate *me*. She'd read about
Bartlett's lawsuit in the paper, and that very evening
she'd called me to ask for help in finding a house for
her and Jack. Even though, up to then, Amy and Jack
had been working with another agent.

Amy, in fact, had set me up just as her father had
done.

There must be something to be said for genetics.

Once Amy had decided to implicate me, I guess it
would've been an easy thing to find out which listings
in town were mine. She could've either phoned the
office, or driven around the Highlands neighborhood,
looking for my name on a sign.

Once she'd located the Carrico house, she'd simply
watched to see how to get inside.

And then, that evening, she'd asked me to see that
specific listing the next day, already knowing that it
was a listing of mine. So that, when I came in the next
day and found Bartlett's body in the living room, my
name would be on the sign outside.

Amy, in fact, had practically signed my name to
the murder.

What a sweetheart.

Amy's odd half smile was slowly becoming a grin.
"It's really just fate that you're involved," she said.
"Like tonight. I'd already left—in fact, I was heading
for my car when I saw you pull up. So I hid in the
shrubbery."

Her grin grew wider. "Then I realized, why, this is
just like the newspaper article. It's too good an opportunity to pass up."

What could I say? How *glad* I was to help out?

"I guess you're wondering what's going to happen
now," Amy said.

I immediately shook my head. "Oh no," I said, "not
at all. In fact, I don't think it's even crossed my mind
to—"

Amy interrupted me. "Well, since you just shot Porter, you're feeling remorseful over what you've done, and you're going to take your own life."

It's funny. When you hear something like that, you don't react the way you think you might. Wouldn't you think that if somebody said something like that to you, you'd scream or start begging for your life or something on that order?

What I did was none of that.

In fact, it was almost as if somebody else was listening to what Amy had just said. Somebody extremely detached from the entire proceedings. Somebody who didn't particularly care.

"Oh really?" I said. "Am I going to shoot myself?" From my casual tone, you might've thought I was asking Amy how a movie ended.

Amy nodded. "You certainly are," she said. Her tone was remarkably cheerful.

"You know," I said, "they can do tests. To find out if I was the one who pulled the trigger."

Amy didn't even blink. "Those tests just tell whether you've shot a gun recently," she said. "Believe me, by the time they find you, you will have shot a gun, all right."

I found myself nodding. Because I realized right away what she meant by this. Amy intended to place her gun in my hand and fire it.

After, of course, I was quite dead.

So, let me see, what was there to do to get out of this little predicament? I was still feeling oddly detached as I considered my options, and rapidly came to a conclusion.

I didn't have any options.

In fact, it seemed to me as I stood there, with my Dooney & Bourke purse slung over my shoulder, waiting for bullets to head my way, that there was really only one thing I could do.

I dropped my purse.

The contents of that huge Black Hole scattered all across the hardwood floor of Porter's living room.

Amy looked annoyed. "What the hell did you do that for?" she asked.

I tried to look as if my dropping my purse had been a pure accident—no doubt, a reaction to the prospect of imminent death—but, as everything began skidding across the floor, I was too busy looking frantically for my keys.

On the ring. With the Mace.

I spotted my key ring right away. As my lipsticks and comb and brush and compact and purse-sized toiletries all bounced merrily at my feet, I saw my key ring slide in Amy's direction.

And, without even a moment's hesitation, I dove for it.

Unfortunately, Amy saw the key ring the exact second I did. She also saw the Mace. You couldn't miss it, really—it looked like a very large, silver phallic symbol.

Just the sort of thing a single woman ought to be carrying around on her person.

Amy went for my keys the instant I did. As she went for my keys, she aimed a shot in my direction.

I heard the gun go off. But I felt nothing.

Either Amy had missed, or else I had one of those wounds that was so bad you couldn't feel it.

Chapter 22

Almost immediately, I realized I had good news and bad news.

The good news was that Amy had clearly missed me when she'd shot in my direction.

The bad news was that Amy was definitely going to get to my keys before I did.

In what seemed like less than a second later, in fact, Amy had grabbed my keys up off the hardwood floor and tossed them over in a corner. Way out of my reach.

As she did this, Amy gave a little shout of victory.

I, on the other hand, greeted that little maneuver with a little moan of despair.

I suppose Amy might've managed to get to my keys before me because she *was*, after all, only about twenty years younger than I am.

That could've been the reason. Amy was younger. And quicker.

I prefer to think, however, that Amy was just luckier.

At least, she was luckier for a split second. In the same moment, however, that I saw Amy grab up my keys, I also saw, rolling past my feet, my bottle of purse-sized hair spray.

I reached down and grabbed it. I took a giant step toward Amy, and just as she was tossing my keys away, I aimed the hair spray directly into her eyes.

Amy let out a shriek of pure pain, and squeezed her eyes shut.

Shutting her eyes, however, was not a good idea. In the moment while she could no longer see, I moved even closer to her.

And knocked the gun out of her hand.

I must not be as strong as I thought I was, however. The gun didn't exactly fly across the room like I hoped it would. In fact, it fell with a thud not far from Amy's feet.

And momentum alone caused the thing to skid across the hardwood floor at an angle away from both of us.

Unfortunately, by the time the gun hit the floor, Amy had rubbed her eyes, and they were open again.

She immediately went for the gun.

I, of course, immediately went for the gun, too.

At that point, a lot of things seemed to happen at once.

Porter's front door suddenly opened, and Matthias came running in. Yelling "Schuyler! Schuy—"

Matthias's voice sort of choked off as he took in Porter on the floor.

And then he saw me and Amy, moving rapidly toward the gun still skidding across the room.

I was, I thought, making real headway, but Matthias's arrival distracted me a little. It also slowed me down a fraction of a second.

I had just enough time to think, What on earth was Matthias doing here? And, *Oh God, he's in terrible danger.*

And then, I saw that Amy was almost to the gun.

Lord, that girl could move. For crying out loud, she was going to beat me *again*.

Matthias had not stopped running when he came in the front door, and as it happened, Amy was now closer to him than she was to me.

Matthias was on her immediate right. All he had to do was take a little leap toward her, draw back one of his big hands, and knock her out of the way.

"Matthias," I yelled, "*hit* her!"

Would you believe, Matthias actually hesitated?

From where I was at that instant, still moving as fast as I could toward the gun, it seemed as if Matthias hesitated for a very, very *long* moment.

It was, in fact, a terribly strange thing. Right after I yelled, everything seemed to slip into slow motion.

I was in a car accident once, and this was just like that. Suddenly, I seemed to have all the time in the world.

I had time to give Matthias a disgusted look. Time to think, Oh, for God's sake. That old rule about how a man should never hit a woman seems to actually be giving Matthias *pause!*

I also seemed to have more than enough time to reach down, and in one smooth motion, grab up one of my lipsticks off the floor.

Unlike Matthias, *I* did not have a problem with hitting a woman.

With my fist curled around the lipstick, I gave up on getting to the gun. Instead, I stepped sideways in front of Amy, and blocked her path.

Amy's eyes had been on the gun on the floor, but now her eyes swiveled to mine.

I looked her straight in the eye, drew back my fist, and clobbered her right in the mouth as hard as I could.

Amy dropped like a rock.

Lord. She must've had a glass jaw.

In fact, she went down so easy, that once she was lying at my feet, unconscious, I almost felt like a bully standing over her. I actually had to remind myself that this little, fluffy-haired, blond person had actually shot two people.

What's more, I had to keep reminding myself of that. While Matthias called 911. While we waited for them to show up. And while they handcuffed a still-groggy Amy and led her away.

Little, fluffy-haired, blond Amy had shot and killed two people.

And today she is where she certainly deserves to be—in a less than cozy jail cell in downtown Louisville, awaiting trial for the murders of Edward Bartlett and Porter Meredith.

These days, can you believe it, I'm still reminding myself that Amy is a murderer. Because, let's face it, I really do feel sorry for Amy. It is an undeniable fact that her natural parents did some pretty awful things to her when she was a child.

On the other hand, it is also an undeniable fact that no matter what was done to you as a child, it doesn't give you the right to do even worse things when you've grown up to be an adult yourself.

At some point it's not your parents, or the world you grew up in, or any other excuse—it's just you and the choices you've made.

Still, knowing all this, I can't help it. Every time the *Courier-Journal* runs yet another article about Amy's upcoming day in court, it's all I can do to keep from crying for a little, dark-haired girl named Jenny.

You'd think that lately I'd be anything but sad. After all, I do seem to be everybody's favorite person these days. Jarvis Arndoerfer—believe it or not—has been singing my praises to everybody in the office.

And, joining him in the chorus, amazingly enough, are the Carricos.

Will wonders never cease.

Amazingly enough, Jarvis and the Carricos are all deliriously happy with me because the week after Amy was arrested, I actually sold the Carrico house.

I sold the place to, of all the people, the Pattersons.

As Mrs. Patterson told Denise Carrico, when I was taking the Pattersons through the house for a second look, "I've always wanted to live in a place that's haunted." The occult, according to the Munchkins, had been a hobby of theirs for years.

After Mrs. Patterson told Denise about hers and her husband's little hobby, Denise and Marvin, oddly enough, decided to hold out for their asking price.

Which, between you and me, was already a little inflated.

The Pattersons ended up actually paying it, though. Every red cent.

So the Carricos and the Pattersons and even Jarvis has ended up happy.

According to Mrs. Patterson, Edward Bartlett has ended up happy, too. Shortly after the Pattersons moved into their new home, Mrs. Patterson phoned to tell me that she's seen Edward Bartlett several times, standing in the middle of her living room.

Smiling at her.

Uh-huh.

It would be nice to think that the little weasel really is happy—maybe because he left behind a significant chunk of life insurance to Gloria Thurman. Who has, of course, moved out of that rundown house in Vista Gardens, and is now residing in the Willowcrest down the hall from Candy Cherry.

Those two must be congenial neighbors.

Like I said, it would be nice to think that's why old Edward is smiling away in the Pattersons' living room.

I'm not sure, however, that I actually believe in ghosts.

Still, I believe in them enough so that here lately I've actually been wondering if maybe I shouldn't advertise that other house—the one out in Eastridge that's been on the market for the last two years—as "possibly haunted."

I wouldn't say it really *was* haunted.

I'd just say it was possible.

Come to think of it, the way things are going between Matthias and me these days, just about anything seems possible.

Shortly after Amy was arrested, Matthias admitted to me that the reason he'd been at Porter's apartment that night was that he had followed me.

I can't say I was surprised to hear it.

Matthias went on to say that he'd been following me from the time I'd left Arndoerfer Realty to go meet the Munchkins at the Carrico house. He'd followed me from there to Porter's, and Matthias had even watched Amy and me from the parking lot.

Amy's back had been to him, however, and he had not been able to see that Amy had been holding a gun on me. In fact, it was only after Amy and I had both been inside Porter's apartment for some time that Matthias had finally begun to worry about what was going on inside and had decided to investigate.

Matthias told me, "Schuyler, I was following you because I didn't want to leave things like they were between us. I was looking for a chance to talk to you."

Uh-huh.

"And, of course, I wanted to make sure nothing happened to you."

Matthias has told me this last again and again.

Right.

It's not that I don't believe him. I do. I know, without a doubt, that all the things that Matthias has told me are absolutely true—that Matthias was probably indeed feeling very protective, and that he most certainly wanted to settle our differences—I do know all that.

I do also, however, have a sneaking suspicion that Matthias was following me in order to accomplish one more thing that he hasn't quite got around to mentioning. He was following me in order to make up his mind once and for all whether I really was as guilty as everybody else in the world seemed to think.

After going over all this in my mind, however, I've decided that this is not all that bad a thing. Even if Matthias *had* begun to doubt me a little—and perhaps even briefly wonder if I really could be capable of murder—he still continued to believe that he was in love with me.

Which, when you think about it, is a major ego-boost.

In fact, this is—without a doubt—even better than Matthias continuing to date me even though I can't cook.

I don't think I've ever been so flattered.

What's more, I realized something when Matthias came running in the door of Porter's apartment. I realized how precious he is to me.

And how huge a hole in my life it would make if Matthias were suddenly no longer around.

So maybe I was wrong. Maybe being in love has got something to do with holes, after all.

Last night, after Matthias cooked dinner for us and we moved out to my screen porch to sit and look at the stars, I finally managed to say it.

"I love you, Matthias."

Hey, if Matthias can take a risk with me, I guess I can do the same with him.

And, my goodness, if I'd known the kind of reaction I was going to get, I probably would've said it earlier. Lord. It's amazing how much impact one little statement can have.

Matthias's face just lit up.

So I said it again. For emphasis.

Don't miss the next
Schuyler Ridgway mystery,
A Killing in Real Estate,
coming from Signet
in 1996.

I wouldn't have felt so bad about what happened if I'd liked Trudi Vittitoe. I know that sounds a little strange, but it's true. It was as if, even before awful things started happening, the way I felt about Trudi had already given my silent vote of approval.

I've never thought of myself as a particularly vindictive person, either. In fact, until Trudi became the newest real estate agent working out of Arndoerfer Realty, I'd been under the impression that I could get along with anybody.

Trudi helped me see the error in that kind of thinking. But then again, Trudi could've made Mother Teresa want to punch her out.

Even now—can you believe it?—Trudi still has the power to make me angry. I'm angry now because I can't stop feeling guilty. I've told myself over and over that none of it was really my fault, and that it certainly wasn't as if I were personally plotting against anybody or anything. And yet I still feel incredibly guilty.

It doesn't help to recall that I spent a good portion of that last day looking forward to raking Trudi over the coals.

I'd been gearing myself up to do a little Trudi-raking ever since shortly after one that afternoon.

That was the time I'd returned to Arndoerfer Realty after showing a house way out in Louisville's south end.

Once I pulled into the office parking lot, it hadn't taken Trudi ten seconds to make me furious, and Trudi wasn't even *there,* for God's sake.

Of course, her not being there was the problem. That, and it being ass-freezing cold, to put it—as we genteel Southern ladies always do—delicately.

Even though the temperature had been in the seventies just the day before, on that particular Monday, it was thirty-five. With a wind chill of minus ten. This kind of sudden temperature change is not all that unusual for Louisville in early November. Around that time of year, Kentucky weather has all the ups and downs of a roller coaster. Only it's not as much fun.

You'd think, having lived here all my life, I would've gotten used to the roller coaster weather. That by now I'd be tuning into the Weather Channel every single morning before I got dressed. But no, I admit it, I'm not that smart. That Monday, for some odd reason, I'd actually been expecting another nice day just like the one before. So I was wearing a lightweight wool suit. No coat, no boots, no gloves. Not even a sweater under my suit.

The wind felt like tiny knives cutting into me as I all but ran across the parking lot from my car to the front door.

Which was, not at all incidentally, shut tight.

A bad sign if I ever saw one.

Jarvis Arndoerfer—co-owner, along with his wife, Arlene, of Arndoerfer Realty—has always insisted that his front door be left standing wide open during the day. Whether it's cold or hot, the only thing that's supposed to separate the front office from the elements is a storm door. Jarvis appears to be under the impression that if he doesn't make it incredibly easy for potential clients to walk in, they might just decide that having to reach out and turn a doorknob was too much of a strain.

I think I knew the instant I saw the front door shut that it was locked, too, but I gave it a try anyway.

I believe the phrase "a complete waste of time" describes it best.

"Damn you, Trudi." As I said this, I realized I was looking straight at the small brass plaque located to the left of the door. It said, 9 TO 5:00, MONDAY THROUGH FRIDAY, AND 10 TO 2, SATURDAY. In plain English that even Trudi ought to be able to understand.

So where the hell was she?

Even if she hadn't been able to read the sign, I believe I'd made myself abundantly clear when I left. "Trudi, a client just phoned and she wants to see one of my listings right away. So, even though this is my floor-duty day, would you mind staying here until one of the others show up?"

This wasn't an odd thing to ask. In fact, since Arndoerfer Realty is fairly small, with only four agents working here other than the Arndoerfers themselves, we cover for each other all the time. Trudi herself had asked me to do the exact same thing just last week, and I'd agreed. I'd even lied. I'd said, "Glad to." As I recalled, she'd totally forgotten to thank me.

Now, judging from the look on her face, she'd not only totally forgotten to thank me, she'd totally forgotten the entire incident.

"What?" Trudi said, looking up from the latest issue of *Vogue* and brushing a wisp of blond hair off her forehead.

Trudi is one of the few women left on the planet who's still wearing her hair in a Farrah Fawcett tumble to her shoulders. I suspect that the reason Trudi still wears her hair this way is that, to be painfully honest, with her hair cut like that, Trudi looks *a lot* like Farrah Fawcett. Trudi certainly has all the necessary Farrah Fawcett attributes: thick blond hair, curvy figure, big brown eyes, and let us not forget, great teeth.

Before anybody starts thinking that the main reason I disliked Trudi was because she was gorgeous, let me hasten to add that I'm not that shallow. Okay, Okay, so maybe I *am* that shallow, but her being gorgeous was not the main reason I disliked her. It was only one thing in a long, long list.

To tell you the truth, sometimes it seemed as if everything about her irritated me. There was the way Trudi told everybody she was "thirtysomething," when I'd seen her driver's license, and she was two years older than my own forty-two. There was also the way Trudi spelled her name, the way Trudi always lowered her voice to a breathy whisper whenever she answered the phone, and the way Trudi always dotted her *i*'s with little hearts. It even irritated me the way Trudi always wore scarves color coordinated to every outfit.

She was fiddling with the end of a burgundy print scarf that exactly matched her burgundy suit as she said, "You mean, I'm going to be the only one here?" She looked around the office as if she was just noticing that she and I were alone.

Like I said before, there were two other agents—Barbi Lundergan and Charlotte Ackersen—who worked here besides Trudi, me, and the Arndoerfers, but none of these people had been into the office so far. That meant that Trudi and I had been here all by ourselves since nine. And *now* she was actually acting as if it hadn't yet occurred to her that nobody else was here?

"Well, that's really going to be a problem," Trudi said, her tone testy. "I wasn't planning on staying here *all* day, Shooler."

I just looked at her. I'd worked with the woman all of six months and every so often, she still called me "Shooler." Just as if I hadn't told her quite a few times already that, although my name is spelled *Schuyler,* the *u* is silent. So you pronounce it "Skyler."

Oddly enough, Trudi always seemed to make this little mistake when I was asking her to do something. The last time she'd called me Shooler, for example, she'd been on her way to the Xerox. Already late for a closing, I'd asked her to make one quick copy of a single page for me. From the look she'd given me, you'd have thought I'd asked her to Xerox the phone book. "Oh, I couldn't possibly," she'd said, handing the page back to me, "but I tell you what, I'll let you go before me. Okay, Shooler?"

That time, even though I was late—and I still had a damn copy to make—I'd taken the time to remind her exactly how my name should be pronounced.

This time, though, I decided to skip it. Mainly because this time I detected an unmistakable gleam in Trudi's brown eyes. As if she were actually looking forward to my having to go through it one more time.

I went smoothly on, as if I hadn't even noticed her mispronunciation, "Do you have an appointment this afternoon to show a house, or—"

The gleam went out of Trudi's eyes. "Well, no, but I certainly don't want to get tied down here *all*—"

I interrupted her. "You only have to stay until one of the others get back."

Trudi's eyes got wider, and her voice got higher. "But, *Schooler*"—this time she put a little extra emphasis on the name as her eyes darted to mine (I didn't even blink—apparently, I'd developed a hearing problem)—"I'm not sure I can handle everything all by myself."

If I were male, the little girl voice, the wide-eyed look of innocence, and the tone of abject helplessness might've worked. I was not, however, male. As a matter of fact, I've used the I'm-so-dumb-you'll-have-to-do-it gambit myself. I use it every time I have a flat tire.

Not to mention, wasn't this the same woman who, whenever the phone rang, nearly broke a leg getting to it before anybody else did? Wasn't this also the same woman who immediately pounced on any walk-ins, with no regard whatsoever to who might possibly have floor duty on any particular day?

This was yet another thing I'd tried to explain to Trudi. How the policy at Arndoerfer Realty is that whoever has floor duty on a given day is supposed to greet all the walk-ins. The person on floor duty then has the opportunity of taking on the walk-ins personally as clients, or passing them on to another available realtor. This was, I'd tried to make clear, pretty much how floor duty was supposed to work. It was not supposed to be a footrace, with every agent in the place trying to beat each other to any prospective clients.

In fact, it was to avoid footraces that all of the realtors at Arndoerfer Realty alternate floor duty days. This way we could *all* have an equal opportunity to acquire new clients.

After I'd finished explaining the policy to her, Trudi had assumed the wide-eyed innocent look she was so good at. "I hope you're not suggesting that *I* would deliberately try to take somebody else's prospect." Trudi had actually looked close to tears when she'd added, "I'm just trying to be of service, you know. I'm just trying to make Arndoerfer Realty the best goshdarn real estate agency Louisville has ever seen. *That's* all."

Jarvis, coincidentally enough, had been coming down the stairs at that particular moment. I couldn't help but notice that Trudi had raised her voice quite a bit toward the last. So that Jarvis couldn't miss a word.

Jarvis had beamed at Trudi as he went by.

I, on the other hand, had felt an almost overpowering urge to give Trudi the best goshdarn punch in the face Trudi had ever seen.

Earlier this morning, asking Trudi to watch the office in my absence, I was once again fighting the urge. "You can handle the responsibility," I'd told her. "I've got real faith in you."

Trudi had not looked delighted by my vote of confidence. "Well, I'll *try*," she'd finally said.

Now, as I stood freezing to death in front of a locked door, I realized that Trudi's last little statement should've tipped me off. People never say "I'll try" when they're sure of success. "I'll try" is what they say when they know they're going to fail.

"Trudi, you asshole," I said, taking my purse off my shoulder and unzipping the main pocket. I'd dropped my keys in there right after I'd locked my car. Believe me, I'd never have done such a thing if I'd had any idea that the door was not going to be open. Because dropping anything into my purse is like tossing it into a black hole.

My keys had apparently been instantly sucked into a parallel universe because they certainly didn't seem to be in my purse anymore.

As I began going through every inch of the damn thing, I also began calling Trudi every name I knew. While, of course, my extremities quietly turned blue.

In the interest of variety, I'd been reduced to calling Trudi a nerd bird by the time I finally located my keys and got the front door open.

Once I was inside, my mood did not improve.

On my desk, printed in blue ink, was a note. It must've been torn off the pad in a big hurry because a good quarter inch of the top of the paper was missing. Torn diagonally across, the note began TO S.R.

After this warm salutation, Trudi must've decided that it was going to take too long to print the entire thing. Even though the rest of the note continued in blue ink, it was no longer printed. Written in a bold, familiar scrawl, it said: *A client called you, wanting to see the new listing on Elm. Since you weren't here, I thought I'd help you out. Back soon. Trudi.*

The *i* in the name Trudi, as usual, was dotted with a little heart.

I barely noticed that, though. What I was staring at was the second sentence. I knew very well what Trudi meant was not "I thought I'd help you out," but "I thought I'd help myself to your commission."

This was, of course, not the first time Trudi had taken another agent's lead. Barbi Lundergan had complained to me more than once that she was sure Trudi had been stealing messages off her desk. And Charlotte Ackersen, who rarely had a bad word to say about anybody, had actually started referring to Trudi as "that thieving bitch."

Under the guise of being helpful, Trudi had walked

off with several clients who'd initially come into the office, looking *specifically* for either Charlotte, Barbi, or me. All three of us had complained to Jarvis about it, and yet his only response had been to say that he found Trudi "inspiring." But then again, I noticed that Trudi had always been very careful never to steal one of Jarvis's clients—or any clients, for that matter, belonging to Jarvis's wife, Arlene.

Trudi, in my opinion, was not dumb.

Leaving me this little note, however, had to be the height of arrogance. Apparently, she'd decided to become outright brazen in what she was doing.

This turn of events was not a complete surprise. I was already aware that Trudi wasn't the least bit apologetic about her behavior. In fact, when I'd taken it upon myself to discuss it with her, Trudi had acted totally bewildered that anybody would even *think* that she was doing something wrong.

I'd even gone so far as to point out to her the exact section of the Arndoerfer Realty manual that specifically prohibits one realtor from going after another realtor's clients. Trudi, however, didn't seem to get it. She'd told me, with a straight face, "I have never, *ever* gone after anybody else's clients." I had to hand it to her, too. When she told me this, she actually managed to look hurt that anyone would even accuse her of such a dastardly deed.

According to Trudi, what few times she'd ended up with a client who used to work with another agent, it was the client himself who initiated the switch.

Uh-huh. Right. And, if I believed that, Trudi, no doubt, had a bridge she wanted to sell me.

What made things worse for me was that up until Trudi got here, I had been Arndoerfer Realty's best-selling agent. Now Trudi and I were neck-and-neck for the title.

Trudi's success was all the more amazing since Trudi had only gotten her real estate license a scant two weeks before she came on board, and it usually takes months, at the very least, for a new agent to build up a client base.

Of course, you can acquire a client base *a lot* more quickly if you make a habit of stealing other agents' clients.

Now, standing there at my desk, staring at Trudi's note, I took one of those deep, cleansing breaths that all the talk shows say is supposed to reduce stress.

It didn't help.

There was no indication on the note as to what time Trudi had left the office, so there was no telling how long the office has been unmanned. I myself had been out over two hours, so for all I knew, Trudi could've easily left right after I did.

Other than Trudi's note, there were no other messages on my desk. Either none of my clients had phoned or else there had been nobody here to take their calls.

I was suddenly so positively furious that my hand shook as I crumpled the note up and tossed it in the garbage can under my desk.

I guess I was so mad, I only barely registered that Barbi Lundergan had just walked through the front door and was headed toward her desk.

As the crumpled note hit the wastebasket, Barbi glanced my way. I must've looked exactly like I felt, because Barbi's eyes widened. "Did Shitty-toe steal another one of your leads?"

"Shitty-toe" was Barbi's less-than-fond nickname for Trudi Vittitoe. Barbi was not exactly a rocket scientist—she'd once asked me how many quarters there were in a football game—but in this one instance, I thought she'd shown real creativity. A couple of times, Barbi had even been so bold as to call Trudi "Shitty-toe" to her face. Both times, strangely enough, Trudi had acted as if she hadn't heard a word.

For somebody I'd never thought was particularly smart, Barbi had certainly had Trudi's number long before I did. In fact, Barbi seemed to dislike Trudi from the moment Trudi had walked in the front door.

At first Barbi had told me that she didn't much care for Trudi because Trudi also ended her name with an *i*. At the time I'd found this a little hard to believe, but Barbi kept insisting that she "hated copycats."

Of course, one reason I found Barbi's sudden aversion to copycats a bit difficult to swallow was that I already knew the real reason for Barbi's animosity. It was the same reason Barbi had often been rude to me. Particularly if an eligible male was anywhere in the vicinity.

Ever since the day Barbi turned thirty-nine, Barbi has been on the Great Man Hunt. That means if you were an attractive female over the age of twelve within a five-mile radius of Barbi, Barbi was going to view you as competition. And she was not going to be treating you kindly.

It didn't exactly take a private detective to deduce why on earth Barbi might not care for someone who looked like Farrah Fawcett.

Then again, after Trudi had been an Arndoerfer Realty agent for about a week, Barbi had even more reason to dislike Trudi.

Barbi had announced on her thirty-ninth birthday that she was going to marry a wealthy man before she turned forty, and until Trudi showed up, it looked as if Barbi was right on target.

The day Trudi signed on with Arndoerfer Realty, Barbi had actually been dating two wealthy men at the same time—Samuel Whitney of Whitney Construction, Inc., and Mason Vandervere of Vandervere Design Corporation. I myself always referred to Samuel and Mason as S&M.

Back then Barbi had been trying to make up her mind whether S or M was the better catch—meaning, of course, who had the most money—when Trudi put an end to both relationships.

By telling S about M. And M about S.

Trudi's story has always been that she had no idea that Barbi had not *already* told both men herself, or she would never have said anything. I, however, am not so sure. Trudi's revelations to S&M came exactly one day after Barbi called Trudi "Shitty-toe" to her face. Although at the time Trudi had acted as if she hadn't heard, I believe I've already demonstrated how easy it is to fake such a thing. Besides, I myself was in the office when Barbi called Trudi that, and I was sure that Trudi could not possibly have missed it.

I was also sure that I detected a triumphant look flash across Trudi's face when both men called Barbi—at the office—and broke it off with her.

Trudi, though, kept right on saying it had all been a mistake. According to Trudi, she just couldn't *believe* that "Barbi had not been completely honest with the two men all along, because *everybody* knows that good relationships are built on trust."

Trudi said this several times in Barbi's presence. Every time Trudi said it, she immediately took the opportunity to describe at length what a wonderful relationship she and her own husband, Derek, happened to have. According to Trudi, she and Derek had a marriage made in heaven because she and Derek had always been completely honest with each other. "Derek and I have a special closeness that most married couples just don't seem to have," Trudi told everybody in the office. More than once.

Barbi, on the other hand, told everybody in the office more than once that she'd like to give Trudi a special closeness to a hot poker.

Trudi did seem to be speaking the truth about her husband, however. Derek has had flowers delivered to the Arndoerfer real estate office on Monday afternoon of every week since the day Trudi first came to work there.

You really couldn't miss the flowers' arrival, because every single time Trudi squealed, as if it was a big surprise. "Oh, that Derek! He is such a doll! He spoils me!" Then she would all but strut around the office for the rest of the day.

Barbi had been known to try to trip her.

Now I wish she'd succeeded. "Oh, yeah," I said to Barbi, looking holes through the crumpled note in my garbage can, "Trudi has just stolen one of my leads, all right. And when she gets back, I'm going to break her face."

I meant that figuratively rather than literally, but that must've been a nuance totally lost on Barbi. She looked startled.

"What I mean is, I'm going to give Trudi a piece of my mind."

After I said this, Barbi actually looked a little disappointed. As if maybe she'd already been looking forward to Trudi's upcoming face-breaking.

As the day wore on, I realized that I myself was looking forward to telling Trudi at last exactly what I thought of her. I even found myself going over it in my mind again and again. Exactly what I intended to say to her the second she walked in the door.

As it turned out, there was only one problem with my little plan.

Trudi never did return.